A THREAD OF LIGHT

ALSO BY NEEMA SHAH

Kololo Hill

Neema Shah

A THREAD
OF LIGHT

PICADOR

First published 2025 by Picador
an imprint of Pan Macmillan
The Smithson, 6 Briset Street, London EC1M 5NR
EU representative: Macmillan Publishers Ireland Ltd, 1st Floor,
The Liffey Trust Centre, 117–126 Sheriff Street Upper,
Dublin 1 D01 YC43
Associated companies throughout the world

ISBN 978-1-5290-3055-6 HB
ISBN 978-1-5290-3056-3 TPB

1 3 5 7 9 8 6 4 2

A CIP catalogue record for this book is available from the British Library.

Typeset in Bell by Six Red Marbles UK, Thetford, Norfolk
Printed and bound in the UK using 100% Renewable Electricity by CPI Group (UK) Ltd

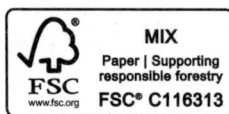

FSC
www.fsc.org

MIX
Paper | Supporting
responsible forestry
FSC® C116313

Visit **www.picador.com** to read more about all our books
and to buy them.

For Mum and Dad

Go, passers-by
And do if you can as he did
A man's part
In defence of liberty

Epitaph on the gravestone of IAF Squadron Leader Karun Krishna Majumdar
(1923–1945) who flew reconnaissance during the Normandy landings

PART ONE

PART ONE

1941

1

Ruby

First thing she did was check for bodies. Crawling through what used to be the front hallway, a carpet of debris crunching beneath her palms.

A faint drip-drip of liquid somewhere. 'Hello, is anyone in here?' Ruby edged her way further along, warden's helmet slipped off her head, strap catching on her neck.

No answer.

Drip-drip.

Along here, the hallway was still intact, leading to a kitchen. A brass lamp lay on the wooden floor, chain handle askew, as though it had already surrendered to the enemy. Her torchlight flitted around the shell of the house as she looked for signs of life.

Ruby stood up, the orb of light cutting through the dark. Above, there was a large break in the hallway ceiling, revealing the night sky. Or at least, she thought it was sky. Maybe the black smoke from one of the neighbouring buildings? They'd all seen the oil bomb fall outside, the way it had turned and twisted in the air, wailing in deathly agony.

'Can you hear me, Major Richardson?' Smoke snagged at her throat. 'Mrs Richardson? It's Miss Thacker here.'

She felt her way along the hallway, then stood up as she reached the kitchen. Edging carefully, in case there was a hand or a foot hidden among the rubble. When had thoughts like this started coming into her head so easily? The Richardsons rarely went to shelter at King's Cross station. Maybe they were in the basement? Ruby tried the back door in the kitchen. Jammed. She shoved harder this time. Some plaster from above came crumbling down, but the door gave way. She fought the urge to move faster because she knew better; had to be careful, in case the house fell down around you. Outside and down the steps to the basement. Ruby opened the door and something soft yielded under her foot. Please not a limb. She looked down: it was an empty pair of leather shoes. They were laid out neat and snug, side by side, like a courting couple sitting on a bench. Trust the rich to have 'shelter shoes'. No one was here though, just a folded blanket, a spring bed, the mouldy smell of old brick.

They must be at the Tube station after all, thank God. Although, of course, Mrs Richardson wouldn't have liked that; breathing in the recycled air of strangers. Ruby had exchanged civilities with Major Richardson on her rounds. He at least tried to spread a fine layer of politeness onto his thick slice of snobbery. Mrs Richardson, on the other hand, was all turps and vinegar. A scrawny thing, she was, with a face like a wrung-out cloth.

Ruby hurried back inside, ignoring the sting in her finger; she must have cut it when she was crawling. The staircase was still intact, save for a gap on one of the steps where the wood had fallen away. She edged her way up, torchlight scouring the gloom.

Standing on the first-floor landing, she moved the light across the ornate painting on the wall. Maybe it was all right, she thought. The Richardsons wouldn't have taken their chances and stayed upstairs during a bombing raid. No, if they weren't in the basement then they were likely safe elsewhere;

perhaps Major Richardson was even secretly enjoying the bawdy songs in the shelter?

Once more for luck. 'Hello, can you hear me?'

Outside Ruby could hear people shouting, trying to put the fires out down the street. But here in the gloom it was quiet, as though the bomb had blasted away the noise.

All clear.

Ruby remembered coming to inspect this house, doing her usual air-raid checks for any traitorous light that might have escaped through gaps in the blackout curtains. Dolly, the Richardson's housekeeper who worked at the house during the day, showed her around while Mrs Richardson looked on. The main bedroom and a bathroom were on this floor, while the floor above housed two small guest bedrooms. Ruby had seen this place dressed up in all its finery: lace curtains as fine as dragon-fly wings, a vomit of chintzy cushions on every soft surface, a flourish of white plaster framing the ceiling roses. Now here she was, creeping around its skeletal frame and clambering over its broken innards.

The whine of a fire engine, coming closer. She'd need to be quick if she was going to take her chance.

Ruby headed straight to the main bedroom, remembering the dressing table where Mrs Richardson probably preened in the mirror. She ran her fingers along the mahogany, the surface covered in a coating of mortar dust so fine it could be talcum powder. When she opened the black-lacquered jewellery box, it was almost empty, holding only some cheap costume jewellery. Damn it. People had grown wary: too many opportunities for looters to scavenge through the rubble.

She heard a man's voice coming from somewhere near the entrance of the house. 'Ruby? You still in there?' It was Errol, back from reporting the incident at their warden post.

'I'm coming out now,' she called, but Ruby doubted whether

Errol would have heard her over the roar of the fires down the street and the gossiping neighbours outside.

A quick scan of the drawers. She sighed. Nothing but a hairbrush, a fancy gold-cased lipstick and a jar of Pond's Cold Cream. The jewellery box that Ruby had spotted on her rounds was nowhere to be seen.

One last thing to try. Ruby ran her hands under the drawers. Yes, here it was.

Something had been taped smooth against the wood. She peeled it away, listening out for the shouts of the fire brigade or footsteps up the staircase. The sharp edges and smooth facets of something expensive. Ruby rammed the necklace down her brassiere, the corners digging into her cleavage, and carefully stepped downstairs. She made her way down the stairs, then clambered on hands and knees along the collapsed front hallway.

'There you are,' said Errol, wincing as her torchlight flashed in his face. 'Here.' He held his rough hand out through the opening where the front door used to be.

'Stop fussing, Errol!' She needed to move without the jewellery falling out.

Over the last of the rubble, she scrambled through the doorway and out into the night. Charred air, acrid on her tongue. Looking out onto Regent's Square, she tried to catch her breath. The house next door was on fire. What use was a blackout when there was still a bloody great blaze lighting up the street?

An old man was trying to stop a fireman using the stirrup pump, despite the crown of flames along the roof. Ruby couldn't see the point herself, the furniture would be ruined whether it burned or drowned.

An ambulance was parked near the green space of the square, the iron railings that used to surround the grass stripped away for war works. Down the street, St Peter's Church had taken a hit, but somehow the pillared tower above was still intact. For now.

A large, lumbering animal twitched its back: an older lady with a crust of blood and plaster dust along her forehead, helped away by an ambulance woman.

A few of the neighbours were milling about, talking in tones that verged on glee. They might as well as have said it out loud: 'At least it wasn't us.'

'I'll finish up here,' said Errol. 'You go and get yourself a brew back at the post.' Errol, like many others, thought a nice cup of tea with lots of sugar after any kind of catastrophe was a help, but Ruby thought it was like putting a small plaster on your leg when it had turned gangrenous. She didn't argue today, though. The jewellery cut into her skin whenever she moved and she needed to hide the necklace somewhere.

'No one inside. Must have gone to the Tube shelter,' she said, tucking a strand of hair that had come loose behind her ear.

'You should have waited for us, you know?' Errol said. His cheeks glowed raw-sausage pink in the light of the flames, and it made her think of something being boiled alive. 'It's all very well acting brave, but you're just putting yourself at more risk.'

Ruby ignored him and lit a Player's. The smoke in her lungs might as well have some company.

'Oh look, I think that's the Richardsons,' he said. Further down the road some of the neighbours were gathering around the couple as they walked towards the house.

'I better get back to the post and file a report,' said Ruby, quickly.

'But they'll want to thank—'

'I'll check on them tomorrow,' she said, already moving away.

The frame of the house next to the Richardson's began to creak and crumble in the fire, drowning out Errol. He'd never understand; it was easy to be brave when you weren't quite sure about living.

2

Kitty

Kitty was as surprised as ever to see that the India Forum was still standing. The bombers were fond of this part of London. After being caught up waiting in the queue for rations, she'd hurried through the streets of Bloomsbury as quickly as she could, the spectral white paint on lamp-posts and kerbs guiding her way as dusk gave way to night. The fall of light today took her back briefly to the countless sunsets she'd seen in Bombay, amber hues surrendering to the shadows of night.

Now, with the raids, you could never be sure from one day to the next what you would find around the corner. One of the old grey Victorian homes down the street had been bombed to the foundations, leaving behind a gap-toothed grin of houses along the road.

This building that housed the India Forum must have been impressive once upon a time, but now it was more like a palace courtesan clinging onto her glory days. There were layers of crusty paint on the window frames and the flower beds had been reincarnated as vegetable patches. Evidently someone had dug for victory and found it lacking. Kitty knew better than to linger outside the Forum. She hurried inside, away from prying *Angrez* eyes.

Kitty was greeted with the sight of Mandalji, standing at

the foot of the wide, dishevelled staircase, his grey-speckled head bowed. From the angle she was standing at, it looked as though he was talking to himself. It wouldn't have been the first time. But then there was another voice. 'You'll be fined next time, you know?' said a young woman.

'Ah, Keerthanaben,' Mandalji called out to Kitty. He always called her by her real name, but it still sometimes took her by surprise. She didn't like it; it made her think of her father.

'This is Miss Ruby Thacker,' said Mandalji. Then he waved his hand vaguely towards Kitty, oblivious to the mention of a fine. 'Keerthanaben here will be able to help you.' Before he'd even finished his sentence, he was halfway down the hall and disappearing into his office.

As she moved towards Kitty, the hallway light caught the curve of the young woman's tin helmet and the forest of bobbled wool on her ARP uniform. 'Yes, Miss . . .' The warden held out her hand.

'Mrs Akhtar. Is there something wrong?' said Kitty. She caught herself and ironed out the hint of irritation in her voice. She could feel the pull of the work waiting for her in the library room. They were behind on the preparation for tomorrow's big India Forum meeting as it was. Mandalji, as the president of the India Forum, always left the preparation until the last minute, in case any late news or updates came in from India, and they'd be up for hours now putting together an agenda and writing his final speeches. 'One of your colleagues came to inspect the building a few weeks ago.' She unbuttoned her tweed coat. 'He said we had followed all the air-raid precautions correctly.' Everyone found the ARP wardens annoying; 'jobsworths', Kitty's neighbour called them.

'Well, as I was telling Mr Mandal, it's the front room,' she said, walking towards the library, gas mask hanging in her left hand. As she passed by, Kitty caught the scent of rose and lemon, incongruous with her fusty uniform. 'The light's leaking out.'

'Oh, I see.' Kitty joined her at the library door, hoping this would be wrapped up quickly. 'Well, I will make sure it's fixed.'

'It's quite all right. Best I show you myself. It's regulations.' The warden pushed the door open as if she owned the place and walked in. The hinges squeaked with reluctance. Didn't these ARP busybodies have anything better to do? They'd been so careful to follow the precautions, the last thing the India Forum needed was unwanted attention.

'Do the lights need to be on in this room? Where d'you all usually shelter?' Today was the day, Kitty thought: it won't be a bomb that kills me, it will be a long, slow death by ARP interrogation.

'Mr Mandal might have been using the library earlier, but he has gone into his office now.' Kitty kept her voice as even as she could. 'He usually stays there, or in one of the rooms upstairs, even after the raids begin. He prefers it to shelter-ing in the basement.' So did Kitty, for that matter, taking her chances here on the ground floor rather than sitting for hours surrounded by damp bricks and the coarse smell of coal with nothing but the mice for company. She and her hus-band Haseeb – who was still at work – rarely went to the Underground shelter, where sleep was broken by noise and fetid human odours, or by people eyeing Haseeb, talking – loud enough that they could hear – about people taking bloody liberties or leaving space for British women and children, 'not the bloody Italians'. Even that had long since stopped being funny.

The warden looked at her, eyes wide with – she wasn't sure

what exactly. Apathy, contempt? 'There, you see,' Miss Thacker said, pointing upwards as she moved across the room.

Someone at the India Forum had pinned black paper across every sash window, but a corner had come loose. How had she missed that? As a child back in Bombay she'd been scared of the dark, glad when it was warm enough to sleep on the balcony, out in the open air, but now it was light that was the enemy. The danger of a shard of candlelight, the peril of an errant bulb left on.

Just then Mandalji rushed back into the library, oblivious to either of them. 'Where's my pen?' Miss Thacker gave him a bemused look as he tornadoed around the two of them, turning over papers on the large mahogany table that took up most of the floor space, scanning the edges of the bookshelves and grumbling under his breath. Kitty found the pen in its usual place, lying on one of the chairs, and handed it back to him. He nodded vaguely by way of thanks and hurried out again.

Outside, the air-raid sirens started to wail.

Across the other side of the table, Miss Thacker was taking in the art on the walls. Kitty watched her as she looked at the patchwork of the cultures and languages of India. Kitty had helped to select some of them: a Thanjavur piece from the South featuring Lord Krishna and his consort Rukhmuni, both drenched in gold foil; a Rajput painting donated by the Maharaja of Baroda, filled with doe-eyed women who looked on patiently; a photograph of a Calcutta courtyard filled with rows of saris hung on washing lines like fallen kites.

'You're new to the warden post?' said Kitty, stacking the papers back into a neat pile.

'Yes, still learning the ropes.' Miss Thacker's eyes moved to the mishmash of leatherbound books on the old shelves, battened to stop them falling out during bombing. As she looked down to the lowest volumes, the pale nape of her neck peeked out from her collar.

Kitty climbed onto a chair and reached towards the window, hoping that it would be enough to convince the warden to leave, but instead she stood and watched. Kitty managed to stretch up and pin the black paper back into place, then stepped back down.

The young woman's gaze had turned towards the table, where there was a pile of the latest political pamphlets that Mandalji had written and printed, emblazoned with rousing headlines: *'United Towards India's Democratic Freedom!' 'The Compelling Case for Independence!'*

'What is it that you do here, Mrs Akhtar?' The warden pronounced her name 'Actor'.

'We lobby for Indian Independence, mainly. Help Indians in England when they need it.' Kitty didn't elaborate further. They welcomed help from British and Indians alike here, but she knew to be wary when strangers asked questions. Indians were one thing, but Angrez were another. The India Forum was scrutinized by the authorities, everyone knew it. War or not, everyone was a potential traitor.

Kitty went and stood by the library door, hoping the warden would take the hint. Outside the ack-ack guns rattled in the distance. She swallowed her fear, wondering whether Haseeb had made it home or taken shelter elsewhere. She'd be stuck here for the night now, but at least she had work to keep her mind busy and Mandalji nearby. 'Well, I'm sure you'll be wanting to get back to your post, Miss Thacker. Sounds like we're not alone.' Kitty forced the corners of her mouth into a smile, then made a point of walking back into the hallway to hurry her unwanted guest along.

Opening the heavy front door a crack and letting in the cutting January cold, she hoped Miss Thacker would take her cue to go, but instead she held Kitty's gaze. 'Well, good night, Mrs Akhtar.'

'Good night,' Kitty said, as she watched her walk away into the darkness.

*

The next day, Kitty was glad to see that despite the cold and the recent raids, there was a good turnout for the India Forum meeting.

'*Dekho*, Mrs Sucking-on-Lemons is here again,' Haseeb whispered to Kitty, brushing his hand against hers. They looked over at Mrs Symington-Lamont, who was standing in the middle of the India Forum hallway. Kitty watched as the woman bathed Mandalji in simpering words, ignoring everyone else.

'Do you think she'll realize that Mandalji has the same level of interest in her as he does in his right shoe?' Kitty stifled a yawn. The raids had gone on for hours last night.

Haseeb smiled.

'*Chaal*,' Kitty said to her husband. Together they showed the last of the visitors into Mandalji's office. It was actually two rooms knocked into one and could seat up to thirty, or forty if they were feeling particularly ambitious. There were other India Forums all over the country but this one was the headquarters, and its meetings usually drew a crowd. An assortment of Indian and English people: dock workers, politicians, civil servants, students, writers, professionals, BBC Overseas programmers; even the occasional Indian prince had been known to show up. Today was no exception, the room a swathe of suits and dhotis, saris and wool coats. People took their seats on the mismatched and maltreated chairs.

Haseeb headed to the front of the room, ready to help anyone who needed assistance or to translate questions from

Hindi and Urdu into English. Even here in the formal setting of the meeting, there was an urgency to his long strides, as though every step took him closer to freedom. Kitty believed in the fight just as he did, though sometimes it was hard not to wonder what impact their work was going to have in the middle of a war. She put on her spectacles, ready to take the minutes. Despite the crowd, a chill clung to the air; she tugged at the silk scarf at her neck, wishing she'd worn a sweater instead of a blouse. Mandalji stood at his lectern waiting for everyone to settle, his tall frame expanding into the space, his jaw set so firmly you'd need pliers to prise it apart.

'Good afternoon. I am Jayant Mandal, president of the India Forum. Thank you all for coming today,' he began in English. 'I know it is getting difficult to travel with all the raids, but our fight for *swaraj* – Home Rule for India – must continue regardless.'

As Mandalji carried on his speech, Kitty heard the panelled door at the back of the room open. A young woman in a half-length fur coat and green pillbox hat came into the room, dark locks framing her face.

It took Kitty a moment before she realized: the ARP warden from the night before, clearly off duty now. Miss Thacker, that was it. She watched the woman take a seat at the back. In her civilian clothes she looked younger tonight. Funny how that stiff ARP uniform could make anyone look old. Kitty glanced down at her notebook, annoyed to see a drip of blue ink blotting her clean page.

'Now to the order of the day,' said Mandalji. 'Our dear brother Shehab Hashim – a journalist by day, Indian freedom fighter by night – has been imprisoned at Canterbury for two weeks. What is his crime, you might ask?' Mandalji took off his thick-framed glasses, looking each attendee in the eye. 'Merely refusing to join the war effort. He came here to London to report the news, to help his home country. Now he finds himself locked up by a British government which asks Indians to fight alongside them in war, in the name of democracy, when they will not afford India the same rights. As Mahatma Gandhi and Jawaharlal Nehru rightly say, this is most definitely an imperial war.' Murmurs of agreement from the audience.

Kitty shifted in her seat as the crowd whispered around her. While Mandalji headed up the fight in Britain, he had close contact with Gandhi and Nehru back in India. It should not have worked, the two leaders of the Independence fight: Nehru, the Anglophile and firebrand, brought up with servants and boarding schools, and Gandhi, the middle-class lawyer turned loin-clothed ascetic. Yet somehow, they had led the country closer to freedom than ever.

'Just like Shehab Hashim, anyone from the Commonwealth who has been in the country for more than two years will be conscripted.' Kitty's mouth went dry. She caught Haseeb's eye a moment, then turned away, worried that her face would betray her concern. They had both been in England for almost two years now; they knew it was only a matter of time before he would be called up too.

'Why should any Indian have to give their lives for the Empire's battle?' Mandalji continued. 'No matter. We have weapons of our own. Those of us who are able must continue to write to Shehab's Member of Parliament; the details will be provided after the meeting.'

Mandalji called on the attendees to donate if they could, write letters if they couldn't. If the British government wanted to make an example of Shehab, then so would they. The India Forum would show the authorities that they couldn't force them to fight.

Out of the corner of her eye, Kitty saw Miss Thacker lean

forward, listening attentively. Kitty's gaze collided with hers and they each smiled politely before looking away.

After the meeting ended with questions from the audience, many of the group left, hurrying home or to shelters before the blackout began. Kitty and Haseeb were usually the last to leave; luckily their flat was only a short walk away.

'It was a good turnout today,' said Haseeb, brushing her arm as he came over. 'In the middle of all this.' 'All this' was the way he tended to describe the bombing raids, as though he couldn't bring himself to admit that they were in an actual war zone.

'It shows that people are dedicated. Almost as dedicated as you.' Kitty gave a tired smile.

She scanned the room, surprised to see that Miss Thacker hadn't rushed off after the meeting but was instead standing in a corner sipping her drink. 'Did you see that lady over there?'

Haseeb followed Kitty's gaze. 'She's new?' he said.

'She's a new ARP warden for the area.' Kitty explained how Miss Thacker had come to the Forum the night before. Her eyes narrowed. 'Why's she suddenly decided she wants to help us?'

'She's probably bored. Or curious. Or both,' he said, looking around the room.

'Perhaps . . .'

'I should go and speak to Councillor Naismith,' Haseeb said, wandering off before she had a chance to gather her thoughts.

Kitty walked over to the tea table. 'Miss Thacker, hello.'

'Oh, hello,' the young woman said flatly.

On the table there were cups and saucers, sugar and milk, mismatched teapots filled with chai. Kitty poured herself a cup of the weak tea. They had to reboil the whole spices from previous batches and use powdered milk which gave it a chalky taste, but it was better than nothing. 'Please don't tell me we have fallen foul of another air-raid precaution?' She aimed for amiable but landed at awkward.

Miss Thacker peered at her over the brim of her cup. 'No.'

'You decided to come to one of our meetings, then?'

'I wanted to hear more about the India Forum's efforts,' she replied, slipping her gloved hand into her handbag and showing Kitty the pamphlet. She must have taken it from the desk the other night.

'You're interested in the work we do here, for Indian Independence?' Kitty took a sip, catching her lip on a small chip in the china.

'You seem surprised.' Miss Thacker looked around. 'But there seem to be all kinds of British people here, just like me.'

'That's true. But it's just that these are difficult times. You must be busy with your warden work? It's important, no?'

'Well, so is freedom.' Miss Thacker gave a tight smile.

Outside, it had started to rain, rattling like grains of rice on the windowpane. Less chance of a bombing raid if there was a lot of cloud, at least.

Kitty took the woman in. She wasn't classically pretty. Her eyes were a fraction too small, her figure just a little abundant to be fashionable. But she had smooth skin, and good make-up could carry you far in youth. And more than that, there was a raw, even visceral energy to her. The fur on her coat was luxurious with a slick sheen to it, not the matted, cheap sort she sometimes saw; a smartly tailored skirt, real silk stockings. Perhaps she came from family money, although she didn't *sound* as though she did. Kitty had spent enough time with her fellow Oxford chums to know the difference.

'Has this young lady passed the test?' said Satyajit, putting out his hand as he came towards them. 'Hello, I am Satyajit Deol, pleased to meet you.'

'Miss Thacker,' she smiled politely. 'The test?' she said, glancing at Kitty in confusion.

Kitty didn't know Satyajit well. He had only come to the India Forum a couple of times, months apart, because he was apparently a travelling pedlar. No one seemed to know much about him, and they were too polite to ask him why he had a Hindu first name and a Sikh surname. There was a rumour that he had a middle name, Muslim at that; unusual, almost unheard of, in a culture where names often denoted religion. Even his age was difficult to discern. Kitty suspected he was in his early twenties like her, but the dark circles around his eyes aged him a little. Not only that, but he spoke excellent English. Most of the pedlars came from poor, rural areas of India, with broken English at best, picked up on their travels.

Kitty looked at the young woman and said, 'He's just joking.'

'Am I?' he said playfully.

'We always try to spend more time with people who are new to the meetings,' Kitty said quickly. Why was he trying to give the game away? The whole point was to be subtle. Across the room, Haseeb was still deep in conversation with Councillor Naismith.

'I've been made to feel very welcome so far,' Miss Thacker said, encouragingly. Kitty arched her eyebrow.

'We've got to make sure people are here for the right reasons too,' said Satyajit, smoothing his tie. Satyajit dressed like a gentleman. Even though his jacket had seen better days and the tweed was a little bobbled, his handkerchief was always neatly folded in his breast pocket to a sharp point, his shoes polished to a gleam.

Miss Thacker blinked. 'What d'you mean?'

'Well,' said Kitty. 'The British authorities regard us as threats, especially with the war. So we tend to be wary . . .' She played with the edge of the saucer with her thumb.

Miss Thacker blushed. 'You're trying to work out if I'm a government spy?' She gave a laugh that wasn't entirely convincing.

'But of course you're not, are you?' Satyajit's tone was warm but there was something darker beneath.

Miss Thacker looked at him, then at Kitty. Flashing a smile, she said, 'No, of course not, I'm just here for the free tea.'

'I'm not sure I believe you,' said Satyajit with a grin, 'the tea's awful.' His eyes glinted.

Miss Thacker regarded him with an unreadable expression. 'I came here the other day on my warden rounds and thought the pamphlet on Independence was interesting,' She finally shrugged. 'But if you'd rather I left . . .'

'No,' said Satyajit, 'of course you can stay.' He turned to Kitty. 'As long as you don't object?'

She gave a tight smile of condescension.

'So, you're an ARP warden?' Satyajit said.

'Yes, that's right, my post's a few streets away.'

'And you live around here too?' he asked.

Miss Thacker explained that she lived off the Caledonian Road.

'And where did you say you lived again, Satyajitbhai?' said Kitty. She'd asked him once before and he had waved his hand around vaguely and muttered something about 'the east'.

'Hmm? Oh, my work takes me all over.' Before Kitty had a chance to probe further, he'd already moved things on. 'So, Miss Thacker, what did you think about the meeting?'

'You mean all that about the conscription call for Indians?' she said, then gave a sigh. 'Doesn't really surprise me. The government's been happy enough to let the docks and the East End get the worst of the bombs on the front line.' With all the essential goods coming in and out by the river, the Nazis had found their sweet spot for dropping firebombs.

'Mr Mandal wants to support those people as well, though,' said Kitty, a firm tone in her voice. Mandalji was a socialist at heart, so far to the left he was practically lopsided. From the slum dwellers down by the docks to those in Bombay or Delhi, he fought for them all. 'But there is another reason we don't want to fight. Mahatma Gandhi and the Indian Congress have been clear, non-violence is the path to freedom. It's what we call *ahimsa.*'

'Oh yes, that's *their* strategy,' Satyajit scoffed. 'Doesn't mean it's the right one.'

'Well, Mandalji agrees—'

'We've been down this non-violent route before.' Satyajit spoke over her. 'Yet here we are, fighting conscription into someone else's war.'

Kitty stared at him. Why did he even bother to come to the Forum if that's how he felt?

He smiled, addressing Miss Thacker. 'Just try to come to the meetings with an open mind.'

Kitty found herself following suit, as though they were both in court pleading their cases to this young woman. 'Our way has worked so far, though. We're closer to Independence than we've ever been.'

Satyajit gave a cool laugh. 'It's working? Restrictions on our press – even before the war began. People dying for protesting against the British. Indians expected to take every *lathi* strike and blow against them.'

'Lathi?' Miss Thacker asked.

'Bamboo sticks.' His eyes darkened. 'Good for building things, not so good for bones.'

Kitty found herself trying to catch Miss Thacker's attention. The Englishwoman seemed to find this entanglement quite amusing.

'Well, perhaps now's not the time for this discussion,' Kitty said, glancing at Miss Thacker. Airing Forum differences in front of strangers was never wise.

'I should probably be going anyway,' said Miss Thacker. 'I've just finished the last of the free tea.' There was a playful glint in her eye, waving her empty cup in the air towards Satyajit, who conceded with a good-natured nod.

The young woman gathered her coat and bag, saying her goodbyes. Kitty and Satyajit stood awkwardly together as she left.

'Do you believe her?' said Kitty, continuing in English. She still wasn't sure which Indian language Satyajit spoke.

'She hasn't given me a reason not to,' he said, straightening the cuffs of his jacket. 'Besides, she could be quite useful.'

Kitty watched him walk away. Useful for what, exactly?

3

Ruby

Ruby's ARP post was practically Buckingham Palace compared to some: a metro-tiled basement in a requisitioned insurance building. Some unlucky wardens worked in nothing better than a glorified pine bus shelter.

'Here she comes,' said Stub, the head warden. 'Ruby with the emerald eyes.'

'And the diamond tongue that'll cut through anything,' said Errol, pulling darts off the board, his grin showing off his tea-stained teeth.

'Evening, Stub. Errol. Left all your good jokes at home again, did you?'

'Oooh,' said Errol, putting on a high-pitched voice, 'who pinched all the elastic out of your knickers, then?'

Ruby ignored him, pouring from her thermos liquid that looked and smelled more like boiled cigarette ash than coffee into a mug and warming her hands against it. She took a seat next to Stub at the small table in the middle of the basement.

'Anything we should be aware of before we start?' she said. Always worth checking whether the buildings were where they'd last left them.

'It was a quiet one last night,' said Stub, picking another card for his solitaire game.

Errol gave a laugh. 'I'll say. I haven't slept so well since the ARP training lectures.'

The wireless was on low volume as usual. It had been damaged in a recent raid, and now every bloody presenter sounded like they had a fifty-a-day-smoking habit, wheezing the news out. The songs were muffled, too. On the wall there was a large map for their post, another spanning the whole of London. When the raids had first started, they'd marked all the incidents on the maps with pins, but there'd been so many now that they'd fallen behind. They barely got the details down into the scruffy logbook if they were lucky, a task usually left to Ruby.

She opened the book to check if the day wardens had left any notes for them. Gone were the long, drawn-out nights of the early months of the war, before the raids had started, with nothing to worry about except who would win at whist and when the only thing you were likely to die of was boredom.

'You and Errol cover north of the Euston Road,' said Stub. 'Think you two can manage that without ballsing it up?'

Ruby rolled her eyes, though at least here at the post the men never gave you bother. She had worked in a typing pool when she'd first left school, learnt the best way to manoeuvre a pile of paper close to your chest when passing men in the office, check behind you before you bent down to pick up a pen, make sure you were never caught in the corridor on your own with Mr Simpson.

When Ruby had first arrived at the post, you could see it all over their faces. A bloody woman. Someone else to take care of while the world burned. Ruby soon put paid to that, getting stuck in with the work as well as the swearing. Then, of course, on her warden rounds, some people couldn't imagine a woman coming to help them, even after they saw her diving into bombed buildings right alongside Stub and Errol.

'I'll take the easterly streets once George finally turns up,' Stub continued. Not that George would be much use, he was all talk, usually dodging the real danger for a cup of tea.

She rubbed her hands together, taking the rough wool blanket from the back of the chair and draping it over her legs. Though she always wore a jumper under her shirt, the authorities didn't bother to provide a warm winter coat or anything else that would stop you catching your death.

'That lazy bomb's been cleared from Ossulston Street,' said Stub. Lazy bombs were their nickname for unexploded HEs, another delight of the blitzkrieg.

The mention of the bomb reminded her about the Richardsons. She still had that necklace, hidden away in the back of her wardrobe. Maybe for some the guilt would have taken hold, but not for Ruby. She had a rule: only take from people that had too much of everything.

'Fancy a game?' said Errol, pulling up a chair on the opposite side to Stub.

'No,' said Stub. 'I'll beat you and then you'll get in a right strop and I'll have to look at your face gawping at me, like a ruddy wet tea-towel.'

'Suit yourself.' Errol took a slurp of his drink, wiping the corner of his thin moustache with the back of his hand. It was the only thing he had in common with Errol Flynn but somehow the nickname had stuck. Errol the warden had about as much star presence as a ration coupon.

A man called out from upstairs. 'I'll go,' Stub sighed, rubbing his hand across his rubbery face. He climbed up the steps.

Ruby pulled out the pamphlet she'd taken last week from the India Forum. It talked about the fight for swaraj – or

Home Rule for India – and set out the case for a free country run by Indians. She'd never paid much attention to whatever was going on in India, even before the war. Nothing to do with her.

'What's that, then?' Errol asked, speckles of tea landing on the pamphlet as he blew into his mug.

'From the India Forum, that building over on Endsleigh Street. D'you know it?'

Stub came back down the stairs and grabbed the tools from the cupboard. 'Got to go and help someone get into their shelter.' The doors sometimes got jammed during raids; half the time they ended up helping people get out of them rather than into them.

'The Indians? Keep themselves to themselves,' Errol shrugged. 'What do they do over there exactly?' he said, taking the pamphlet.

'They lobby the government for Independence. Fundraising, that kind of thing.'

'Good luck to 'em, I say. But I don't think much of their timing. We're being blown to bits and that Gandhi fella with his loincloth and his mate Nehru are just stood around going on about Independence. That Indian National Congress need to wait their turn.'

Ruby stared at him, surprised by how much he knew about it all. 'They seem to have quite a lot of support, though. The Forum, I mean.'

'Hmm. Not that many Indians over here, mind.'

She gripped her mug, swirling the dark pool of liquid around. 'Not just Indians, though, fair few British men were there too. A couple of wives and all.'

The telephone rang just as the air-raid sirens began their wail. Errol stood up, chair scraping along the floor, and walked over to answer it. Ruby put her mug of coffee down with a thunk, leaving a dirty half-crescent on the pine table. Time to get to work.

The traitorous moon was full that night, the skies cloudless. Easier for the enemy to find its target. They made their way along the street, waiting for their eyes to adjust to the dimness. Ruby's fingertips scuffed along rough red brick and cool plaster as she walked the pavement. Errol pedalled slowly on his bike beside her.

Sometimes it felt as though the city was no longer theirs, as though they were the invaders, the ones who were squatting, with buildings boarded up and unfamiliar buses, brown and grey and dark like dried blood, loaned to the city from all over the country to support the hard work of the good old red double-deckers.

'Let's go down here,' said Errol, when they reached the front of St Pancras Old Church. The air was tainted with sulphur from the nearby coal depot.

They carried on until they reached the basement shelter on King Street. Ruby gave him a nod and stood in the doorway, Errol perched behind her on the steps.

'Oh, here's Ruby. Look, and Errol too.' They heard a familiar call from the gloom inside.

'Evening, Mrs Fernsby,' she said. Ruby tried to ignore the smell; stagnant water and warm bodies.

'How are you then?' Errol piped up from over Ruby's shoulder.

They could see the glow from Mrs Fernsby's cigarette now. In her other hand she held her granddaughter, who'd been born in the shelter two months before.

'Can't complain, love. Although this little one's been making more of a racket than all the Luftwaffe combined,' she said.

'That dark fella was here, weren't he?' said a young man who sat in the corner. He was referring to a man from Jamaica, Gilbert, who was an ARP warden in the ward next to theirs. Some people were less than keen to take orders from anyone, let alone someone who wasn't white. Gilbert had told Ruby he didn't know whether he was coming or going sometimes. In some of his local shelters, Gilbert had said, they treated him like a lucky omen: 'But at least then they listen when I tell them to get into their shelters.'

Ruby didn't say anything as the man in the corner carried on. 'Trying to get us to make room for more. The cheek. It's already cramped enough as it is.'

In this part of the city, they were used to the East Enders drifting their way, with nothing in their suitcases but a few clothes and a lifetime of grief; hair aged with dust, or shock, they couldn't always tell. People like Mrs Fernsby had become territorial about their shelters, like football fans who only care whether their own team succeeds. Although they were concerned about the other boroughs, they became blinkered. Weren't so understanding when you helped people on the boundaries of their wardens' post, in case it took you away from saving them. As far as they were concerned, they were definitely not 'all in it together'.

Errol exchanged some tips with Mrs Fernsby about the races, both liking a little flutter down the Walthamstow dogs when they could. 'Put a shilling on Royal Aurora,' he said with a mischievous tap of his nose. 'But you didn't hear it from me.'

'Royal Aurora it is,' said Mrs Fernsby with a wink.

Across the city, the faint but sporadic drone of bombers and gunfire continued.

'We'd better get on,' said Ruby. Errol nodded.

As they made it back to street level, multiple ambulance sirens began bellowing over each other in the distance, and then the silhouette of a single plane, getting closer. They looked up. 'Is it one of ours?' She had to raise her voice over the noise of the engine, so close it thrummed in her chest.

'Come on,' he shouted, mounting his bike and dashing towards a narrow alleyway.

Ruby ran behind, the sound of the engine getting louder as they ducked into the passage.

An explosion.

Crouching in the alleyway, Ruby looked up just as phosphorescent gunfire burned holes in the sky. A blaze had erupted, the sky alight with flames and flashes. It looked like the end of the world.

'Quick,' she said, dashing from the alleyway in time to see the bombs fall; a domino effect as the explosion from each one lit the pilot's way for the next.

The noise of the plane ebbed away. 'It's heading eastwards,' said Errol. 'Ruby, wait until—' Ruby ignored Errol's shouts and ran. There was no time to wait. Those homes had families in them, she knew that, but in her panic she couldn't remember who they were or whether they usually sheltered at the Tube station. The sky was ablaze with light now, the whirr of more planes, the shrieking hiss of bombs as they plunged onto houses down the way. Tracer bullets, flashes of red firing up into the sky.

Ruby raced down the street, her eyes following the dark shadow of another bomber as it flew over a house. The building seemed to hold its breath, then expand as the bomb exploded. So much broken glass that it chimed as it crashed onto the pavement.

Errol was there now, and they ran towards the house, blowing their whistles as they'd been taught to do in training, warning others of fire, for all the good it did. The planes seemed to have disappeared.

'There's no chance of getting in there,' said Errol, when they reached the blaze. Some people had come out of their houses, huddling together in thick coats, hands over mouths, murmuring comments.

'The house down the road, though, I think I saw a bomb fall behind it,' said Ruby, looking at number 68. She turned towards the neighbours who were clustered in a little group. 'Did they shelter here tonight?' she asked, remembering the Anderson shelter in the garden. She tried to recall the family. A surly grandfather and his daughter Iris, wasn't it?

An older woman, curlers in her hair, huddled in her night-gown, came over. 'They had some visitors too,' she said, breathlessly. Ruby had seen this sometimes, people bordering on euphoric from the excitement of a raid, the nerves racing through their bodies. It was almost indecent, the way they got a thrill from it.

'What about the other side?'

The woman shook her head.

'We could try and get in?' Ruby said to Errol.

'Well, it'll be a while before any of the other services get here,' he said, putting his hand to his chin and leaving a char-coal mark. The least of his problems. 'All right then, let's give it a try.'

They first checked the houses either side, knocking on doors, asking those across the street if anyone had seen the inhabitants, if they knew whether anyone was sheltering there, or in the gardens. They knocked hard at number 68. No answer.

They couldn't see into the house because of the blacked-out windows. Usually around here people didn't tend to lock their doors, though the reasoning had changed over the years. Before, it had been safe enough not to have to; now it made it easier for ambulance services and dispersal units to get people out.

The door wouldn't budge. Errol took his coat and wrapped it around his hand. He smashed the small window at the top of the door, then carefully put his arm in and opened the latch.

Before they went in, their torches scanned the front room. Nothing looked like it had been disturbed. Good sign.

'I'll go and check upstairs,' said Errol.

Ruby would usually look for clues as to whether anyone was there. Was the kettle on the hob, was it still warm? Was there a pram in the hallway?

But before she had a chance to think about it, she saw that the wall at the back of the house had caved in. Ruby could just make out the silhouettes of the shrubs outside because of the light from the surrounding fires. She moved closer, then lifted a torch to the bricks that remained standing. A glint, something like a thick sludge, oozing down the wall. She touched it with her hand and it congealed on her finger. The texture of jam, she thought, absentmindedly.

No.

She stepped back in shock, her foot giving way on something soft.

On the floor was a bundle wrapped up like a gift, in layers of lace. A baby. Except that it collapsed when she tried to lift it. The tiny body inside was broken. It felt damp underneath. Her first thought was that it had wet itself, but no, it wasn't urine, it was blood.

Ruby's throat closed up. There was a stench, metallic and sulphuric; she could almost taste it on her tongue. She retched, thinking that she mustn't throw up here, not in this place with these poor people.

She took a deep breath, tried to calm her runaway heartbeat. She was scared to scan the area with her torch now. The beam of light never more unwelcome.

'How's the back of the . . .' Errol's voice trailed off. She couldn't believe how glad she was to hear his voice.

An ambulance siren grew louder outside. Too late.

'There was a baby,' she said quietly. 'Reenie, wasn't it?'

'Are you all right, Rube?' he said. His eyes looked hollowed out in the shadows.

She felt as though something was squeezing her lungs so tightly they might burst. Ruby pushed past him and stumbled out the house. She tried to gulp in fresh air, but the smouldering fires made her choke. Standing with her back against the wall across the street, she tried to steady herself. Bricks cool beneath her hands, she slowed her breathing. The cloud had descended, or perhaps it was bomb smoke; the gauzy moonlight struggled to break through now.

Errol came outside.

'I'm all right,' she said, before he had a chance to ask her again. Before he tried to say something nice and Ruby fell apart right there.

The ambulance crew arrived and Errol did his best to tell them what had happened.

'Here you go, love,' said a woman with dusty spectacles, who'd miraculously boiled a kettle in the midst of all the chaos. Ruby gazed at the tea, wishing that she'd poured her a cup of something far stronger.

'That was just so daring of you.' The woman beamed at her as if she was her own daughter. 'Going into these houses, never knowing if they'll come down around you.'

Ruby reached for her cigarettes but then stopped, remembering the smell of gas. The woman carried on talking but Ruby had to ball her fist to stop the impulse of her fingers reaching for a cigarette, the taste of it in her mouth, the spectre of smoke that wasn't there. She couldn't face even the smallest sip of tea.

After a few minutes, Errol came back over. The lady had disappeared.

*

Many hours later, after her shift had finally ended, Ruby reached home. The climb up the stairs to her flat took her an age, her muscles leaden, her jacket stiff with blood. Her flat-mate Alma had already left for work; the faint scent of toast lingered in the air.

Ruby took off her clothes by the front door, not wanting to be in them a minute longer. She had a wash and changed into her pyjamas. It took her three goes to light a cigarette, her hands were shaking so much. Finally she lit the tip, taking a long drag. Through the window, which she'd left ajar, she could hear a horse-drawn milk cart clattering past, two women having a chat.

She stretched her legs out on top of the bedcover, leaning up against a pillow. Towards the end of her shift, Errol, Stub, George and she had all gone back to help at number 68. For the two they could identify, the baby and her grandfather, she spoke to neighbours and wrote out their names on luggage tags. But then her pen ran out and she had to use a lipstick on the arms of the other victims, a mid-pink shade, so it wouldn't be mistaken for blood. For the rest they had to piece together the bodies, a morbid jigsaw. She had found a torso, broad at the chest; a slender leg, the stocking snagged; a left hand with a gold ring on it.

The rest they'd had to collect up with shovels and buckets.

Eyes scrunched tight, trying to barricade herself against the worst of her memories. She tried not to think about her brother Freddie, but he trespassed into her mind all the same: his sleek wooden coffin, velvet-lined, open casket, smaller than the length of her bed.

A voice rang out in her head, a memory from earlier. That woman with the spectacles who'd handed her the tea and said, 'That was just so daring of you.'

No, the bravest thing was living, wasn't it? Fear that the ones you care about could be taken away from you. Was that worse than the silence of death?

Ruby almost wished she was back on duty at the post now. You didn't have time to dwell on anything in a raid, even the war itself.

4

Kitty

Kitty finished scanning the shelves of the Bombay Empor-
ium. The sign outside the shop on Grafton Street said it sold
'fresh' spices, but she doubted that with the war restrictions.
The shelves were half empty but what was there – Kashmiri
chilli, nutmeg, black pepper, saffron – had taken her back to
childhood evenings, the table piled high with *daar bhaat* – or
biriyani if it was a special occasion – *samosa*, *bhajia* and *rotli*. She
quickly picked up the *jeeru* and *elchi* and paid for it, not wanting
to linger with the memories.

As she made her way home, Kitty ran through her mind all
the things she would have to do tomorrow. There were India
Forum meeting minutes to write up, for a start. She remembered that young warden woman who had turned up at the last
meeting, the sudden way that Miss Thacker began showing
an interest in the Forum. And then there was Satyajit's curious comment about her 'being useful'. Either way, the entire
exchange had left Kitty unsettled.

Dusk was falling, but the low cloud made the day look
darker still. By the time she arrived on her street, Cartwright
Gardens, she had to put her torch on to see the rest of the
way. Kitty followed the crescent of the road round, past the
small half-moon green where the railings had long since been
removed.

She approached her building. Kitty and Haseeb's Blooms-bury flat was sandwiched between two others, in what would once have been a large Victorian family home. The red bricks and black slates, the framed arch windows, all reminded her of the Dickensian houses she'd read about as a young girl back in Bombay.

The air-raid sirens started up. Kitty hurried up the steps. Sometimes Haseeb left work early to avoid the blackout; per-haps he was safe inside already?

She climbed the stairs, clutching her cloth shopping bag filled with rations and spices.

'Haseeb?' she called out from the hallway, but there was no answer. Trying to ignore the prickle of worry in her stomach, she went into the sitting room. Drawing the blackout curtains, Kitty waited as the wireless wheezed and crackled slowly to life. There was an item from the BBC's Eastern Service on; a man gave a book review in Hindi. Since the war began, more programmes had been run in a host of Indian languages, intended to bring the Commonwealth together, although sometimes it just made India feel further away than ever.

It hadn't been easy to find this flat. The first time Haseeb had gone out on his own looking for places to live, one woman had told him, as kindly as though she was declining a second cup of tea, 'I'm ever so sorry but we don't have blacks here.' The next time, he had taken Kitty along, draped in her finest clothes and best cut-glass accent. They had probably paid over the odds, the mink coat and Schiaparelli skirt suit con-vincing the landlords and ladies these were Indians who could afford the finer things, perhaps one of those modern maharajas and maharanis they'd seen in the newspapers who travelled around Europe on their royal jaunts.

Once she'd put the food away and started the fire, she gath-ered up the pages of the letter she'd written earlier, scanning the words again. All her news of England, first addressing her father, then adding a section at the end to her grandmother. Kitty used a ruler to fold it exactly in half, tucked it into a blank bond paper envelope and put it on top of the neat stack of all the other letters she'd never sent. Would her father ever want to contact her again? She wondered what they were both doing now, whether they were thinking of her, too. Kitty shut the drawer sharply.

She sat down on the sofa, pulling a blanket over her and staring into the fire. There'd been raids two nights in a row. The bombers seemed to be catching their breath now, just as London was, though everyone had to pray that they didn't come back twice as hard next time. One of the houses down the road had been bombed and a man had lost his legs. She'd walked past and heard people talking about it, but beneath the sadness, there was also a frayed edge of relief. *It wasn't me.* She'd swept the feeling away as quickly as she could. Kitty had thought about it for far longer than anyone should have to: that if there was a bomb, the flat above would come crashing down on them and they could be buried in an instant.

The air-raid siren stopped. She tensed, clutching the edge of the blanket. Was Haseeb still at work at his barristers' chambers?

She tried to listen to the radio, but it was impossible to follow the thread. Should she have gone to King's Cross station? Perhaps Haseeb went to a shelter near work?

If she was like this now, what would happen if he really was called up for military service and they weren't able to resist it? The months, perhaps years, they might spend apart. Kitty looked around the room, trying to find something else to focus on. Though it was filled with furniture, it felt cold and empty. There was an uncomfortable low-backed two-seater, made of mahogany with velvet upholstery, cross-hatched with age where the fabric had worn. The dining table was actually a desk, with legs at either end too narrow to tuck your legs under. Kitty had collected a bouquet of bruises where her knees had knocked against the hard wood whenever they'd had guests over for dinner and she and Haseeb had to perch at either end. There was a mother-of-pearl photo frame with a picture of them taken on their wedding day. There were no photos of family. They were too painful to look at.

She went over to the side table, where they kept their chess set. Anything to distract herself from wondering about Haseeb. It had been Kitty who had taught Haseeb how to play Shatranj, an early form of the game that had originated in India, not that you'd know it from the way the Oxford dons went on about it. Her father had the original version in his study, the pieces based on ancient army divisions: cavalry, infantry, elephantry and chariotry. Kitty and Haseeb had the modern, Western version. They would play each other regularly back in Bombay, but once the war started in London, inevitable delays to the day, from ration queues to bus route changes due to bombs, meant they could rarely play a game together. Kitty would make her move when Haseeb was at work, and the chessboard would lie untouched until the evening, when he could make his next play. When Kitty returned from a meeting at the India Forum, she would ponder her options. She stared at the pieces now but nothing came to her.

There was the familiar creak of the door, followed by the clink of keys in the enamel tray in the hallway, announcing Haseeb's return home.

He hurried in and kissed her, his lips cold against her cheek.

Kitty's gratitude fell away. 'You should have come home earlier, Haseeb,' she called out, as he went to the kitchen and washed his hands.

'I can't keep bringing all those heavy files back and forth, meri Kitabi,' he said, calling her by her nickname, meaning bookish, a play on her English name.

'I was worried.'

'Sorry, I lost track of time.'

She sighed, turning off the radio. There was no point pressing the issue. The main thing was that he was home. 'I'm going to make a *pulao* tonight.'

'With what?' he laughed, coming back into the room and pulling a jumper on over his work shirt and tie.

She nearly answered back 'rice and vegetables' but realized he meant, with which spices. '*Jeeru neh hardar*,' she replied in Gujarati.

'*Jeera aur haldi*,' he playfully corrected in Hindi. It was a joke between them, her Bombay Gujarati versus his Delhi Hindi, but today it simply served to annoy her more.

'The spices are probably older than me, but it should be fine.' The fact that she could make any food edible was miracle enough; she'd only learnt to cook since their marriage. Kitty had grown up with a cook and servants, so whatever she did manage was an achievement in itself.

She went and got him a glass of water. Then she opened the curtain a fraction and peeked out of the window. The buzz of faraway planes cut through the air; the chaotic beams of searchlights moved across the sky.

'Still working on the Masterson case?' she asked, trying to distract from the sounds outside.

'It's been postponed.' Haseeb took a sip of his drink. 'Masterson has absconded.' He shook his head wearily.

'Over a petty theft?' She raised her eyebrow.

'It's his fourth offence. Perhaps he didn't want to risk the jail time. Or he was simply drunk and forgot,' he shrugged.

Mostly Haseeb did magistrate court work: criminal damage, common assault and the like. It was not the type of work he wanted to do or had trained for at Middle Temple, but they both understood how things worked. Some older Indian lawyers like Womesh Chunder Bonerjee had made it all the way to the Privy Council, but it required far more experience. No one could be sure how an Indian face defending in a Crown Court case would fare, so Haseeb took whatever he could get.

'And of course, the Old Bailey case that came up yesterday went to Whittaker,' he said, referring to his English colleague. 'As usual.'

Kitty wished things were different, but a part of her was envious. She had the same training, the same qualifications, except that she had studied at Oxford and he at Cambridge, following in the footsteps of many wealthy Indians, Nehru and Gandhi included. Trying to practise law in England was pointless, though. It would be doubly hard for a woman. India wasn't much different, as she'd discovered before they'd left.

'Anything else coming through?' she said, watching Haseeb as he got up from the table and went into the kitchen.

'Maybe tomorrow,' said Haseeb quietly. 'I'll check with the clerk.'

She knew that it was wearing on him, the way she asked him about his work all the time. But Kitty missed it, and this was the only way to keep up with the law. She worried that if she didn't keep engaging her brain, applying all the things she'd worked so long and hard to learn, she'd forget it all. She held onto the hope that, somehow, she'd be able to practise again, in a free India. But what then? Would she even be free to be who she wanted?

5

Ruby

Usually, you'd pass by the four-floor India Forum building on Endsleigh Street without a second glance. You'd barely take in the worn-out rose bush or the black door, have no idea that, inside, it was all talk of rebellion and revolution. But as Ruby stood across the street and stubbed out her cigarette with her court shoe, there was something about this house; its black-eyed windows, its patchwork roof, the way it imposed over the street, as though it was glowering at her.

Inside the entrance, the stoic grandfather clock judged each visitor as they passed. Ruby went down the hallway into Mr Mandal's office, where all the meetings were apparently held. The house had dark wooden floors with the dull sheen of an onion skin, the rooms tinged with the toasted smell of old books.

She sat at the back of the room. Ruby had nothing else to do that evening; she'd finished a day shift at the warden post and had been bored sitting at home. She could have tried to get an early night, but every time she closed her eyes, the room spun and she could smell the stench of blood at number 68 again.

Rest in peace. *But what about the rest of us?*

Even before the war started, what they had lived in was not really peace, but denial. The sense that death was something that happened to other people, with foreign ways, who had

41

nothing to do with them. But the war had raised the dead, her brother Freddie included.

At least here at the India Forum, the way they talked about freedom and India, it was almost as if there was no war going on, and you could join in that make-believe that death was kept at bay. And besides, she hadn't forgotten about all those donations that Mr Mandal had talked about in his speech last time.

That Mrs Akhtar she'd spoken to was standing at the front of the room wearing a navy suit, a striped white-and-navy silk scarf tied with a flourish around her neck. Her make-up was pristine yet somehow appeared effortless. A slick of scarlet lipstick, a swish of liner. On some people it might have all looked like a costume, as though they were dressing up and pretending, but the Indian woman looked like she was born to it. It was funny, that; the way Mrs Akhtar acted like gentry. As though she was white.

The young man Ruby had also spoken to the other day, Mr Deol, sat on the other side of the room, the light glinting on the pomade in his dark hair as he talked to the man next to him. She couldn't work him out; had he really been worried that she was a spy, or was he just toying with her?

The meeting began as Mr Mandal shared the latest news from India, explaining how something called 'satyagraha' was still going on. 'The freedom of speech for Indians was curtailed long before the war. But why should we not converse in public about Independence? Our brave friends in India, personally selected by Gandhi, are undertaking *satyagraha* – civil disobedience – holding speeches in public spaces, practically inviting arrest in the name of freedom of speech. We will prevail. We will never be silenced!'

Murmurs of approval broke out around her. It was strange, Ruby thought, the way they all happily broke the law and

Indians seemed to support it. Everything she'd been taught growing up was flipped on its head. In India it was fine, even encouraged, to go against the authorities, to speak out against them, to openly risk arrest.

The discussion moved on to fundraising events that were going on in other parts of the country and upcoming meetings with prominent government figures. Mr Mandal also provided an update on the young man that he'd talked about last time, Shehab Hashim, stating that they were close to the target to pay for a lawyer. Hashim was still in prison for refusing conscription. 'We will never give up. We will strengthen our resolve even as the shadow of war hangs over us all,' said Mr Mandal, wrapping up his speech. A swell of clapping and cheering. Ruby looked on, bemused. Who in their right mind would take up a cause like this with a war going on?

Ruby watched as a young Indian woman in a green sari and a sad grey cardigan walked around the room with a cloth bag, as people dipped into pockets or handbags for a few shillings or pennies.

People milled about: there were a couple of finely dressed English gentlemen, as stiff as their starched collars; a group of young men in turbans, possibly students; some other Indian men who looked like dock workers, in dark wool trousers and threadbare pea coats.

Ruby poured herself some Indian tea and took a sip. The heat of the spice caught in the back of her throat.

She looked around for Mrs Akhtar, mainly to make sure she could avoid her. Ruby knew the lady still wasn't entirely convinced about her, wondering whether Ruby was about to expose the entire India Forum as fifth columnists. What a laugh. If the poor woman only knew how far from the truth she really was.

Mr Deol was deep in conversation across the room. He was chatting with a slim English gent in a pinstriped suit, all wiry fingers and bony wrists.

Just then, she saw Mr Mandal take the bag of collection money from the young woman. Ruby put down her cup and followed him into the hallway. She watched as he headed up the stairs. What was up there – more rooms, lodging for Mr Mandal, more money?

She heard him coming back down, his footsteps echoing on the stairs. Ruby stole back into the office and stood at the doorway as he passed. She scanned the room. Good, everyone was still immersed in conversation. Mrs Akhtar had her back to Ruby, pouring tea for someone.

Before she knew it, Ruby found herself moving through the empty hallway and hurrying up the stairs. No light on in the upstairs landing, only a row of three panelled doors, all closed. Breathless now, exhilaration spurring her on. She glanced downstairs; the hallway was still empty. Ruby tried the first door. Locked. She waited a moment, in case someone came to open it. Nothing.

Next door, same problem. As she moved along the hallway it got darker still, light from below fading into the recesses.

'Can I help you?'

Mrs Akhtar's voice.

Ruby turned around to see her standing halfway up the stairs, peering up at her. Think quickly.

She gently leant over the banister and took a deep breath to steady her voice. 'Oh, maybe you can help me. I was looking for the bathroom?'

Mrs Akhtar didn't say anything for a moment and simply stared. 'There's a toilet outside in the garden.'

Ruby gave an awkward nod and headed downstairs.

'Next time, do come and ask me if you're not sure about

something,' said Mrs Akhtar, and though her tone was measured, the look she gave Ruby was anything but.

Ruby went out into the back garden, glad of the chill in the air to cool her flushed cheeks. She lit a cigarette, reassured by the snap of the lighter. But it was dark outside and her hand wouldn't hold steady; she clung onto the cigarette with all her fingers to make sure she didn't drop it. Nerves fired through her body; the way she'd nearly been caught by Mrs Akhtar. Taking a purse or a necklace was one thing, but this? She threw the butt away and brought her heel down hard, stamping out her thoughts.

Ruby went back inside, and was about to take her coat from the stand and leave when Mr Deol called out, 'Miss Thacker?'

'Hello,' she said.

'Leaving already?'

'It's been a long day,' she said, glancing down at the floor.

'Please, do stay a little longer.' His tongue soft on the 'd' because of his accent. 'You will be doing me a great favour. There are only so many times I can hear Mr Dhaliwal's story about how he fought off an entire army of German officers single-handedly on the Western Front.'

She looked around. Even after the encounter with Mrs Akhtar, wasn't a roomful of strangers preferable to going out into the darkness? To being alone?

In the library, Mr Deol handed her a tea. 'Have you been in England long?' said Ruby. She put the cup down, not yet trusting herself to hold it steady.

'A while,' he murmured. 'When I first arrived here, none of us thought that Europe would actually go to war.'

'No, I suppose not.' People had thought the Führer was some kind of '*eine kleine*' Charlie Chaplin at first. Some said it crept up on them. As though Hitler had put his hand out like a pickpocket when no one was looking and just snatched up

Austria, Czechoslovakia and Poland. But everyone could see it just suited them better to look the other way. Before, the world, even France, had been a faraway place. She could barely point out Germany on a map back then. But once the war began, even with the might of the British Empire behind the country, the world compressed. Their neighbours, welcome or not, were inching ever closer.

'And you didn't think about going home, after France fell?' she said, thinking back to last summer, the despair across the nation as their ally was forced to surrender. The French had joined the conflict as a proud Great War victor, but all that bluster had soon disappeared. Like the adolescent who lied about his age, shipped off and armed with little more than a rifle and all the swagger he could manage.

'I have things to do here in England,' he said, looking around the room. 'Besides, the war might be over soon.' Ruby wanted him to be right, but she'd also heard enough stories of the Great War from her parents to know that they could have a long road ahead of them yet.

Across the room, Mrs Akhtar was looking at her, but her eyes darted away as soon as Ruby caught her gaze. 'And you could be conscripted soon,' Ruby said, turning back towards Mr Deol, 'like that man they were talking about earlier.'

'Well, of course.' He gave a cool laugh. 'But we don't have freedom in India, so why would I fight in your war?'

'Not all of us British are the same, you know,' she said, curtly. After all, the rich were fighting for themselves, the rest were fighting for everyone's freedom.

'No, of course not.' Mr Deol's tone softened. 'I didn't mean that.'

She decided not to dwell on it. 'So, this whole conscription business. You'd risk prison and—' The rest of the question came to a halt on Ruby's tongue: *risk being called a conchie and treated like a traitor?* It didn't matter what the cause was, all conscientious objectors were lumped together.

'It is no worse than the risks we take back in India to fight for freedom.'

She nodded, looking down at the table.

'What do you think of the work we do here?' he said, putting his cup down.

She glanced at him. He seemed more relaxed this evening, not trying to catch her out. A faint speckle of stubble along his jaw, the full mouth, that large nose – a confident nose, you might say. For all his charm, there was nothing polite about his face.

Ruby's mind went blank. She hadn't given it much thought. 'To be honest, Mr Deol, it seems like hard work. All that lobbying you do.'

He laughed, eyes narrowing. 'Not *all* of us do that. Mandalji thinks that's the way to get what we want. But there are other means. And you can call me Satyajit. Jit, for short.'

'Jit,' she repeated with a nod. 'What kind of other means?'

Just then a young man with round spectacles came over and said something to Mr Deol in whatever language they shared. Though neither of them looked at her, something about the hard tone of their laughter made her unsure. Were they talking about her?

'I'm sorry,' he said, as the bespectacled man walked away.

'It's all right.' She glanced towards the door. 'Anyway, I should make a dash for it while the skies are clear.'

'And will we see you here again?'

She stared at him. 'Perhaps, yes.'

6

Kitty

Kitty had marvelled like a child when she'd seen snow for the first time. She had been in her room at Oxford when the sparkling white crystals had begun to fall. She hurried outside and forgot to put a coat on; it had tingled on her tongue and melted in her palm. Now, standing outside the India Forum in the dull afternoon light, she had the same feeling of wonder. But the large flakes looked grey, like ash. As with everything, her mind was brought back to war. How even the thick clumps of snow looked as though the clouds had burst open during a bombing.

The raids had been relentless. London set alight might otherwise have been beautiful: a saffron glow across the buildings, flashes of fire across the sky. Kitty's mind was growing accustomed to the sights. That morning, as she'd walked past a building sliced in half like a birthday cake, barrage balloons glinting in the sunlight, she'd seen a trail of long red hair poured across a pile of rubble in the street. Workers were trying to recover the woman's body, brick by brick, uncovering a lifeless hand, a cold limb. It was only when Kitty had been walking for a few minutes that she realized how effortlessly she had banished it from her thoughts, as though what she'd seen was nothing more remarkable than a sparrow perched on a tree branch.

The India Forum was for the most part a haven from the

ravages of war. Mandalji's energy was infectious and they could see the light of Independence ahead of them, when peace came. If it came. For now, they'd created their own little India in London. Kitty stood on the steps thinking of all that they'd achieved.

'Are you trying to catch a cold?' A tall, turbaned man with a peppered beard paused beside her. 'Come now,' he smiled, holding the door open for her.

Kitty put down her things in the hallway, wrestling with the weight of winter – heavy Harris tweed coat, itchy scarf, thick wool jumper. The hallway was still festooned with colourful saris that had been hung up to cover the walls after the Holi festival celebrations. Back in Bombay, they would have been out in the streets or even at the beach, playfully throwing coloured powder at each other; here they settled for coloured fabric.

She went into the kitchen where two other women were bustling around. Despite the fact that women were fighting for freedom just as the men were, some things were still drawn along traditional lines. The women were both sari-clad, with thick sweaters over their blouses, hard leather boots sticking out beneath the softly draped fabric. One was stirring the tea, hand on hip, while the other put the milk in. Though she'd seen them once or twice during meetings, Kitty had never spoken to them before.

'Here, I'll take out the cups and saucers,' said Kitty, diving into one of the cupboards. When she stood up, the two women were looking at her. 'I'm Kitty,' she said with a smile. Smiles were not in ample supply, however.

'*Mera naam Raksha hai,*' the first woman said slowly in Hindi, pointing at herself by way of introduction. '*Iska naam Madhu hai,*' she said, pointing at her kohl-lined companion, who looked Kitty up and down, taking in her worsted-wool skirt and rolled hair.

'*Accha*,' said Kitty, replying pointedly in Hindi. The women looked at her as though she was an imbecile. Kitty knew that she was unusual, choosing not to wear traditional clothes or use her Indian name. For her, like some of the other Indians who had arrived on British shores, it had been a way to survive, to assimilate, even a way to understand the very people India was negotiating with. But the more like the British she became, the less some Indians wanted to do with her.

She took the cups and saucers out to the gnarled mahogany table in the library. The *dhol* – double-sided barrel drums – from the Holi celebrations were still settled in the corner. The memory of her family, celebrating back in Bombay without her, tugged at her heart.

The grandfather clock outside in the hallway chimed three. It was a smaller, informal meeting today. Even though it was a Sunday afternoon, the snow made it too difficult to travel far on public transport.

She sat down at the table, regretting her choice of chair almost immediately as it creaked with every movement. There was a chill in the air and she noticed that no one had bothered to light the fire. Mandalji, who spent so much time at the Forum, had probably not even noticed; even now he was holed up in his office. The turbaned man she'd spoken to outside had already taken his seat, pouring some chai into a saucer, and taking a slurp. The two women who'd been in the kitchen sat with their respective husbands. No English people today, which was unusual; they were usually joined by someone from the civil service or local government, or perhaps a left-wing writer compelled to add their support.

Mandalji strode in with his head down, muttering under his breath, absorbed in some papers. It was only when he was at his chair that he looked around, as though suddenly remembering there were other people here.

'Welcome, everyone,' he nodded with a brief smile. And then he was back to his notes, scribbling furiously with a fountain pen, pen scratching paper.

Kitty was used to Mandalji's erratic tendencies. His ideas were so numerous, and his mind flitted from one thought to another; trying to keep up was like trying to catch a moth. Just yesterday Kitty had made a silly joke, and Mandalji's expression had become deadly serious. Kitty had stopped what she was saying in case she'd offended him, but it was just that Mandalji's mind had moved on to something else long before the conversation had. Still, in his speeches and his writing, the president of the India Forum could focus on a cause as though it were a single grain of salt.

'I'm not too late?' Haseeb said as he walked into the room, wrapped in his thick tweed coat and scarf. They all nodded and smiled at him. He pulled up the chair next to Kitty.

'Practically early for you,' she leant over and whispered. He gave her a wry smile. Kitty's chair creaked loudly again and she resolved to stay as still as possible.

'Namaste,' said Mandalji, suddenly in a different mode, putting down his pen, looking each person in the eye as he spoke. 'Will it suit you all if we speak Hindi?' he asked. Murmurs and nods of agreement. Although Hindi was one of the official languages of India, not everyone necessarily spoke it. In South India, local languages such as Kannada and Tamil prevailed. English was the other option, but some, particularly those who were poorer or hadn't learnt it at school, would not understand the detail and nuance of the discussions Mandalji held. Usually, there would be translators during his speeches, but as this was a smaller meeting, Hindi was agreed upon.

'Keerthanaben, you can take the minutes?' said Mandalji. Kitty was certain that, like her, many of the men in attendance could also write quickly and translate the notes into

English, but as with serving chai, it would fall to her for one very particular reason. Despite the efforts of great freedom-fighting women such as Sarojini Naidu and Annie Besant, who had led large meetings and influenced many well-known men in the swaraj movement on Independence and Indian women's suffrage, when it came down to it, some things were still decided solely by gender. Women were allies because now the men needed them. Yet these very men who said they were fighting the British 'divide and rule' policies didn't seem to realize that their own actions had separated women from men all these centuries, long before the British set foot on their land.

'Thank you for making it here despite the snow. We have a number of matters to discuss today,' said Mandalji. 'Firstly, Shehab Hashim will have his case heard in court next week. But I will add that there are many others fighting conscription who also need our help. I've received letters from Indian men across the UK who don't want to take up arms in an imperial war. We must support them too.'

Just then the door of the library opened. 'I'm sorry I'm late.' It was Satyajit, hands raised by way of apology.

'Don't worry at all. Please,' said Mandalji, gesturing with his hand towards an empty chair, 'do sit.'

Satyajit smoothed his silk tie as he settled into his chair.

'Now where was I?' Mandalji looked at his notes, thick brows meeting in concentration.

'The fight against conscription,' said Kitty.

'Ah yes. In fact, Haseebbhai, I thought that you could help us advocate for the cases at the tribunals?'

Haseeb glanced at Kitty, then back at Mandalji. 'I would – I'm sorry, Mandalji, as much as I would like to help with these cases, work is keeping me very busy. That's why I was late, in fact,' he said, his Adam's apple dipping as he swallowed.

'That's a shame,' said Mandalji, not bothering to hide his disappointment.

Kitty waited a moment for Haseeb to say something. She looked over at him but he wouldn't meet her eye.

'I could do it,' she said. 'It's only been two years since I was called to the bar in Bombay, but it means the law is still fresh in my mind.'

Mandalji brought his hands together with a loud clap. 'That would be wonderful, Keerthanaben. Yes, yes. Most wonderful. Well, this has worked out well, then, hasn't it?'

Haseeb gave a small smile.

'But Mandalji, there is Shamji Haria, who lives up in Muswell Hill, he is a solicitor. He could be of help?' said the turbaned man, looking warily at Kitty.

'Yes, Palvinderji,' said Mandalji, gazing back at him. 'We need all the help we can get. But Keerthanaben here is a barrister, she has spoken in court, a very useful skill for the tribunals where the cases are heard.'

The people at the table regarded her, including Satyajit. One of the men sat forward in his seat with curiosity. Kitty was used to it now. She quite enjoyed subverting expectations.

'I'll take a look at the letters we have so far and see how we can help,' said Kitty. She stole a glance at Haseeb. Why had he been so quiet?

'Accha!' said Mandalji, before moving on to other matters: a musical fundraiser that they were organizing at the India Forum, volunteers needed for distributing pamphlets, the latest matters from India.

'Now, if there are no further matters to discuss, I suggest we adjourn the meeting.'

'Will we not discuss Netaji?' said Satyajit, sitting back and placing his elbows on the armrests of his chair. There was something nonchalant, even arrogant, in his bearing.

Mandalji waited for an elaboration. Subhas Chandra Bose – or Netaji, as he was often known – had been a leading voice at the Indian Congress with Nehru and Gandhi for years. They'd seem aligned at the start, but now had very different views on how to secure freedom. Though he had been thrown into house arrest by the British in India, the wily Bose had contradicted that mild-mannered and bespectacled face of his and apparently disappeared.

'Do you think he'll succeed?' said Satyajit. The rumour was that he wanted to ally with the Axis powers as a way of gaining support for Independence against the British.

'In joining Hitler and his friends, you mean?' Mandalji put his palms together, resting his chin upon them. Rivulets of black ink had caught in the skin around his fingernails.

Satyajit nodded.

Before Mandalji could answer, Palvinderji piped up, 'It is madness,' waving his arm furiously in the air. 'Why would the *pagal* Nazis help India?'

Kitty shifted in her seat.

'Netaji always argued that we should take a stronger stand against the British when war broke out. This could be it.' Satyajit was perfectly calm, looking the man straight in the eye.

His coolness annoyed Kitty, the way he talked about it as if it was nothing more than a game of cricket. Had he not seen the pictures, all the Jews harassed and beaten in Germany? And what would the Nazis do to people like them if they managed to invade? Indians who were clearly not part of their 'Aryan' race? Her heart fell at the thought of what it could mean for all of them, for her and Haseeb. The ever-present night bombers in full force and the Nazis gathering pace in Europe; how could anyone be so relaxed about it?

'We really have to listen to this nonsense?' Palvinderji

grabbed the wooden armrests on his chair, knuckles white with tension.

'*Chalo bhaiyo.*' Mandalji raised his hand to calm them both. 'Bose has made his choices. He is no longer acting in the interests of the Congress and we don't know where he is. That means it's no longer our concern.'

Before anyone else could say anything, and to Kitty's relief, he wrapped up the meeting and thanked them for their time.

Later, when Mandalji had rushed back to whatever urgent matter awaited him in his office and everyone else had begun gathering their things, Palvinderji was still mumbling under his breath about 'that madman Bose'. He kept huffing away, muttering about how 'our way is working, we are closer to freedom than ever and he could ruin it all'.

Satyajit stopped doing up the buttons of his coat and stared at him. 'And where exactly is that freedom you've been fighting for all these years?'

Palvinderji glared at him. 'You young people think you can just do this –' the man banged his hand down hard on the table, making Kitty start – 'and it all comes to you?'

'And just how long are we supposed to sit obediently and wait for it?' Satyajit gave a cold laugh.

Palvinderji's voice was sharp with fury. 'It takes patience as well as courage to win freedom. Why can't you understand that?' He shook his head, barely able to look at Satyajit now, and hurried out of the room.

'If India helps Hitler and his army, then perhaps we can finally stop talking about freedom and actually live it,' Satyajit said, to no one in particular.

'So you think India should simply go from one imperialist ruler to another?' said Kitty, thinking of Czechoslovakia and all the countries that had gone before. 'While Hitler gulps down countries like a cobra?'

'He only cares about Germans,' Haseeb added, then quieter, 'Aryan Germans.'

'The Germans have allied with the Japanese and they're hardly blue-eyed and blond-haired,' said Satyajit. 'Netaji's way is better, no? Hindu, Muslim, Sikh, Parsi, Jain, Christian, all the other religions running India together, for swaraj. Maybe fighting on the German side could be a means to an end.'

'But to what end exactly?' Kitty said, failing to hide the exasperation in her voice. 'I can't listen to this any more,' she said to Haseeb, pulling her belt tight around her waist. 'Let's go.'

Outside in the snow, Kitty and Haseeb took tentative steps. It was lucky they lived close to the India Forum; the blackout and the ice could be a lethal combination.

'Here, take my arm,' said Haseeb. She was glad of his warmth.

They trudged carefully along the dim white pathway. Snow fell into the tops of her court shoes, melting onto her toes.

Perhaps she was clutching Haseeb's arm tighter than she'd realized, because he said, 'It's all right. You did your best with Satyajit but he's the type who can only see his own view.'

Kitty glanced at him. Satyajit was the last thing on her mind right now. 'Why didn't you say something, Haseeb? You know I could help with the conscription cases just as well as you can.'

Haseeb looked down at the ground, stepping carefully.

'Or is it because you don't think I'm capable?'

'You know that's not what I think,' he said, quietly.

'You seem quite happy for me to make a home for us. Is that all I'm good for?' A dark figure came towards them, torchlight scanning the ground. They moved towards a shopfront so that they could pass by.

'I've always supported your career,' he said.

'You supported me in India, before we were married, yes. But now . . .' Kitty's torch beam collided with his along the pavement.

Haseeb stopped walking and turned to her then, faint moonlight catching his sharp features. He held her gently by the shoulders. 'I don't want you to have go through what you did in India. We're at the bottom, despite the fact that we have exactly the same skills as they do.'

She could hear the resentment in his voice. He had done everything he was supposed to: worn the right clothes, spoken the right kind of English, read the right kinds of books, and still it was not enough. It wasn't easy for him to accept that assimilation was a threat to some, that the more Indians emulated the British, the more that some British people looked down on them for wanting to be like them.

Kitty knew exactly what it was like to keep knocking at a door that wouldn't let you in. 'You don't need to tell me—'

'And I'm sorry,' he said, 'but you know it's true that an Indian woman—'

'Will find it doubly difficult. I know, Haseeb, but this is different. It's a tribunal and people need my help.' The snow caught on their coats and hats now, she felt the soft chill of it as the icy flakes brushed against her face.

He sighed, taking her hand in his. 'You should help them, if that's what they want. But you'll still be arguing in a British system, against British men. You just need to be prepared for what that that means.'

*

When they got back to the flat, Haseeb had gone straight to bed. Kitty was still restless, so she changed into warm clothes, opened the leather top of the gramophone and put a record on.

She tried to savour these rare times when there was no air

raid and the night was still, almost safe, even. There was always something comforting about the familiar crackle of the stylus in the record's groove as the music began. Despite the chill that wouldn't leave her body, she leant back against the headrest of the armchair, letting the music transport her back to Bombay, where she'd first heard the song, and where she'd first met Haseeb.

They used to pass each other in the lancet-arched corridors of the Bombay High Court as they hurried to their cases. Sometimes they'd found themselves seated at the same table at Bombay Bar Association dinners. She had thought him handsome from the first time she had seen him: tall, with hazel eyes. Kitty loved the way the dimple in his chin deepened whenever he smiled, like the pressing of a thumb on a pillow.

It didn't matter what Kitty thought of him, though, because he was Muslim and she was Hindu. There would have been more chance of marrying the Maharaja of Baroda than someone like Haseeb. No one had to tell you, it was something you just knew in your bones: you could be friends with Muslims, Sikhs, Jains or Parsis, but it was forbidden to go further. Looking back, Kitty saw that she had relaxed around him with that knowledge in her heart. There was no expectation, free from questions over whether anything more could happen between them.

Many months later, Haseeb had told her that, yes, he of course knew all the rules of self-imposed romantic segregation. Yet from the very first time he had met her and found out her real name, Keerthana Mehta, a name that, like most, signalled her religion, all he could focus on was finding a solution to this impossible situation. For him, it was simply a wall to be climbed over, or knocked down.

One evening Kitty had gone along to a cocktail party held by one of the most esteemed judges in India. The impressive house in Malabar Hill, one of the wealthiest areas in the city, was made up of a series of circular rooms, each with high, arched windows. But the building paled in comparison to the views looking out over the ocean. The sun hadn't yet set, the sea and sky disappearing into a vast canvas of deep blue.

Most people were enjoying the entertainment as one of the young barristers gave an impromptu turn on the piano. Kitty and Haseeb stood out on the terrace, sipping sweet *nimbu pani*, the pale green of the lime juice in the glass gently glowing in the early-evening light.

'What brought you to Bombay?' Kitty had asked. She had heard that his family were from Delhi. Later, he would tell her that he had had to bite his tongue. What he really wanted to say was that his subconscious must have known that he was about to fall in love with a beautiful woman. She had replied with a laugh, saying she was glad he hadn't because such a nauseating line might have put her off right there and then.

'I wanted a taste of Bombay life,' he had said, sipping his drink and giving her a smile. 'Besides, Delhi's arid air is as dry as an elephant's skin, you have something rare here called "a breeze".'

'So you're just here for the weather, then?' She raised an eyebrow.

'Among other things,' he said quietly. His smile fell and he looked out towards the ocean. She'd learnt later that Haseeb had become a barrister because his father's export business was on the brink of collapse. Suppliers had reneged on their deals and he had thought that learning the law to defend the contracts would help. But while Haseeb was in his final year at Cambridge, the business had collapsed and they had lost everything. Though Haseeb was determined to earn some money that he could send back home, he couldn't face going back to Delhi, his mother and father reduced to sleeping in a one-bedroom apartment in a rough part of the city.

'It's unusual to see a female barrister at the High Court,' he said, suddenly remembering himself and brightening again.

'Well, most of the time I'm only helping out with the senior cases.'

'Still, it can't have been easy for you. It certainly hasn't been for me.'

Kitty stared at him; she found his honesty refreshing. Most men put on a brave face, no matter how they felt. She found herself following suit. 'No, I suppose it wasn't. I didn't even really want to study law.'

'No?'

'I was following in the family tradition. My father's a lawyer. He said I should go to Oxford and study law just like him. To truly understand the systems and culture we were pitted against. It wasn't really presented as a choice.' She looked down at her glass. She knew that in some respects she was lucky, that most women didn't get the luxury of higher education, but it had been hard to put her own dreams aside. She had wanted to be a writer, a journalist, perhaps. Kitty had been lucky, though, there were things she enjoyed about the law: putting together arguments, the methodical way that cases were set out, standing up in court and defending a point of view.

'Are your family active in the Independence movement?'

Kitty nodded. 'They always have been.'

'And in learning about British law, the hunter becomes the prey,' he said in English. 'Isn't that how they say it?'

She smiled. 'Yes. And you, what do you think about Independence?'

'I think we should all be free to do whatever we want,' said Haseeb, his eyes narrowing. He had a deep voice, at odds with his lean physique. 'Don't you?'

Kitty felt her cheeks flush. She was no longer sure whether he was talking about India.

She hadn't seen Haseeb for quite a few weeks after that, as she'd been stuck at the office preparing for a trial. Then, one bright November day when the Bombay weather was at its best, she had bumped into him at the end of a long day in court.

'You're not going home, are you?' he said, clutching his leather case in his hand as he walked with her out of the stone-arched entranceway and down the broad steps.

'It's what I usually do, yes,' she smiled.

'On a beautiful day like this? When you have the beach just a step away.' It certainly wasn't a step away but she humoured him all the same. 'Come on, let's go,' he said, as though the matter was settled.

'But I said I'd be home—'

'Remind your family how lovely it is outside today.'

The driver was already waiting for her across the street. 'I . . .' she trailed off, and willingly let herself be swept along on Haseeb's adventure. She gave the driver a message, a vague story about working late, and then sent him on his way.

They took a chaotic rickshaw ride part of the way to the beach. Sharing the cramped space, Kitty tried her best to keep her legs well away from Haseeb's for the sake of propriety, but the way the *rikshawallah* stopped and started it was quite the challenge. Or at least, that's what she told herself.

Chowpatty Beach opened up to them, endless water as far as the eye could see. Kitty kept an eye out for people she knew, but her well-to-do relatives and family friends usually went to Juhu Beach. She and Haseeb talked for hours about all the things they had in common: studying law at Oxbridge, the freedom movement, their love of music, the complications of torts (thankfully, they didn't linger on this subject for too long); and all the things that were different about them: her love of literature versus his love of food, their upbringings, their faiths, their languages (she spoke Gujarati at home, he spoke Urdu and Hindi). They stopped and ate roasted corn and *pav bhaji*, using pieces of the fresh bread rolls that glistened with butter and coriander to mop up the spicy vegetable mash. The salt-tinged air caressed their skin beneath pomegranate skies. As they walked, children played cricket in the sand, men dozed under coconut trees. And as dusk fell, she knew all was lost. They were falling in love with each other.

7

Ruby

Ruby came to a halt in the street. It was Mrs Richardson, standing further along Regent Square, talking to a man outside her bombed-out house. She had hoped that Mrs Richardson might not recognize her in her off-duty fur coat and maroon pillbox hat, but just as Ruby had gone to cross the road she had called out for her: 'Miss Thacker!'

Ruby did her best to act surprised as she came closer. 'Mrs Richardson? Oh, hello.'

'This is one of the wardens who was here when the house was bombed, Mr Carthew.' Her eyes were red and she was clutching a handkerchief.

Mr Carthew held a notebook and gave her a nod in greeting. He was likely from the insurance company or Camden council. 'I'll just go and take a closer look now, Mrs Richardson,' he said, heading gingerly towards the blackened house. Though the snow had cleared, there were still a few puddles of sludge here and there.

Ruby scrabbled for something to say. 'I heard you were staying with family in Hertfordshire?' An army goods van trundled past, turning left at the corner of the square, past the brittle-branched plane trees.

'It's very strange, really.' Mrs Richardson stared at her, ignoring Ruby's question.

When Ruby realized she wasn't going to elaborate, she said, 'Sorry, what do you mean?'

'Well, a lot of the furniture had been destroyed, of course, but almost everything was accounted for,' she said, eyes narrowing. 'Except for a necklace.'

Ruby felt her cheeks flush. She hoped Mrs Richardson would put it down to the cold. 'Oh yes?'

'It was kept in a very specific place.' Her grey eyes were observing Ruby, waiting to see how she would react.

Ruby kept her voice calm. 'It's always chaos in these situations, I've seen it many times now. Perhaps it could still turn up.'

'It's definitely *not* there.' Mrs Richardson's tone was sharp, eyes still fixed on Ruby. 'It's been stolen.'

Ruby tutted sympathetically. 'Oh no, do you think so? Well, there's so many people coming in and out.' It had started spitting with rain. The sky was mottled like a tarnished spoon and the clouds were drawing in.

'You were inside, weren't you? Your colleague Mr Gastrell mentioned it to me.'

'Briefly,' then Ruby added with emphasis, 'when I was looking for you and Major Richardson.' She carried on, 'And what with the bomb disposal team and the firemen, lots of people will have been in there. Then, of course, when they've left, anyone can walk in off the street, can't they?'

'We're going to speak to the police.' Mrs Richardson put her handkerchief away and snapped her handbag shut.

'Oh, you should, of course you should. Maybe you'll have more luck than others have had. Now, I won't keep you with this rain starting up,' she said, and began to walk away. 'Take care of yourself, Mrs Richardson.'

Ruby pushed open her umbrella, resisting the urge to turn

around. Lots of people had been in and out of there, she told herself. There was no way they could pin it on her, a respectable ARP warden, was there?

*

It was still pouring, the sort of rain that couldn't make up its mind, falling in every direction. Ruby hurried inside the Hare and Hounds, shaking off the rain from her wool coat and putting her umbrella in the stand. The pub was dishevelled, probably hadn't been redecorated since Queen Victoria's days, with patterned carpet and peeling flock wallpaper. Small pictures were placed in a haphazard way, as though the main aim was to hide the terrible state of the walls behind them. Lucky that the glass panes had been taken out in case of bombing raids, so the only thing they could assault was your gaze, and not your head.

Ruby stood at the bar, taking in the curves and loops of the brass fittings. Two soldiers were standing and having a pint together. A thought seized her heart: would her little brother Freddie have been one of them had he lived?

Ruby turned away. A couple of older men were huddled at a round table. They gave her a look that said that the only place young women should be sitting was at home by the stove with their aprons on, polishing their husbands' shoes.

'Evening, gentleman,' said Ruby, giving them her best smile. That always took them by surprise. They mumbled something to each other, suddenly fascinated by whatever was in the bottom of their pint glasses.

'Fleet about?' she said to the bald man who was pulling a pint behind the bar.

'Give me a minute, I'll check. Do you want a drink?'

Ruby shook her head and looked around. Three elderly gents were having a jovial argument about their scores at the dartboard. Other punters were having an out-of-tune singsong matched by the out-of-tune piano, laughing away as they did. The whole city was knackered and in need of a good bath, but the bad weather meant there probably wouldn't be a raid tonight. The air fizzed with the urge to have fun. *I'm alive*, said London, *for now, I'm alive and I want to make the most of it.*

'And to what do we owe this pleasure?' Fleet came and stood opposite her, Welsh accent pressing gently on each word.

'Got a moment, Fleet?'

'For you, of course I do,' he said, putting his hand to his chest, as if he was really doing it out of the goodness of his own heart. He gave a flick of his head to follow him upstairs.

He took Ruby through to the front room, filled, as it always seemed to be, with washing – all white this time – hanging on wooden racks. The rest was draped over the chair backs. In the corner, it even hung from a shelf, pinned down by two sturdy china dairymaids.

'Sorry,' said Fleet, shaking his head. 'With the rain the way it's been, Ma's decided to turn the whole bloody house into a laundry. So, what have you got for me?' he said, gazing at her. He was much older than Ruby, tufted edges of grey hair framing his bald head, and was lean except for the slight paunch that hung over his belt.

Ruby produced the necklace from her handbag, then pulled out a gold cigarette case and an art deco brooch.

Fleet sighed. 'Nothing else?'

She shook her head, annoyed at the way he acted as if it was so easy. She had been on shift the last night, a particularly heavy assault. She'd watched the flares and flashes across all of London. The entire city violated.

On the street where Ruby was patrolling, past the gasworks, an incendiary had fallen, making a huge crater in the middle of the road. At one house, all of the windows had crashed to the floor, even the door had been blasted away, but strangely, the rest of the house was entirely intact. She felt the anger burn through her, fists clenching, wanting to do something, anything, to give herself some control.

There was no sign of people inside, but of course Ruby called out anyway. The house was decorated in an old-fashioned way, though only the finest materials had been used: walnut, velvet, brass and marble. She hurried through, checking the high-ceilinged rooms with large art deco furniture, making sure that no one was cowering under a bed, as she'd once found a woman doing. She noticed the jewellery box on a side table. Most people had the sense to hide their valuables or take them with them, but some people had so much they could hardly keep track. She'd found the gold brooch, decorated with sleek green enamel geometric lines, and put it in her pocket; something that was hers. Something she had just a little power over.

Fleet took a closer look at the goods on the table and they agreed a price. Less than she should have got, but then it was money for nothing, after all.

She waited for a pang of guilt to hit, but as usual it never came. Wasn't as though she stole from everyone. She had rules; Ruby only took from those who could afford to lose some money one day and drape themselves in fur stoles and airs and graces the next. Her future was right there for the taking, as they say. So she took it.

'Back next week?' Fleet glanced at her, trying his luck as they headed back downstairs.

'We'll see,' she said, as they walked towards the bar. 'It's not that easy now.' A flicker of worry scurried across her chest as she remembered her encounter with Mrs Richardson.

'Oh now,' said Fleet, rubbing his hands together and looking across the pub, 'this *is* good timing.'

Ruby followed his gaze towards the door. It took a moment for her mind to catch up.

The man from the India Forum.

'Sunny! How are you, old fella?' said Fleet. Sunny: not the name he'd introduced himself with the other day. Mr Deol, wasn't it? In fact, hadn't he told Ruby to call him Jit?

Jit, or Sunny, whatever his name was, walked over to them, a look of recognition slowly passing over his face. He smiled at Ruby, and if she wasn't mistaken, he seemed a little amused.

'Managing to avoid the bombs so far,' Jit said to Fleet. 'Will you give me a small moment, Fleet, then we will talk?'

'Right you are,' replied the landlord. 'See you soon, then, Ruby,' he said, a look of curiosity on his face as he tried to work out how they knew each other. He went over to serve a customer.

'Hello, Miss Thacker,' said Jit, putting down a large, battered leather case that he'd brought with him.

'Hello.' Ruby scrabbled in her bag for a cigarette. She would have to find a new Fleet, she realized immediately. This pub had been fine when she was over at her old warden post by the Caledonian Road, far away from the Forum, but now it was too close for comfort.

Jit struck a match and held it towards her.

'Well, if there was any doubt about you working for the government, that has definitely been put to rest now.' Jit gave a broad smile.

'What d'you mean?' she said, pulling an ashtray towards her as she exhaled. She resisted the urge to undo her coat, even though she could feel the blood rushing up her neck.

'Whatever you're buying or selling from Fleet, you won't get it with a ration book,' said Jit, raising an eyebrow.

Ruby saw something familiar in him now. Recklessness. That was it. As though he enjoyed it, watching her squirm, and he didn't care about the consequences. But then again, Jit wasn't as innocent as he made out either, not if he knew Fleet.

'And what about you . . . Sunny? Is that your name?' She couldn't resist adding, 'For today, at least.'

'Fleet finds it easier to say Sunny than Satyajit.' He gave a nonchalant shrug. 'Most people do.'

Rubbish. He'd told Ruby to call him Jit; that was easy enough to say. No need for a different name. The thrill of having caught him out surprised her. Maybe because it put them on more of a level footing. Whatever it was, lingering now wasn't doing her any good. 'Well, I really should be off.'

'That's a shame. Perhaps we'll see each other again. It seemed like you were quite interested in our work at the India Forum. Or was it simply some of the wealthy patrons that held your attention?' he smiled. It was unnerving; like he saw right through her.

'I came because I was curious.'

'Oh, I'm sure you were very curious about something. Whether it had anything to do with India, though . . .' That knowing smile again.

Before she could ask him what he meant, Fleet came over to them. 'Sunny, are you ready?' There was a faint look of concern on his face. Probably worried they were about to cut out the middleman.

Jit nodded. 'Well, as I say, I hope I'll see you again sometime, Miss Thacker.'

Ruby didn't answer. She watched him as he followed Fleet, their two shadows disappearing down the hallway.

8
Kitty

'This takes me back to my childhood,' said Kitty, as she served some *suji halwa* into a bowl for Haseeb. They were at the Indian Fort restaurant off Piccadilly, owned by one of the patrons of the South London India Forum based in Brixton, Farhad Aziz. With the two Forums so far apart from one another, Mandalji had agreed that they should instead meet in the middle, and the Indian Fort provided the perfect location.

Kitty took a mouthful of the halwa. It was made of sweetened semolina – an ingredient that was reasonably easy to find during rationing – and bound with a mixture of butter and oil (although back in India it would have been ghee). The whole thing was topped off with a few raisins and the thinnest slivers of almonds. In Bombay, they often ate *suji halwa* on special occasions like Diwali and Holi, when it would be served on a vast platter. The taste made Kitty think of her grandmother, who hated the stuff and would wince whenever she was offered it.

'It's not bad,' said Haseeb, taking another spoonful. It was quite a treat to eat Indian food that they hadn't had to cook themselves or scavenge for ingredients to make.

The restaurant was decorated in old colonial style, with a red carpet, brass lamps and intricate *jali*-cut panelling which threw beautiful shapes around the room, all intended to attract

British people who had lived in India over the years as much as it was to entice the small middle-class community of Indians in London.

Music from a harmonium rang out around the room. The player – one of the waiters – sat on the floor, pumping air into the accordion-like bellows, back and forth with his left hand, while playing the keys with his other. It was a sound Kitty associated so closely with home that it was somehow incongruous in the middle of London, even in this ornate setting.

The owner of the restaurant, who they knew as Azizji, came over from the kitchen where he'd been overseeing the food and sat down next to Haseeb. 'Enjoying the food?' he said heartily.

He and Kitty nodded and gave their compliments.

'How long have you owned the restaurant?' Kitty asked.

'Fifteen years. Long years,' he laughed. 'I started by working in a lascars' cafe on Percy Street and worked my way up.' Lascars were Indian sailors. Enterprising people like Azizji had lost no time in catering to homesick men who were seeking their own little portion of India, offering hearty food at affordable prices. Restaurants like this were rarer now, particularly with the war, but there were still a couple of stalwarts, including the Indian Fort.

'Well, I can see why you've been so successful.' Haseeb gave a contented smile, gently pushing away his empty bowl.

'Nothing makes me happier than people enjoying my food.'

'It's quite a treat, really,' said Kitty. 'Almost makes me homesick,' she said, and though she tried to infuse her tone with joviality, she couldn't help but feel a little sad.

'You've been here since before the war?' Azizji had heavy, drooping eyes that gave him a sorrowful look, as though the question was a lament.

Kitty nodded.

'You can't have been married long, though?' said Azizji.

'Just over two years,' said Haseeb.

'What a way to start a marriage,' Azizji said, shaking his head. 'This war looks like it has no end . . . And your parents, they were accepting of your union?'

Kitty braced herself; though most Indians were too polite to comment on their highly unusual marriage, there were others who had been known to cut conversations short when they found out, as though Kitty and Haseeb's choice of spouse would somehow contaminate those around them.

Haseeb explained as quickly and discreetly as he could that it was hard for their parents to accept the situation but that they hoped to reconcile one day. Kitty couldn't bear to look at him then, the lump in her throat threatening to take hold. Haseeb made it sound like a minor family rift. Though at least the great loss they'd both felt had brought them closer in marriage.

Kitty had agreed to come to London in part because there was little left for her in India then. Of course, the irony was not lost on her: leaving the very country she was fighting for.

'We Indians all need to stand together now. None of this talk of a separate state for Muslims,' said Azizji.

Haseeb shifted uncomfortably in his seat. 'Jinnah seems quite adamant,' he said quietly. How could they possibly agree with the Muslim League leader in India, Muhammad Ali Jinnah, who wanted to split the country into two after Independence?

Kitty looked down at her plate. What would freedom look like for her and Haseeb if Jinnah got his way?

'Well, what better symbol of religious unity than your marriage,' Azizji said, in an apparent attempt to buoy them all.

Kitty looked at him. 'Our marriage was not a political act.'

Azizji smiled, though he still looked sad. 'Whether you like it or not you have made a public statement about who you both are, *beta.*'

'Our marriage was a matter between the two of us,' Haseeb said firmly. 'It's only that others think they have a say over our lives. We have enough of that with the British government ruling over us.'

Haseeb's tone put an end to the matter. They fell silent, Azizji nodded and turned to speak to Mandalji. Kitty squeezed Haseeb's hand under the table. She was glad that they'd not shied away from the conversation. And while Aziz had been ultimately supportive of the union, and she knew they had nothing to feel ashamed of, after so many years of being taught to believe that you must not step out of the clearly drawn borders of love, years of being told by others that who you chose to marry was more of a concern to them than it was to you, it was hard to shake those old feelings.

Once the plates were cleared away and the harmonium fell silent again, Mandalji began the meeting with some updates from India, then opened the floor to other agenda items.

'Mandalji, I have something I'd like to raise with you,' said a man so drenched in hair oil that Kitty was surprised it wasn't dripping down his temples. Mandalji nodded at him to go ahead.

'*Shukriya.*' The man then took out a letter and put on some half-moon spectacles. 'You stated last week that the Indians must work as one and refuse to give our blood for a war between two imperial powers.' The man spoke in a surprisingly double-barrelled English accent with only a pinch of *mirch* in his inflections. 'I agree with this opinion except for three crucial amendments. Firstly, that if the Germans invade Britain, we Indians should cast aside ahimsa – our non-violence strategy – and defend ourselves against a fascist enemy.'

The man then proceeded to spend the next ten minutes

working his way meticulously through not one but four sheets of paper (double-sided). Though Mandalji tried to speak whenever the man took a breath, he was too polite to interrupt.

'To summarize, then, I agree with your opinion except –' the man pointed a finger up to the ceiling and Kitty prayed he wasn't about to go through them all again – 'for these three matters.'

The audience members, many of whom had ended up half-slumped in their chairs during the man's soliloquy, suddenly perked up.

'Thank you for your . . . comments,' said Mandalji, resting his elbow on the table and leaning forward. 'I fully understand your concerns. We at the India Forum are clear in our mandate: we will not fight with the British. If Indians can't have freedom, we can't help them protect theirs.' The room held its breath. What would happen to the Indians if they didn't stand up for themselves against an invasion by the 'great Aryan race'? Surely they couldn't surrender?

'However, fascism has no place in the world,' Mandalji went on, 'especially when it is dressed up as nationalism. If it is a choice between the British and the Germans, I choose the British every time. And if the worst happens, we would be right to defend ourselves in the case of an invasion.'

There were murmurs of agreement and then the discussion moved on to other matters, but Kitty's mind kept wandering. That morning, she had been standing in the queue at the grocer's, when her attention had been caught by a conversation between two older women standing in front of her.

'I just want the war over with now,' said the taller of the two women, hair rollered and wrapped in a scarf.

'And you think the rest of us are all enjoying ourselves and having a great old time, do you?' The other woman had given a gruff laugh.

'Not going to do us any good carrying it all on, though. Look at all this, for a start.' The woman with the rollers had waved her arm vaguely towards the queue in front of her.

'You'd rather give up and have Mosley and his lot?' said her friend. Oswald Mosley was the leader of the British Union of Fascists; Hitler had been guest of honour at his wedding. The mere uttering of Mosley's name gave Kitty the chills. Nothing but a fragile thread held them back from a fascist peace.

'Wouldn't much change things for us,' the woman in the rollers had shrugged.

Kitty had heard similar opinions since the war started. Not everyone was all for 'fighting the Jerries'. What would it be like, Kitty had wondered, to sit on the fence, not to have to worry about what happened to your country because you believed it wouldn't affect you?

After a final discussion about a fundraiser they were planning for May, Mandalji drew the meeting to a close. A waiter brought over a tray of steaming cups of chai.

'I'm glad that we were able to reach a conclusion on self-defence, Mandalji.' The man with the hair oil patted him on the arm.

'Hmm?' said Mandalji, then blew on his tea. His mind had inevitably moved on to something else. 'Oh yes.'

'Well, some of us might have to join the war soon anyway.' Haseeb leant back in his chair. 'Conscription letters are coming.'

Mandalji, who at fifty-two was too old to be called up, and who would undoubtedly have refused no matter the consequences, gazed at Haseeb. 'That is something I can say with 100 per cent certainty that I will continue to oppose, no matter what.'

'I think we can make strong cases,' Kitty said. She had spent the past week going over the first of the letters and working out how to help the men who had already been called up. 'For some, we can make the argument that Indians are pacifists on religious grounds and for others, we can argue that they are only living here temporarily.'

Mandalji nodded with approval. 'Good, good. Why should they have to join someone else's war?'

'Though it's interesting that there are some Indians who think we should join the Allies,' Haseeb said, propping his elbow on the table.

'You mean the communists?' asked Mandalji.

Haseeb nodded. 'They wanted to make a stand against fascism by joining the war, didn't they?'

Kitty stared at him; this was typical of Haseeb, it was what made him a good lawyer, trying to see things from every possible perspective. But there were some things that required single-minded resolution no matter what.

She remembered the fall of France last summer: first invaded, then picked at by Germany like a hyena. Churchill's speech still rang in her ears: '. . . And even if, which I do not for a moment believe, this island or a large part of it were subjugated and starving, then our Empire beyond the seas, armed and guarded by the British Fleet, would carry on the struggle.'

The good old colonies would save the British Isles, apparently. What *bakwas*. For a 'great' ruler, Churchill could be quite naive. Or perhaps, wilfully ignorant, when it suited his oratory. It was easy to muster bravado with an empire behind you. She'd heard the men and women at bus stops and in ration queues, going on about how they weren't scared, that they'd fight on alone now. Kitty had bitten her tongue so hard it might have bled.

Mandalji sighed. 'We can help the Jewish refugees here. Volunteer, donate. But as for fighting in the army, the navy, the air force? No.' He lightly drummed the side of his fist on the tableclothed table to emphasize each word: 'The only rationale for violence is self-defence.'

'Yes,' murmured Haseeb, rubbing the edge of his plate with his finger, 'I suppose you're right.'

The group went back to India Forum matters, but Kitty was distracted. Perhaps it was the threat of conscription hanging over them, perhaps it was the Indian music and food, but she couldn't help thinking about Bombay.

Kitty's family home was called *Lal Bhavan* – Red House. Although it was actually white, that would have been a too on-the-nose name for Kitty's grandfather, a fierce anti-Britisher. But just before Kitty was born he had changed the name to *Kush Bhavan*, meaning the house of Lord Rama's son, in some vain hope that simply changing a name could change a destiny.

Kitty grew up there with her father and grandmother – her dadi – along with her uncle, aunt and their three sons. Not that her uncle's family were around much, off to meetings or trips to do with the Independence cause, sometimes even serving brief stints in jail for protesting, while their children were tucked away at boarding school in the North.

Kitty had never known her own mother. She had died during childbirth. Kitty was the first and only. Though Kitty was aware of a kind of loss, it was not exactly her mother she missed.

In a way, her death wasn't what took up all the space; it was her father's grief. Kitty's view of her mother was always coloured, on the occasions she'd come up in conversation with guests, by what he said, what he thought, what he recollected about her. Even the memories Kitty had of her mother were not her own. And so, in a way, her mother was not her own either.

The house was split in two, the kitchen divided for English cooking and Indian cuisine, with two drawing rooms, one in the English style with straight-backed mahogany chairs and the Indian room with comfortable loom-woven *asan* so they could sit on the floor.

Her father's study too, was divided in half. English books on one side, Indian on the other, with Dickens and Voltaire staring out across the divide towards Tagore and Kalidasa.

Kitty had found herself between them all one January afternoon, standing there while her father's head was buried in papers at his desk. The air was sharp, with a metallic tang that warned of a storm, as though the sky was holding its breath. The sky would soon crack open, the fault line rupturing the clouds apart.

'Papa, I need to talk to you,' she said, feeling herself suddenly regress into adolescence, as she stood there asking for an audience with him.

'Hmmm?' he said, though he was still engrossed in his papers.

'I've met someone,' Kitty began, 'and we'd like to get married.'

He looked up at her in an instant. 'What do you mean?' He sat back, clutching the armrests with his hands. A love marriage was unusual by any standards. 'How did you meet?'

'He's a lawyer,' she ventured. Law was common ground, it demonstrated a good education, a sign of a prize suitor.

'Yes?' he said, taking some tobacco from a pot and rolling it into a *bidi* with his thick fingers. He stared at her over the top of his spectacles.

'I know it's not an arranged marriage . . .'

He gave a brittle laugh. 'My choices not good enough for you?' Kitty's father had tried in vain. It had been a near-clean sweep of fleeing suitors: she was too tall, too intelligent, too lacking in culinary skills. Education was desirable in a prospective bride, unnecessary in a wife.

Despite the spectacular lack of love interest, really she knew it was simply that she was too Keerthana, too Kitty. 'It's not that—'

'Keerthana, it is easy to miss the wheatfields when you are looking at the poppies.' Her father lit his bidi and took a long drag.

'What does that mean, Papa?' Though Kitty said it gently, she was in no mood to decipher these cryptic – and often non-sensical – comments that he came out with time and time again.

Her father looked at her, smoke curling in knots around his throat.

'That you are not giving the young men I've picked for you a chance. When I was young, women had no say at all. Your mother's path was chosen for her, though we were both lucky in the end,' he said, his voice faltering a moment. Kitty knew: while there had been no love in the beginning, it was certainly there by the time she died. 'Do you know how lucky you are?'

Kitty stared at the corner of the desk. There was nothing for it. 'His name is Haseeb.'

Her stomach dropped, her father's eyes still on her. 'No. End of discussion,' he said, making a slicing movement in the air with his hand.

'I am going to marry him,' she said, mustering courage from somewhere deep in her heart. She'd chosen a path now; no choice but to carry on. Back then, some small part of her had believed that her father would see sense over time. It had taken her a long time to see that belief for what it was; the naivety and arrogance of youth.

He stood up from his chair. 'I spoilt you, Keerthana! You think you can come in here and make statements like that. You haven't even had the respect to ask me.'

'At least meet him.' She knew she was on the rockiest of ground now. There were parents who would have beaten their daughters for even daring to bring up a Muslim marriage.

'Meet him?' He stared at her incredulously. 'Why are you even still standing there?'

Her heart hurt at the ice in his tone. 'Papa—'

'What would people say?' he said, voice taut as a tabla skin. 'Your Muslim husband will never set foot in this house.'

Kitty could taste the salt of her tears in the corner of her mouth. 'We fight for freedom, our freedom, but other people still get a say in what part of us is free? How can that be right?'

'You want to turn your back on me, and your dadi? Well, you have all the freedom you want, Keerthana,' he said, glaring at her. 'Now you are free to choose.'

Why couldn't he see it? He had been the one to educate a daughter and send her to England though it was not the usual tradition. Hadn't he been the one that her set on her on this course: to live your life as though yours was the only opinion that mattered?

'I won't have people saying you brought shame on this house and I allowed it,' he continued. 'If you choose this man, you will leave my house and never come back.'

Kitty rubbed her cheek with her palm, skin stinging. She took a deep breath, calming herself as best as she could. She looked at her papa, then whispered, 'Can't you see, Papa? If we live our lives by what everyone else thinks we should do, they are no longer our lives.'

The laughter in the restaurant jolted Kitty out of the past. Everyone was relaxed now, drinking the last of their chai. She tried to muster a smile, to join in, but her mind still lingered in Bombay.

Time had created a border between her memories and reality. Why was it that the memories you wanted to forget were the ones that clung on the hardest, while those that were precious were the first to fall? Some days the loss of her family snatched her heart clean away, other days it was subdued and she'd barely have thought about it. Others still, an incessant needle pricking at her heart. But it was always there, springing up when she least expected it.

She thought of what Azizji had said, what others had said about their marriage ever since she'd met Haseeb. Had part of marrying him been about showing how small-minded some people were, and how broad-minded she could be, that no one should make decisions about their life based solely on chance, a soul that had been born into a Muslim body rather than a Hindu one?

Yet it spurred her on; the more they said it would be a disaster, that she was throwing away her caste as though it were nothing, the more determined she became to marry him and face everything that followed.

9

Ruby

'Quick, come inside, then.' Ruby's mum held the door ajar. Her grey-blonde hair was in rollers, piled up on the top of her head like an acorn. She quickly shut the door once they were in. God forbid the neighbours saw her. Out here in the Enfield suburbs, gossip was the only light that cut through the drear.

She gave Ruby a weak hug and she took in that familiar smell of hers: hot cocoa and apathy.

Ruby followed her through to the front room. Dad got out of his tartan armchair and swept her up in his arms. Despite his years, he nearly lifted Ruby off the ground.

'My little *manika*,' he said, using the Hindi word for 'jewel' as he always did. His tar-black moustache curled up at the corners into a smile; the dark-brown skin under his eyes had taken on a purplish hue through lack of sleep. 'Sit, sit, please.' He always treated Ruby like a revered guest, even though it used to be her home too. She slipped off her coat and draped it over the moss-green sofa.

'That'll crease, hang it up,' said her mum.

'Let her be,' said Ruby's dad gently, Indian accent woven into his words. It made her think of Jit for a moment, but she pushed that thought to the back of her mind.

'She never listens, Amrit. It's new, isn't it? Nice bit of wool, too.'

Ruby avoided her gaze. Her mum hung the coat on the banister in the hallway. The earlier rain had left blotches on the windowpane of the door, as though the houses beyond were scarred with acne.

'How are you keeping, then?' said her mum, leaning on the dinner table as if the answer was about to exhaust her. So much disappointment packed into such a fragile frame.

'I'm fine.' Ruby sat down but her mum didn't join her.

'I've got to go upstairs and take these out in a minute,' she said, pointing at her head. She didn't have any make-up on today, and the flourish of freckles on her cheeks that she usually tried so hard to cover were out on show.

'Have some tea, beta,' said Dad. He looked over at the white teapot on the table, bundled up in a bobbled red-white-and-blue tea cosy.

'Don't worry about me,' said Ruby. 'How are you both, anyway?' A hint of relief escaped with her words. They were both here, flesh and blood, still intact, despite their tired bodies, their weary faces, always alert to the threat.

'Can't complain, manika,' said Dad, with a spring in his voice.

Her mum – who, unlike Ruby's dad, could most definitely complain – did so for a good few minutes, telling Ruby all about Mr Morgan the butcher's lack of manners and the latest on her various ailments, from chilblains to a bad back. Ruby found it curious. Despite the ever-present fear of death just around the corner, people like her mum forgot, retreating to more familiar gripes and minor grudges.

'Dad,' said Ruby, taking her chance when her mum stopped for breath, 'I wanted to ask you something, about when you first came to England.' Ruby knew very little about his life before she'd been born, other than the story he often told about landing on British shores as a young Gujarati man, hoping that his nose would sniff out money and his heart would find him the love of a good woman. When Ruby was a kid, she never cared, never bothered to ask him much. When you were too young to have a history of your own, you weren't interested in anyone else's. Besides, he'd never seemed to want to talk about it. Convenient for the both of them.

'Oh, you don't want me boring you with all that.' Dad waved a hand.

'Yes, good luck with that, Rube.' Mum rose from her arm-chair as she spoke. 'You know you'd have a better chance of raising King George, God rest his soul, from the grave, than you would getting him to talk about India.' Ruby watched her stockinged legs, the colour of weak tea, climb the stairs.

She was right. Though Ruby tried to coax a little informa-tion out of him – what it was like when he first came over, what had happened in all the years before he met Mum – she soon got tired of trying.

'Please, let me hear all your news instead, yes?' Dad knelt down by the fire, which cracked and spat as he added a piece of scrap wood.

Ruby told him stories from her warden post and they covered the obligatory ground of how the world was faring in the war, the never-ending Battle of the Atlantic, the relentless charge of the Germans over the UK.

Later, Ruby helped her mum set the table. She always insisted on napkins, the good cutlery, the 'best' plates with the ring of blue flowers. 'That's a bit crooked, Rube,' she said, adjusting a fork. Ruby moved it back when she wasn't look-ing. It started after Ruby's brother Freddie died. Her mum saved her money for all the nicest magazines, *Vogue* and *Queen*, full of people that were nothing like them, doing things that they never would. Mum liked to point out the way the society women held a drink, the way a model composed herself on a chair. She used dress patterns based on the latest designs from Chanel or Lanvin, found cloche hats just like the ones that the Duchess of York wore. When times were good and there was a bit of spare money, she'd spend it on Chanel No. 5 or Shalimar and douse herself in them, plus maybe a pair of soft kid gloves for Ruby. 'You should behave the way you want the world to treat you,' she told her.

She spent hours with Ruby over the years, teaching her how to sit properly, how to lay the table the way the gentry did, even though they'd never set foot near a silver service in their lives. Mum thought you could become someone else simply by wearing the right clothes, sitting the right way. Never seemed to understand that underneath, you'd still have your old taint.

The three of them sat and ate a dinner of chicken pie – although there was so little meat in it that the closest it had got to chicken was probably when the vegetables had grown on the farm. Ruby listened to Mum going on while she hunted for chopped Brussels sprouts in the filling, as though it was shrapnel in a wound, letting the gloom wrap around her. It was her mum, mainly. Sucking up all the joy, as you wondered if you were about to step on a landmine. She didn't shout, she never hit out. Worse than that. She'd given up on the two of them, disappointment bound around them tight as a ball of a string, squeezing any contentment out of what remained of their family. Mum spoke with her emotions: the way she put her glass down, the sour way she held her body when she talked to you, anger rigid in the small gestures of her hands, in that clenched jaw of a thousand regrets.

They finished eating and cleared up. Dad soon fell asleep in his chair, the open newspaper laid over him like a blanket. Ruby and Mum shared a thin slice of dry carrot cake, the wireless on in the background.

There was a photo of them all on the side table next to the

armchair, a family portrait, Freddie's floppy hair threatening to fall into his eyes any moment. Ruby had fussed her way all through it, apparently, even after the third humbug the photographer had tried to bribe her with. Mum and Dad in their Sunday best. It was one of her earliest memories. A couple of years later and Freddie was gone. Knocked down by a car. An Austin 12. A stupid detail Ruby wished she didn't know. Freddie hadn't been looking, the driver said; he'd walked out from a corner of two streets. There were no witnesses to confirm or deny.

'So did you get anything out of Sleeping Beauty over there?' asked Mum. Ruby shook off the sad memories and stared at her mother. 'About coming here from India?' she said, and Ruby shook her head.

'Those were hard times for him,' said Mum, voice quiet. 'He doesn't like to be reminded of it.'

'What times, though? I don't really know anything about it.'

'It's not my story to tell,' said her mother, fork clinking against the plate as she broke off a scrap of cake.

'Oh, come on, Mum. He's not going to tell me. I don't even know how you met.'

She sighed. 'Well, he'd got a job as a lascar, you know them? An Indian sailor, with the navy, and he came over here from somewhere in Gujarat. Most people were nice enough, asking him questions about India. Wanting to know if he was one of those maharajas and what not. What would a maharaja be doing waltzing around Stepney?' She gave an amused huff. 'Well, like I say, *most* people were nice. Others . . .' She looked down at her cup and saucer framed with a pattern of faded pink roses, voice going quiet. 'Best not to ask him about that. What's brought all this on, anyway?'

'Nothing . . .' said Ruby, summoning the silence. She'd never met her mum's parents; they'd both died when she was little.

All they got was an occasional letter and the obligatory Christmas card with a penny stuck inside from her mum's sister Iris who had moved up to Scotland. 'You're all enough for me,' Ruby's mum used to say, 'our little family.' But then Freddie died and her heart snapped shut.

'Well, I'd better wake your father up.' Although Mum and Dad lived in Enfield, on the outskirts of the city, there were factories nearby which the Jerries saw as fair game. It was just as important to shelter here as it was in central London. Her parents preferred to stick it out in the back-garden shed, though it looked so flimsy that a wolf could have huffed and puffed it down. 'Are you coming?' said Mum.

Ruby shook her head. It had been raining the night before and she knew it'd be damp and waterlogged as usual.

Though Mum and Dad always tried to insist she come out, they knew she hated it out there. Besides, there was no denying her warden work in the city put her at far more risk anyway. She'd stay in the house and take her chances.

Ruby got into bed in the room she'd slept in as a kid. She pulled the old, warm quilt over herself, hoping for the chill to settle. As she waited for the skies to fill with the distant buzz of planes, exhaustion tempered any fear. Though it was pitch black at first, her eyes slowly grew accustomed to the dark room. Eerie objects from her younger years: the mannequin head on the table where she used to practise being a beautician; her old teddy bear, imaginatively called Ted, slumped on a shelf.

And then they came, like the bombers overhead, all the old memories. Why they'd moved away from Stepney, from all her friends, the school she loved; why lying in her childhood bed, with the familiar smell of mothballs and Sunlight soap, took her back to places she didn't want to go.

Ruby often wondered what life might have been like if Freddie had lived to see the start of the war. It was too difficult to imagine him as a man. Uniform too big for him, empty sleeves and trouser legs trailing like octopus tentacles. She didn't just grieve for who he was, she grieved for who he could have been.

And how might her life have been different? Would she be married by now, worrying about a husband who'd gone to war, burying him, grieving for a full-grown man instead of a boy? She wondered about the Ruby who died the day that he died, buried in her guilt and in her parents' grief.

Forcing back her tears and dragging her mind to the present, she thought of Dad. No wonder he didn't want to talk about his old life. That was something they were both good at, pretending that the past didn't happen.

He'd always tried to keep the darkness at bay, though, ignoring the people who called them names. Used to turn it into a game as they walked down the street, his giant hands enfolding Ruby's and Freddie's own, as stupid men called out to them. Dad would muster a smile. 'Oh, ignore him, he thinks I'm Michael Darkie, from down the pub, you know?', giving a squeeze to their fingers. 'Oh yes, he's after his friend from the factory, don't you worry about him. He shouts because he thinks I can't hear him from over there, you see.' It didn't work for long, of course. Ruby and Freddie learnt for themselves that those cruel words meant the same in the street or on the playground. And for Freddie it was worse, because he was darker than she was; no mistaking who his dad was. But still the two of them carried on walking down the street, Freddie peering at her through the mop of hair that forever fell across his eyes, both children nodding their heads and smiling as though they still believed Dad. Sharing in the deceit, all the way home.

She used to look down on Dad for acting that way. Thought him weak for trying to blend in. But as she'd grown older, Ruby could see that he was being strong for her and her brother. For a safer life, not an easier one.

Lying there in her old bed, she remembered when she and Freddie stopped sharing a room. Dad put up a partition board to divide the larger of the two bedrooms and squeezed exactly one single bed and one small wardrobe into each half.

Freddie would still annoy her when she was trying to get to sleep, knocking on the partition door, the hollow sound echoing in her room. She'd shout out, 'Freddie!' But of course he'd just do it again, louder this time.

Sometimes they'd talk before they fell asleep, sound travelling through the small gaps in the partition where it didn't quite reach the carpet. About school, or about how their parents had annoyed them that day, or about what they wanted to do when they grew up.

'You said you wanted to be a vet,' Ruby had said to him, pulling her cover up tighter over her chest.

'No, I never.'

'Yes, you did, right up until that day next door's cat Moggie threw up all over your shoes.' She gave a laugh.

His voice was tentative; she had to strain to hear him. 'No, I want to be a policeman, but . . .'

They'd lain there in silence, then. He didn't need to finish his sentence.

Unlike Freddie, Ruby had been 'lucky'; her skin was just the right side of white. And her name didn't sound Indian. Later, she had a flat miles away where no one knew her family. At first, it had been tricky; even if no one else knew you weren't entirely white, it was hard to shake the old feelings. But over time, it became easier to lose that side of herself, perhaps too easy, until she almost forgot herself. And in a way, other people were complicit. They rarely wanted to know where your mum and dad were from, where they grew up, because the natural assumption was that you fitted in, that everyone was as British as they were.

That's why she was one person with her parents, another when she was on her own. A life divided, backs turned to each other, as though one didn't know the other existed.

Was it the India Forum that made her think of all this now? That man, Jit – Sunny, whatever his real name was. He'd practically encouraged her to go back to the Forum. Those dark eyes of his, framed by thick brows, the determination to make something more for his people. She'd only gone through boredom and to see what she might be able to get out of it. But there was something about him that seemed to draw her in.

Ruby turned onto her side, propping her hand under her head. She'd spent most of her life running away from who she was. Split in two. Could she really step across the border she'd drawn for herself?

When Ruby went downstairs in the morning, her parents had already finished their breakfast.

She walked over to the sideboard and tucked a few shillings inside her dad's one prized possession from India: a mother-of-pearl inlaid box. 'You shouldn't be giving us money,' said Mum, as she went into the kitchen to make a start on the dishes. Ruby finished the sentence in her head. *It should be your brother doing that.*

'Manika,' Dad said, his eyes dark, face serious. 'You know you don't need to do that.'

'Yes, I know, but I want to.' Ruby gave him a quick smile. She saw it in the look he returned to her, the same one he'd given her countless times over the years: *You're hiding something,* it said. Never could keep things from him.

'Dad?' she said, hoping to make him forget. He gave a small smile as he waited for her to continue. 'Thank you.'

'For what?'

For trying to shield us from the worst of the world, she thought. 'For being a good dad,' she said, adding a sunshine to her voice that she didn't quite feel.

He gave a laugh of surprise. 'It's nothing.' The pride in his gaze made her heart swell.

'Well, I'd better be off,' she said, finding her mum and then giving both of them quick pecks on the cheek, committing their faces to memory all over again.

Dad called out his usual goodbye as she opened the door. 'Promise me you'll take care of yourself, my little manika?'

Ruby nodded and caught herself just before she was about to reply, 'Cross my heart and hope to die.'

10

Kitty

Torch beams guided their way as moonlight shimmered through the elm leaves onto the pavement. 'Where are we going?' said Kitty, as Haseeb led her along by the hand. 'Patience,' he whispered.

'Do you even know me at all?' Kitty laughed.

They carried on along Elmore Street, past the three-storey brick houses on either side of the road. The smell of leaf mould and damp sandbags hung in the air from the earlier rain. Finally, they came to a scruffy-looking three-storey house. But rather than knocking on the front door, they took the side entrance.

'Nearly there,' said Haseeb without turning around, probably anticipating another question from Kitty.

The sound of laughter and music carried through the air, getting louder as they approached the back garden. There was a run of small steps down to the basement, but instead of a cold and cavernous shelter, he opened the door to a world of candlelight and dancing. There was a four-piece band playing jazz music; a song she'd never heard before. Two Indian men, one on a clarinet and the other with a large, round drum placed between his legs. Beside him, there was a man on bass and another on saxophone. The place was full of young couples, mainly Indian servicemen, but there were others too, possibly

African or Caribbean. A couple of the women were in WAAF or ATS uniforms, though most wore tea dresses like Kitty's. No one was sitting at the small tables, where lonely white candles burned away on saucers.

'What is this?' Kitty tugged on Haseeb's arm. He moved closer to hear her better, his stubble grazing against her cheek.

'Just somewhere to forget for a while,' he smiled. He took her fur coat and folded it inside his wool jacket, placing them on a chair. His head nearly touched the ceiling and the music was so loud the drums thumped in her chest. He briefly said hello to an Indian man in a tweed jacket who was on his way to the dance floor.

'Is this a shelter?' she asked, standing by the table. She had seen a few places like this during the war: business basements that had been requisitioned, crypts beneath churches, but this was more like a pub under a house.

'Two Indian families rent the house above, they open it up sometimes.'

She tried to take it all in but couldn't quite fathom this picture of mainly Indian men and women, dancing just like the people at Café de Paris.

'And you've come here before? How did you know about it?' she asked. He bent his head again to meet her own, the warmth of his cheek glowing against hers. Smoke floated in halos of light around them.

'One of the barristers at work told me about it,' he said. 'Shall I get us some drinks?'

She watched as Haseeb went and handed some money to a young man standing behind a large table. The man gave him two glasses. Cordial for him, watered-down gin and lemon for her, which was for the best because Kitty could tell from the first sip that it was strong.

The dancers were wrapped up in a fast-beat number,

'Darktown Strutters' Ball', with playful clarinet refrains and an insistent drumbeat.

There was something about live music, a hint of danger that things might go wrong, an errant note, a slipped beat, but also the thrill that the musicians could improvise and create something brand new, more beautiful than ever before. Anything can happen, said the music.

She thought back to the places she used to go to with her father and friends of the family sometimes, the Taj Mahal Hotel in Colaba, one of the few five-star establishments that didn't have a colour bar preventing Indians mingling with the British. In fact, the hotel was said to have been built solely for that reason. The founder, the wealthy industrialist Jamsetji Tata, was fed up with being declined entry to Bombay's Watson's Hotel and decided to build somewhere else. After all, you would never turn yourself away.

All kinds of jazz and swing music could be heard at the Taj Mahal Hotel. American, mostly, big bands who'd come over with the black musicians trying to get away from the segregation back home, but occasionally there were Indians too, like Mickey Correa and Frank Fernand.

Kitty had fond memories of stepping inside the cool, air-conditioned ballroom. It was decadently decorated with vast chandeliers and deep, velvety carpets; they would be greeted by a maître d' with a middle parting sharp as a blade.

They would take their seats, looking around at the women draped in Schiaparelli and Patou, hair freshly washed, permed and waxed, doused in rose and patchouli and amber to stave off the staling sweat, the men in military or civil clothes, always smartly turned out. Then there was the diamond-clad 'fishing expedition': the young women who were fresh off the boat from England, a startled expression their main accessory. They would come along with family members who were already embedded in India, on the hunt for a captain or a plantation owner who could add yet another jewel to their fingers.

'Shall we dance?' Haseeb said. Kitty put her drink down and took his hand. The dance floor was full now, the jaunty clarinets of 'Begin the Beguine' giving way to the urgent, sultry brass of 'Sing, Sing, Sing'. The deep and incessant drum beat so hard she couldn't tell the difference between the percussion and her heart. The band seemed to be enjoying themselves as much as the dancers, heat rising, a sheen of sweat across Kitty's chest; how good it felt to lose herself, to feel Haseeb's hand in hers, his smile reflecting back at her.

Then a change in tempo. A languorous kind of song, the notes wrapping themselves around their bodies, the slow beat brushing their skin.

After a while, the musicians paused for a break, laying down the clarinet and saxophone on chairs as though they were sleeping babies that needed the tenderest care.

Kitty and Haseeb smiled at each other in commiseration and moved to the edge of the room to sit down.

'There's a meeting at the Forum on Monday,' said Haseeb. 'Will you be able to go?'

'Depends on how my trial is going. Conscription will still be the hot topic,' he said, looking out across the makeshift dance floor. Their voices echoed against the bare brick.

She put her hand over his, giving it a tight squeeze. They'd been in the country for two years, so there would be no escaping what was coming for Haseeb.

He swallowed, staring down at the table.

'The India Forum will help you fight it,' she said, rubbing his arm.

'Maybe I won't need any help,' he said quietly.

Kitty looked at him. 'You can't just hope you'll fail the medical test?' She knew of people who had taken their chances, been called up, measured, weighed, prodded, poked and rejected in no time at all, but that was a big risk.

He looked down at the floor. 'However bad it is with the British, it could be far worse under Nazi rule. Other people need help too.'

Her body tensed. She turned towards him. 'So what are you saying? You want to take on all the woes of the world and forget the Independence movement?' she said. 'We have to help ourselves first, Haseeb.'

'But perhaps if we fight with the British, we can use it as a bargaining chip. It could help our cause too. Plenty risk their lives for freedom in India already. What's the difference?'

She gave a cool laugh. 'That was the whole point of coming here. To help our country. Leaving everything behind.' Leaving everyone behind, she thought.

He finally took his eyes off the table and looked at her, stroking her hand. 'I've not made a decision, it's just something to think about.'

'Lots to think about, yes,' she said, quietly. 'Getting yourself killed for a country that won't give you freedom.'

Without the warmth of the jazz music, the basement felt cold and hollow, like the bottom of a well. Kitty and Haseeb stayed where they were as the shrouds of smoke wrapped around them.

11

Ruby

Though parts of London were being cracked open like a skull, the city seemed to impose itself more than ever. Ruby noticed what was lost, the things that had disappeared, becoming more aware of the city than she had been before. On the outskirts of Hyde Park, where drunken sandbags dozed along the perimeters, gaps in the skyline had opened up where once there had been buildings. Ruby walked on, passing the various bins where people dropped their paper and tin cans to be recycled and entered the park at the Marble Arch entrance.

Though she'd lived in London all her life, Ruby had never been to the famous Speaker's Corner. She'd always suspected it was full of political cronies and people who liked the sound of their own voices far too much. But she'd heard via her warden rounds that the India Forum were going to be at the park today, and she couldn't face another weekend sitting around the flat.

Out on the path there was a large gathering of people: mainly men, a few women, with a smattering of Indians among them all. A bit further on, a trestle table had been set up and Ruby could see Mrs Akhtar in a cropped jacket and a teardrop hat, putting out pamphlets.

The barrage balloons watched over them from a distance. Sheep were dotted across the green, grazing in the park and keeping the grass nice and short, as they had done for as long as Ruby could remember.

Mandalji stood on a wooden box, giving a speech. Perhaps it was the outdoor setting, the breeze rustling in the trees, a fresh crowd of new ears, but he seemed more passionate than ever.

'We call on the good people of Britain to support India, your ally now and forever, and to give her democratic freedom.' Mandalji talked of his dreams for India, how British friends could help build a better future for both countries and all the ways they could be of help, through donations, through lobbying, through local groups like the India Forum. Ruby joined in the applause as his speech came to a finish.

Ruby couldn't help but be swept along with it. You could be blown to bits any minute but the India Forum still carried on: fighting for something that wasn't about war. They fought with hope, despite the challenges they faced.

'You're talking about democracy, but that's what our boys are fighting for,' said a younger Englishman in a navy brimmed hat. 'And haven't we been the ones guiding India all this time? What about the railways? All those new buildings?'

Mandalji looked down towards the speaker in the crowd. The breeze picked up and he had to clutch hold of his hat, speaking louder to be heard. 'But sir, we are not Britannia's children. We have our own right to govern, surely?'

'That's what the civil service is for,' said the man in the navy hat. 'Indians have already been given jobs in the civil service to help govern the country, haven't they?'

'And why, sir, do we need to be *given* anything, except our freedom?' said Mandalji. Though his words were pointed, he kept his tone surprisingly calm. 'Is there anything civil about a service that prevents ordinary Indians from working at the highest level of authority?' People in the crowd, both Indian and English, murmured along in agreement. The man in the navy hat gave a non-committal nod of his head but decided not to press his case further.

Ruby scanned the space. Jit had joined the edges of the crowd at some point. She caught his eye and he gave a small doff of his hat.

'We have our own problems trying to keep ourselves safe,' shouted another man, older this time, dressed in a grey suit. Everyone turned to look at him. 'We can't help you and your causes an' all.'

From here it escalated as another voice joined in the jeering, and then another. A couple of Englishmen took offence, shouting at them to show some respect.

Ruby felt the blood rise up her neck. She turned towards Jit, expecting to see her own anger reflected back at her, but it was almost as though he was bemused.

'We've given 'em plenty, and still they're moaning,' the man in the grey suit piped up.

'If you wogs hate us so much, why don't you just go back there?' another man shouted.

The pain came sharp. *You're not like us, you never will be.*

'Eh! We can do without that. We're here to peacefully debate, why don't you listen to 'em?' called out a man with a Scottish accent, breaking Ruby away from her thoughts. He was young and leant on a walking stick.

'It's quite all right,' said Mandalji, raising his voice above the shouts. He had an extraordinarily gracious smile on his face considering what was going on around him. He held his palm up. 'If you would like to find out more about the India Forum, please do come and speak to me and my colleagues. You are all most welcome.'

Someone else from the Forum had taken to the podium now. Mandalji's words seemed to have calmed the hecklers for the time being.

That all-too-familiar feeling of being the outsider shrouded her once again, no matter how hard she tried to escape it. A memory of a photograph she'd seen in the newspaper came back to her now. A picture from Germany, a young man in a hat and thick wool coat, a woman with her hair tucked under a scarf and short fur, all otherwise ordinary, except for the pale six-pointed star on each of their lapels, rippled and clumsy. There was something infantilizing about those cloth stars, the way they just hung there on the black fabric. A mark of difference, of shame even. Just like her dad, except that for him, it was his skin that gave him away.

Ruby thought of the Indians she had sometimes come across, huddled together on buses, or waiting for rations, how they'd largely kept themselves to themselves, not keen to mingle with others, glancing at you with wide, wary eyes. She knew it well, that reluctance to draw attention, to be called out at any moment for not fitting in, or worse still, as an enemy.

She had got away with it. Hiding in plain sight. It sometimes gave Ruby a kind of small, empty thrill to think of it. That unspoken connection that said, *You're allowed because you're just like us.* Of course, nothing could be further from the truth.

'Hello, Miss Thacker,' said Jit, appearing beside her and drawing her out of her thoughts.

'Oh, hello,' she said. 'And what are we calling ourselves today?' Ruby couldn't help herself.

Jit broke into a grin. 'You can still call me Jit, or Satyajit. Just like everyone else here.' Daylight made his brown eyes gleam, like rum in sunlight.

'Well, I suppose you can call me Ruby, in that case. That's my name. Every day.'

He smiled at her.

'Is that normal?' said Ruby, turning her head briefly back towards the crowd. 'All the things they were saying?'

'Which ones – the do-gooders or the bigots?' said Jit, his tone cool now.

'They're so . . . open about it,' she said. 'I'm just surprised, here of all places. Where free speech is supposed to be sacred.'

'Oh, it is,' said Jit and then added, in a matter-of-fact tone, 'that's why anyone can call us wog whenever they feel like it.'

Ruby's breath caught in her throat. Hearing it out loud again. It was just a word, yes, but it was loaded like a gun. 'I'm sorry,' she said quietly.

'We're used to it.' He shrugged it off.

'And when will you be taking the podium?' Ruby gave a small smile, trying to move the conversation to more comfortable ground.

She had expected him to smile back, but instead he said quietly, 'Standing up there isn't a good use of anyone's time.'

'But people listened, at least?'

'Half were too busy shouting to hear a single word.' His voice was curt.

'Then why do you come here and support it all?'

'We can learn from seeing what is not working, just as well as what is,' he said. 'But anyway, I've seen enough. Are you hungry?'

The question took her by surprise. 'Should we not wait for the others?' she asked.

'They can carry on throwing words around if they want,' he shrugged. 'I have better things to do.'

*

Lyons' teashop was busy inside, with the tables and chairs crammed together, a half-empty counter with a forlorn set of ginger cake and iced buns begging to be picked up. The waitress directed them to seats near the window, which had been playfully taped across with noughts and crosses to protect them during a raid.

Jit took off his hat and propped it on a hook on the wall. They ordered iced buns, coffee for Ruby, tea for Jit.

'If you don't mind me saying, you don't seem to have all that much in common with most of the people at the India Forum?' said Ruby.

He looked at her with curiosity, waiting for her to continue.

'It doesn't seem like you agree with what they want to do,' Ruby ventured.

'Well, they keep talking about how we're so close to Independence. But we don't have it, do we?' said Jit, sitting forward in his chair. 'All these decades people have been fighting.'

He explained just how far back the fight went. To the bloody and brutal Indian Sepoy Mutiny of 1857, the Amritsar Massacre of 1919, when thousands of peaceful protestors had been killed by the British Indian Army, to the many years since when Gandhi and his fellow Congressmen and women had carried on the fight.

'There has to be a better way than sitting around waiting for others to make decisions for us. We need to show them that we won't back down.' Jit's eyes lit up as he spoke.

Ruby wondered what it must feel like to muster so much energy for something, anything. Even yourself. 'You're clearly very passionate about it,' she said.

'And you, what do *you* feel passionate about?' Was that a glimmer of flirtation in his eyes?

She leant forward and said in her most earnest voice, 'Saving cats from trees, it's truly my life's work.'

He watched her with the briefest moment of hesitation, then laughed. 'You're doing it again,' he said, his voice crisp, like the last leaves of autumn.

'Doing what?'

'Avoiding questions.'

'That's not true,' she said, her neck flushed. 'I *do* like cats.'

'You're really not going to tell me, are you?' he smiled.

'What's there to tell?'

Jit held her gaze as if to say, *I dare you.*

But in the silence, all she could think about was a coffin, the helpless look on her parents' faces.

'Keeping people safe,' she said, her throat dry. 'There, happy now?' The words were more forceful than she'd intended.

Jit's face was a mix of triumph and surprise. The truth was, Ruby hadn't expected herself to say it out loud any more than he had.

'And that is why you became a warden?' Jit squinted at Ruby. Sun shone through the gaps of the taped windows and illuminated his features. Faint wings of laughter lines appeared in the corners of his eyes.

She nodded her half-lie.

The waitress brought over their orders. Jit took the lid off the teapot, but popped it back on when he saw how weak the liquid looked. He turned his gaze back to her. 'Well, it's admirable.'

'What do you mean?' Ruby blew on her black coffee, still not used to taking it without the usual two sugars. Her dad always said she had a tooth so sweet that it must have been made out of Tate & Lyle.

'Your warden work. It's very brave.'

Ruby didn't say anything. It was useful to let people make assumptions about you, easier to let the lies fall where they wanted.

She took a sip of coffee. Keeping her tone as nonchalant as possible as she put the cup down, she said, 'So what were you doing at Fleet's the other day?'

Ruby could feel his eyes on her, wondering how to respond. 'He has a lot of goods for sale. But then you know that already, don't you?'

The blood rushed to her cheeks, and she wondered if she was blushing. There was no point in pushing it; he was clearly smart and he had probably worked out what she was doing. But now it was clear: Jit didn't seem to care either way.

She shifted in her seat. 'How long have you been in England, then?' said Ruby.

'About eighteen months,' he replied, casually flipping his packet of cigarettes round and round on the table.

'And before that you were in India?'

Jit opened his mouth to speak, but it took a moment for him to gather his thoughts. 'On and off.'

He wasn't making this easy. Ruby tried again. 'You speak good English. I thought perhaps you'd been here longer.'

'We were taught it at school, but I studied here too. At the University of London,' he said, pouring out his tea.

'University? But then how come you're . . .' She trailed off, wondering if she was being rude.

'How come I'm working as a pedlar? I was given a scholarship, but I decided that there were better ways to fight for India than sitting around in classrooms listening to British men tell me what to think.' A harder tone in his voice now.

'And you decided to stay here, rather than carry on in India?'

'Life over there is even more restrictive for Indians than it is here.' He gave a scornful laugh. 'In India, the worst thing you can be is an Indian.'

The honesty of his words caught her off guard. She thought of her dad, what his life had been like there, what he'd endured when he'd first come to England. She decided to retreat to safer ground. 'And what do you do when you're not working at the

India Forum?' Ruby tilted her head. 'Or do you eat, drink and sleep revolution?'

Jit smiled. 'Well, it is good to keep busy.'

'True,' said Ruby.

'Keeps your mind off things,' he said. His eyes darkened, before he apparently remembered himself. He straightened up in his chair, a cheerful smile on his face once again. 'And what about you, you grew up here in London?'

'Yes, lived here all my life.' Now it was her turn to hold back.

'And siblings?' he said.

'No, just me,' she said, dropping her gaze and swallowing her lie whole.

After they left the teashop, she took Jit on a tour of Marylebone, which he sweetly pronounced 'Mary-Lebone'.

Like so many who'd given up their professions to fight for their country, buildings had surrendered their old lives too. A community hall now masqueraded as a rest centre for the homeless; a church crypt had been requisitioned and was now a morgue. Ruby tried to distract from the carpets of broken glass, the twisted girders and the blackened premises, still smouldering from the raids, which even the rats were scuttering away from. She told Jit useless trivia about the area, some of which she embellished because she couldn't remember what had stood there before.

They carried on walking. Ruby was grateful when he suggested heading back towards the park, which was nicer than having to face all the reminders of the war. Across the way, they could see the sandbags packed into the entrances of the grand Park Lane hotels.

'That's a pretty ring,' said Jit.

Ruby glanced at him and then down at her finger.

'There's something Indian about it, in the pattern. My mother used to have something like that.'

'Oh, really?' Ruby rubbed her thumb over the filigreed gold, then put her hands down, hoping he'd move on. A brief flash of memory: pulling it out from a drawer in a bomb-wrecked house. 'Don't think it's been further east than Mile End,' she said, with a flash of a smile.

'Did you spend much time around here, growing up?' Jit asked.

'We came on a day trip once or twice. Picnicked in the park.' She thought of the times her mum had brought her and Freddie when they were little, how once they'd played hide-and-seek and Ruby had been stuck behind a tree for what felt like hours. Then she realized that Freddie had fallen asleep next to her mum on the blanket while he'd been counting, his chubby cheeks puffing gently in and out as he dozed. Perhaps grief was a kind of penance; all that joy had to be paid for somehow.

There was a buttery light across the trees. Tulips and daffodils were standing to attention. Squint along this stretch of grass and you could almost pretend that the dugouts weren't there.

'Well, I'd better be going now,' said Jit, looking at his watch.

To her surprise, she found herself a little disappointed.

'It was nice to spend time with you, Ruby. Perhaps we can do it again sometime?'

'Perhaps,' she said. It was an honest answer. She hadn't worked him out yet, although she recognized something of herself in him, that much was true. A holding back. A cage around the heart.

12

Kitty

Something about this street was different. Why was it brighter than usual, despite the ashen clouds above? A building was missing, another crushed down to the foundations, letting light in where once there'd been an army of bricks and mortar protecting the inhabitants inside. Yet nature was fighting back. Plants – weeds, mainly – were springing up between the ruins.

It had been a long day. Kitty had just finished helping out at an India Forum branch near Archway. After crossing Dartmouth Park Hill she'd lost her way, no longer able to keep her bearings among the carcasses of collapsed Victorian houses. Even if they made it through the war, what would be left at the end?

She moved on slowly, winding her way around blocks that looked as worn out as the workers they housed. As Mandalji often said, life for those on the lower rungs of the ladder was hard, whether in India or England.

As dusk fell the clouds turned red, as though steeped in all the anger of the world. The smouldering air and the smell of charred flesh from the night before lingered; she tried to forget how it reminded her of the funeral pyres back home.

Kitty arrived in good time at the shelter, ignoring the usual looks from a few of the people who were waiting to go inside. She couldn't be sure whether they were intrigued by her, her 'exotic skin' coupled with her English clothing, or whether they were suspicious of the foreigner in their midst.

She made her way down the escalators, which had been turned off and would soon be filled with a ladder of sleeping people, to the platform. Some people were in a routine: go to the shelter, get some sleep, then straight to work, and back to the shelter again. It carried on all week, until they could finally get home for a bath at the weekend.

Usually there'd be a few of her fellow countrymen, perhaps a West Indian or African man or two, and she wouldn't feel quite so out of place. She recalled stories of people like them who were treated differently at the shelters. Haseeb had once only been able to get into the Camden Tube shelter after an older gentleman stepped in on his behalf and quietly spoke to the ARP wardens, who were far less welcoming. Being a woman, even an Indian woman, sometimes had its advantages.

Kitty sat on the floor in a gap along the postered wall. Dozens of people had packed in already, while nerves and fear took up every last inch of space along the platform. Next to Kitty, an older couple made some space for her. The fellow was a balding man with postbag eyes; his wife had wrapped her rollered hair in a pink scarf. She gave Kitty a thin smile, then wriggled about, entirely deluded as to how much space was available, as her bottom became well acquainted with Kitty's right thigh.

The sweat-and-breath damp clung to her skin, the reek of the latrines mingling with the fish-paste sandwiches. There'd be another whiff of it whenever there was a whoosh of air from the last of the Tube trains coming in. They emptied out more people, who hurried home as quickly as they could, stepping over those who had already set up camp.

She wondered where Haseeb was now. Did he make it to the shelter near chambers? Had he decided to brave it out instead?

Kitty opened her book, a Hindi translation of Tagore's *Ghare Bhaire*. It would be nice to give her mind a rest from English and retreat back into a familiar language, to read about characters who were caught up in the Independence movement just as she was. She took out the bookmark, an old postcard with an illustrated map of Bombay, trailing her finger over the city that looked like a hand outstretched, a place of opportunity, the word 'Bombay' written across the middle. Above them, the sirens started up.

Along the platform, the fear was catching. Early on in the war, the anticipated thrill of the raid they were about to face, the bravado at finally facing it head on after months of waiting, had run through London like a fever. But there was only so much exhilaration you could take when your heart was worn out by stress. The older woman next to Kitty was chatting away now, apparently addressing her husband but also sneaking a look around, gauging the rest of her audience's response. Kitty pretended to read.

'I love cosying up in a dark shelter with my Ron, don't I?' she said, clutching his arm with her chubby hand.

'Leave it out,' said Ron. Despite the fact that his voice sounded like he'd been gargling with nails, he didn't seem to mind all that much.

'Let me tell you, we're best off down here,' she said, breathless. 'Remember the other night? We'd decided to stay at home, which was just asking for trouble, weren't it? Bomb came down right in the middle of the street outside our house. You've not had such a shock since our wedding night, have you, Ron?' she snorted.

Ron said nothing.

The woman tried to carry on but eventually her voice faded, as she found no comfort in the people around her. Kitty almost said something, but she was tired of dealing with the inevitable questions and comments:

Where are you from then?

You speak very good English for an Indian.

Where'd you get those nice clothes from?

And besides, who was going to comfort Kitty, make *her* feel better?

Down the platform, someone had started up the gramophone. Soon people were singing along with the music, young or old, note perfect or tone deaf. Kitty recognized the song; she'd heard instrumental versions at balls at Oxford and in the grand hotels back in Bombay. She looked down at the postcard again, and sadness expanded inside her, from the top of her throat down to the hollow of her stomach, as she thought about home, as she remembered her adolescent years, spending time with her dadi in the sitting room. The warmth and humidity of the shelter took her back now. To the aniseed scent of the tulsi tea her grandmother always liked to drink filling the air. How they would sit together at the table every afternoon. Dadi's ornately patterned Singer in the corner, surrounded by vermilion fabric and bobbins of thread, the sheesham-wood seating lining the other walls.

One afternoon they had been discussing Kitty's aunt, Anandi Kaki, who lived with them when she and her husband weren't off on some new Independence crusade. Anandi Kaki had been arrested yet again and was due to return home that afternoon.

'We won't get a minute's peace until we go to bed now.' Dadi put her hand to her head, gold bangles clattering against each other as she moved. 'We're going to have to hear every little detail.'

Kitty giggled, trying in vain to get back to her schoolwork. She stretched her feet down, touching the cool floor. Outside, the *qawwals* had begun their determined calls to prayer from the mosques.

Later, Kitty learnt for herself. The way Kaki went on about it, how it had become some kind of competitive sport for her, how Kaki had been the one who had faced the policewallah, how it was she who sat on the cold, hard jail cell floor the longest and without complaint. Perhaps she simply needed to win something, because they certainly weren't winning against the British.

'What's it like in jail, Dadi? Isn't Kaki scared?' Kitty had asked. It was a recent thing, her interest in the freedom fight. When Kitty was little, the adults used to tell her and her younger cousins that her kaki had gone to visit a distant family member, that they were poor and lived in a rural area outside Bombay, which explained the dishevelled state of her aunt when she came home. But her family had decided that Kitty was more than old enough to understand now. For the most part, it was just something the adults did, congregating in the formal sitting room, talking about things she had no interest in. Boring politics. Jail, on the other hand, was fascinating.

'Ask your kaki if she was scared. That will get her going, maybe then she'll finally give me a moment's peace,' she sighed, then pointed at the *paan daan* box on a side table. Kitty understood her cue, getting up and bringing it over to her grandmother. It was a circular box made from perforated silver, decorated with an ornate pattern of lotuses. Lifting the lid, she revealed her treasure of chewing tobacco – *supari* – shaved areca nut, cloves, cardamom and betel nut leaves, which were refilled every day by the housemaid. Dadi pushed the box across to Kitty as she couldn't fold the large leaf – the *paan* – as well as she used to. Dadi never let anyone else make it for her, and so Kitty began the daily ritual. She pulled out the bright-green leaves and, as usual, looked for the one that most resembled a heart.

'Did you used to protest, like Anandi Kaki does? When you were younger?' Kitty cut the top of the stem off and then rolled the leaf into a cone shape.

Dadi gave a grunt of a laugh. 'You think I didn't have better things to do, Keertini?' she said, using her nickname, a shortened version of Keerthanaben.

Kitty put the ingredients into the paan, then folded it into a kind of pouch, sealing the top by tucking it in.

Just as Dadi was about to take a bite, Aditi, one of their servants, barely tapped the door once before rushing in. 'It's the policewallah!'

'At the door?' Dadi put the paan down.

'*Ji.*' Aditi nodded vigorously.

'Those silly books of your aunt's,' Dadi muttered as she left the room. Kitty's aunt often sold or gave out banned books about revolution and Independence to others, but sometimes she had to hide them in the house until she could move them on.

'Stay here,' she said, though Kitty followed her out all the same.

There was a turbaned policewallah at the door, along with a shorter policeman with a wispy moustache who stood behind him.

'Yes, what is it?' said Dadi, staring at the man. Was Dadi really not scared of the police or was she just very good at hiding it?

'We've come to search the house.' The turbaned policewallah's voice was so deep and loud it almost seemed to echo in Kitty's chest.

'For what? There's nothing here,' said Dadi in a curt tone.

'We have a warrant.' There was a hint of smugness in his voice now.

Dadi huffed. 'Fine. But don't you dare make a mess.' She

turned around and then Kitty saw a flash of alarm on her face, but it was gone as soon as it came.

They followed the police around the rooms as they looked in trunks and cupboards, scanned the bookshelves and peered under beds. Kitty hated the way they ran their hands over their belongings, the things that held all their memories.

She could hear Dadi's annoyance as the other policeman searched the sitting room down the hallway: 'Careful with that!', 'No, put that back over there where you found it.'

Kitty watched as the turbaned policewallah stepped into her bedroom, arms clasped behind his back. He turned his head slowly from side to side, taking in the bed, the simple teak desk and chair and the traditional carved mango-wood wardrobe.

Kitty stayed by the doorway, peeking in. Her heart raced now. The books were hidden under the floorboards beneath her bed. He was standing no more than two feet away from them.

'And whose room is this?' He looked at her with light hazel eyes.

'Mine,' she said, quietly.

'You sleep here?' He pointed at the bed but continued to look at her, eyes travelling down her body. It was one of the first times she'd been truly aware of a man's gaze, the danger two eyes could hold.

'It must get lonely at night,' he said, eyes narrowing.

Kitty swallowed. A flash of heat in her cheeks.

'Does it get lonely?' he persisted, and began to move towards her.

'Have you not finished yet?' Dadi pushed past Kitty.

The policewallah stepped back. 'Almost.' He made a show of looking inside the wardrobe and inside the desk, while Dadi glared at him. When he came towards the door, Kitty hurried away, into the safety of the sitting room.

Once the door was securely locked and they'd watched the

policewallah drive away, her dadi said, 'He didn't look under the bed?' Kitty shook her head, heart still racing.

'All this politics nonsense.' Dadi screwed up her face as though she'd stepped in cow dung. 'I have a home to look after, a family to take care of. Why do I have to get caught up in all of it?' she said. 'Those *goonda* have left everything in a state, all over some books.'

It wouldn't be until many years later that Kitty would realize, when she took up the cause herself, that for her grandmother it was easier to let other people do the work for her. Dadi never seemed to understand that she was just as caught up in the politics as the rest of them, in private, at home; what her family were allowed to do, what women were allowed to do. After all, doing nothing was just as political as taking up arms.

Laughter in the Tube station dragged Kitty back into the present. She straightened her back, the brick wall behind her cold against her neck. Kitty longed to speak to Dadi, to feel those bony fingers of hers on her skin, waiting for another gruff comment or dismissive laugh. Yet even now, Kitty couldn't quite place Dadi's voice in her mind; time was smothering her memories, day by day.

The gramophone down the platform was still playing. As the crackling voices echoed through the Tube tunnels, it was as though the ghosts had come out to join them. The tunnel walls filled with the dancing shadows of courting couples in dark corners.

There was a longing in her chest, a pain that caught like a piece of flint. She might never see or speak to Dadi again. And then there was Haseeb.

Her heart charred with loss. How alone she felt, among all these people.

13

Ruby

It had been a sudden onslaught tonight: the bombers hidden amid a black marble sky, taking everyone by surprise. The ground floor of a house on Tavistock Street had collapsed through to the basement. When Ruby had stood there at the top of the mound of rubble, looking down into the black, she'd heard a sound, almost like a mewling kitten. A little boy.

Ruby knew who it was. Archie; he was only seven or eight years old. Most of the children in London had been lined up at train stations at the beginning of the war, gas masks hanging from a long string, the way that mittens used to be, nametags pinned to their clothes, as though they were about to be posted through letter boxes up and down the country. Archie had been sent away too, and he'd hated it, so his mother had brought him back, although Ruby suspected it was also because she couldn't bear to be apart from him. Mrs Joseph wasn't the only parent to let their kids stay in the city. Ruby had heard people in the shelters, with their I'm-just-minding-my-own-business faces, whispering loudly about how selfish it was of parents to keep their children here. All but the youngest children had largely left London, as though the Pied Piper had taken them away.

There'd been nothing for it but for Ruby to go down and try to get him. Someone had fetched a rope to fasten around her body. Errol had tied some of his expert knots – the ones he'd learnt from his boy scout days and never shut up about. Ruby hurriedly tucked her trousers into her socks so they couldn't catch on anything.

Now, she gripped the torch tight in her right hand and held her body as straight as a torpedo as Errol and a couple of other men lowered her down head-first, as though she was diving straight into the debris.

Ruby called out every so often, letting Archie know that they'd get him out safely. Funny how lies were not only acceptable, but positively encouraged, under this kind of pressure.

As she went in, her hips hit the jutted edges of what must have been the ground floor. She was at the mercy of the rope and the men's strength, her body swinging haphazardly as she tried to steady herself on the rubble. She fought the urge to turn herself upright and stand; darkness was the only ground beneath her.

'Easy now, Ruby. Get your bearings,' said Errol.

Once her feet had cleared the gap above her, Ruby held the torch out, scanning among the earth and rubble for any sign of life, trying to ignore the smell of smoke and sulphur. She'd watched as the bomb had fallen, the way the bricks and mortar seemed to stretch, as though they were made of elastic.

The crater was like a cave. Then she saw a small movement: Archie was covered in a thick layer of ash, the only colour to him a pinkish cut on his forehead. He was a couple of metres away from her, where the chimney breast had once stood. She could only see his head; the rest of him was buried in the wreckage. He was sobbing so hard that there was no sound from his mouth, except for gasps of air every few seconds.

'It's all right,' Ruby said, another lie. 'Can you try to move a little?'

'My leg . . . It really hurts,' he cried.

A large piece of wood, perhaps a broken tabletop, lay across his body. The blood rushed to Ruby's head. She'd been upside down for a good few minutes now, her vision blurring as she tried to focus on what had happened.

She called to Errol to help her get upright and stand.

'Is it safe?' shouted Errol.

'I'll let you know when you lower me down,' she said, tension surging through her muscles. Couldn't get this wrong. The rope slackened slightly, letting her inch lower until she could reach her arms out into a handstand on the broken bricks below. Next, she rolled her legs down, hoping the debris wouldn't give way beneath her. As she turned herself upright, her head began to spin. That was definitely the smell of sulphur, which meant a gas leak. They needed to hurry.

Once she'd found her footing as well as her nerve, she gingerly stepped across so she could reach the boy, the rope straining at her waist. She tugged it so that Errol and the two men could feed more through and allow her to move across. She rested the torch on what looked like a piece of plaster and Errol did his best to give her some light from above, too. The table seemed to have been broken into two pieces but it was still a hefty slab.

'Now, Archie. This might hurt a little, but we're going to get you out, I promise.' What did yet another lie matter now?

She grabbed hold of the piece of wood. It gave way, slipping a little, her curved fingers catching on a dozen splinters. The boy screamed.

'I'm sorry, I'm sorry,' she said, catching her breath as she took in his wounds. She could see now that his leg was at an awkward angle, twisted inwards. No blood there as far as she could tell. Pyjama shirt was a different matter; torn and soaked. Arm looked broken. In the torchlight, the bone reminded her a little of cherry pips, stained with juice.

Ruby called to Errol to throw her down a second length of rope so that she could tie it around Archie. She coughed at the plaster caked in her mouth as she swallowed.

The boy was whimpering from pain now. Though there were no other voices down here, they couldn't be alone. Somewhere beneath all this was his poor mother.

Ruby turned slightly and beamed the torch across the surface, summoning the last grain of hope from her darkest depths. 'Is there anyone else down here? Can you hear me?'

She moved the torch around, surveying the mountains of broken wall and glass, the beam catching on something. There, what was that?

Like a punch to her chest. A single bare foot, skin pale as bone, upright in the debris.

'Hello, can you hear me?' Hope had long left her voice.

Freddie's face flashed through her mind, and she blinked hard. Focus. Errol threw down some bandage and she tried to tie the boy's arm with it. She took the rope, wishing she'd paid more attention to her dad when he'd tried to teach her all the different sailors' knots; all she knew was the double. Ruby wrapped the rope twice around Archie's waist and tied it again, then told Errol to pull the boy up.

Slowly, the rope tightened and Archie's body began to rise in the torch-beam glow. She held onto his torso as long as she could. She was sure she'd never forget the boy's screams as they began to pull. 'Not much longer now, Archie. You've been very brave,' she said, her words echoing in the hollow.

Archie's feet vanished from view, and Ruby was left in near darkness. They might build this house again one day, but the family, as it once was, was gone.

She wanted to pull the rope loose, to run out of there somehow as fast as she could.

Errol was shouting, directing the people above. It felt like an eternity, but finally he called out to her, 'Right, let's get you out. I'm long overdue a cuppa and it's your turn to make it.'

By the time Ruby's shift ended, dawn had come and gone. Her limbs were leaden as she cycled home past ruptured buildings, wounded churches, the steel skeleton of a factory.

Climbing the stairs to her flat felt as though she was scaling Everest. When she got in, Ruby looked down at her clothes. They were covered in a fine lace of mortar dust and her coat reeked of cordite. Sorrow sat at the bottom of her throat like a marble.

As Ruby stood in her hallway now, she shook her head hard, as though she could shake the memories out of it. She went into the bathroom and took off all her clothes, dust scattering across the tiles. Ruby bathed as best as she could, a map of bruises on her stomach, wiping away the horrors of the night from her body, the cloth tinged pink from the traces of Archie's blood on her hands.

Morning light crept through the blackout curtains when she went into her bedroom; it was gone six. The solace of sleep evaded her, events whirling around her mind. She thought about that poor boy, left without his parents. Her own mum and dad, left without their son. Ruby wanted to put them together, like the pieces of a jigsaw puzzle, and mend all their broken hearts.

Her cheeks felt wet and it was only then that she realized she was crying.

Her body curled into a ball, like a clenched fist. She had almost grown to miss that sharp, visceral pain straight after Freddie's death, but now, after all these years with war, it was back. I'm hollowed out, she thought. Broken.

Shake me and I'd rattle.

14

Kitty

It was not yet dark, May bringing longer days, and the sky outside the Forum tinged with an amber glow.

Kitty knew that some visitors just came to the Forum for the food (brought by various members, eked out despite rations, sometimes improvised when a particular ingredient wasn't in supply). *Gajar ka halwa* was a staple. Carrot shredded and cooked in a little sugar and milk, then spiced with cardamom, was a close approximation of the food many had grown up with.

Once the meeting had finished, Mandalji had hurried away as usual to his office as quickly as he could, eager to press on with his work. Kitty briefly spoke to Savitribai, who often joined the meetings along with her husband Dr Chopra, although it was usually Savitribai who had the most to say. Just after she'd finished saying goodbye to her with a wave from the hallway, Kitty caught Satyajit as he was leaving.

'Do you have a moment to discuss conscription?' she asked in Hindi. When they'd first met, she wasn't sure whether he spoke Hindi, like her, but in the past few months it had become apparent that not only did he speak one of the most common languages of India, but Urdu and Bengali too, depending on who he was conversing with.

'I was just about to leave,' he said, glancing ahead to where his friend was standing near the front door. 'Can it wait?'

'We need to get a head start on this,' Kitty responded firmly. She had promised Mandalji that she would take an inventory of all the men who might need their help. When she had first begun the work, it had felt a little beneath her, filling out forms and sitting arguing on someone's behalf at a tribunal, when she had been used to using her years of gruelling legal training in full-blown trials alongside prominent barristers in India. But now, as she heard more of the individual stories of the young men, knowing that she might be saving some of them from terrible fates, she took every case as seriously as the next.

'I haven't even received a conscription letter yet,' he sighed.

'Even better. We can start preparing your case now.'

Satyajit looked over to his friend, who was leaning against the wall, fiddling with his shirt collar.

'It will only take a few minutes,' she added.

'All right, but give me a moment,' he said, as though even saying the words out loud exhausted him. He walked down the hallway, calling out his apologies to his friend; a strand of hair fell in front of the young man's eyes as he nodded.

Kitty headed back into the library to wait. There was a growing worry that twisted in her stomach now. After all this time, there was no guarantee that the war would be won by the Allies. Was it better to live in the shadow of a British empire than the doom of a Nazi one?

At least she could be of use, more thankful than ever for her education, for her papa's commitment to her learning. Though it had not been out of some strong belief that women should be educated. Her father always wanted to keep up with society. If his middle-class friends sent their daughters to school, so would he. While in many other ways the scrutiny and attention that came from their community was a bore, and would later cost her and Haseeb dearly, Kitty could partly thank the pious gossipmongers of Bombay for an education she would not otherwise have had.

And besides, the fact was that her father had pinned all his hopes on her.

There had been a birth before Kitty was born, a boy, a blessing – the terms were almost interchangeable when it came to males – but 'he hadn't survived the journey', that was the way her grandmother had described it. When people heard Papa had only one daughter, they would commiserate. Smiles fading, muttering that 'God blesses us in different ways.' Her father had had no choice; he had been forced to become liberal whether he liked it or not.

Satyajit wandered into the room. He tossed his trilby onto the chair next to him as he sat down. He was wearing some kind of strong and musky cologne that prickled at her nostrils.

Kitty had set herself up earlier that afternoon at the vast table. She took out a leather notepad, a neat stack of printed papers on the relevant law and a beautiful forest-green Mont-blanc fountain pen with gold filigree detailing that Haseeb had given her for their first anniversary.

'*Tum kaisi ho?*' he said, using the informal Hindi for 'how are you?' This immediately annoyed Kitty; they were hardly friends.

'*Main theek hoon,*' she replied, simple, perfunctory. '*Aap kaise hain?*' deliberately switching to the formal Hindi, before quickly directing attention away to more important matters. 'Now we need to confirm when your letter is likely to come through. It's usually around two years after arrival in England,' said Kitty, putting on her spectacles and snapping the glasses case shut.

Satyajit sat back in his chair, waiting for her to continue.

'When did you first arrive in England?' she said, her pen poised over her notebook.

'Sometime in 1939, I think.'

'And can you narrow it down, what month?'

'March. No, perhaps it was May.' He put his hand to his chin.

This was going to take all day, at this rate. 'Do you have your passport?'

'Not with me.'

'Well, I suppose that doesn't matter so much right now,' she said, as she wrote some notes. If he wasn't going to help her, she wasn't going to go out of her way to help him.

'And what's your full name?'

He paused, as if deciding whether to give it to her. 'Satyajit Azad Deol.'

She peered at him over the top of her spectacles. His name gave little away. Satyajit was a Hindu name and Deol a common Sikh name. But Azad? Not only was it a Muslim name, but it also literally meant 'freedom' – '*Azad Hind!*' was a common rallying cry at protests across India. 'That's the name you were born with?'

'It's my name,' he said firmly, then looked at his watch, an expensive-looking gold timepiece. 'I thought this was only going to take a few minutes?'

Kitty went through the same details with Satyajit that she did with everyone else, the details she'd turned over a dozen times in her head at night, thinking about how the time would come when she'd have to use them for Haseeb. Whatever he said, she wouldn't let him go.

'When your call-up comes through, I'll need the letter.' She explained the process and the different religious and political grounds on which they could argue a case. 'We could also say that you're here only temporarily and assure them that you would be happy to take on any noncombat work.'

He stared at her. 'But I wouldn't.'

'Well, we can work out the details when the time comes. And it would help to know what religion you are?'

'That won't matter.'

'But—'

'You don't need to waste your efforts on this,' he sighed. 'They'll get their Indian soldiers one way or another. Don't you know? The British dangle a few decent rations and wages in front of men back home, just so that they can feed their families. The poor won't have any choice.'

Kitty hadn't known that. She wondered how Satyajit seemed so knowledgeable about what was going on back in India. It wasn't the sort of thing that was being reported in the British newspapers. 'Well, what about you, though? You're willing to leave it to fate?'

He fixed his eyes on her. 'We write our own fates.'

'You'll just go and join up, then?' Of every Indian Kitty had met at the Forum, the least likely of them all to join the British in arms was Satyajit. She could see him in prison, but not in military uniform.

'How can I join their war?' He laughed. 'I'm already at war with them.' She tried to ignore the dismissive tone in his voice. 'You can save your form-filling for the others.'

'Is that all you think I do?' Her cheeks flushed with annoyance, but a part of her agreed with him. Conscription notices, tribunal forms. A simple piece of paper to decide whether you might live or die. 'So, what do you suggest?' The heat rose up her neck.

'You can carry on with all this,' he said, waving his hand in the air, 'I can see how important it is to get recognition from Mandalji.'

'What do you mean by that?' But even as she said the words, she knew: he thought it was a vanity exercise.

'Dekho, you write your little forms if you want.' He gave a

smug grin as he stood up, the chair scraping behind him. 'But I don't need your help.'

'But are you really saying you want to—' Kitty stopped herself. *Get yourself killed*, she was going to say. Whatever she thought of him, she wouldn't let any Indian walk willingly into death.

Satyajit moved towards the door, putting on his trilby.

'What are you going to do, then?' she said.

'Let me worry about that.'

Kitty watched the door close behind him. She leant back in her chair, wondering how he could be so fearless, so sure that he wouldn't be made to fight a war that had nothing to do with them. And why Haseeb seemed so willing to run straight towards it.

*

She got home to the flat to find Haseeb asleep on the sofa, his feet dangling over the edge, clutching a case file to his chest. The only sound was the ticking of the clock on the mantelpiece.

Kitty opened the window a fraction to let in the breeze. She looked over at the chessboard. Haseeb had made his move. His bishop had pinned her knight. She'd deal with it tomorrow.

She walked over to Haseeb, sound asleep, the worries of life absent from his face for once.

Satyajit's words came unbidden into her head. *They'll get their soldiers one way or another.*

Kitty bent down and kissed Haseeb gently on the forehead.

'What time is it?' he whispered.

'Just gone half past eight,' she said, crouching down to him and placing her hand on the top of his head. 'I didn't mean to wake you.'

He stretched out, giving a yawn.

'I missed you,' she said, stroking the tips of his hair, soft beneath her palm.

'We only saw each other this morning.' He gave a sleepy smile. Outside, the air-raid siren started up.

'Maybe we can go to the shelter down the road.' Haseeb rubbed his eyes.

'It doesn't matter,' she said, crouching down towards him.

'But—'

'It doesn't matter,' Kitty said again, kissing him deeply on the mouth to stop the conversation. She carried on, hungry kisses across his face and lips, tugging at his shirt. As she ran his fingers along his back, she watched his spine, rippling like piano keys. Her heart thrummed like a double bass, deep and low as he held her close. She clung to him as they moved together now, holding onto him, gripping his back tightly, as though she could always keep him safe.

15
Ruby

Ruby had just finished dusting her room when she found her roommate Alma sitting at the small table by the kitchenette, brown hair in rollers. The tang of vinegar polish lingered in the air. Alma was chewing her thin lips as she often did when concentrating, carefully tearing up a roll of toilet paper, separating it into sheets of four then folding those into a pile to make sure they didn't waste any.

Alma thrived on the rules of wartime. Every night, she made sure she'd turned off the gas, put her valuables away in a tin under the floorboards, checked all the windows and always made sure there was some water in the bathtub. Alma had been rationing all her life; now she just had the joy of coupons.

'What are you up to today, then? I'm going to see my friend in Ealing later. Lovely day for it, isn't it?' said Alma.

Ruby braced herself for small talk. They had little in common: Alma was a bank clerk; she liked the tidy order of numbers, the neat regulation that came with cross-stitching of an evening. And besides all that, it had always suited Ruby to keep people at arm's length. Wasn't it best not to get close to anyone, so you couldn't disappoint them by never being the person they really wanted?

'Got my mum and dad visiting. They'll be here soon,' said

Ruby. She could just imagine the look her mum would give if she saw all that toilet roll out on the table.

'Oh, really? Hopefully I can meet them before I go.' Although Ruby had lived with Alma for over a year, she'd always tended to go home to see her parents rather than having them visit her. It was safer that way, especially with all the black-market goods she had knocking around her bedroom. But her mum had gone on about it so much on her last visit home that Ruby had relented.

'And before I forget, the meter's running low, we'll need to top it up soon.' Alma patted her tightly drawn hair into place. It reminded Ruby of the colour of Tube mice.

'I'll do it tomorrow,' she muttered, retreating back into the bedroom before Alma had a chance to tell her off for some other crime against housework. In her room she tried to settle, but even now that the bombing raids seemed to have stopped, with Hitler apparently turning his attention else-where, it felt as though something was unsaid, undone, that there was something amiss but you were never sure what, like a sentence without a full stop.

Her mum and dad didn't arrive for another hour, by which time Alma had luckily already left to meet her friend.

'Sorry, love,' said her mum, giving her a brief hug as she came into the flat – her scent a confusion of face cream and mothballs. 'Had to take the long way round as some of the roads down by London Road are still wrecked from the raids.'

'Manika.' Her dad gave her a hug.

They stook there a little awkwardly as her mum and dad took in the surroundings. A tired fireplace and old green-checked linoleum. Alma had tried to make the place look a bit nicer with a cosy quilted blanket and a few ornaments. The car-riage clock on the table next to the wireless ticked relentlessly.

'Well, show us around then?' Mum said. Ruby walked

them around the kitchenette and the tiny bathroom without a window.

'And this is my room,' said Ruby, pushing the door open.

Mum took in the room, not that there was much to see. Ruby had been careful to tidy it all away, the silk stockings and furs buried at the back of the wardrobe, the jewellery piled into the lacquered box on the chest of drawers. She'd been on edge after bumping into Mrs Richardson that day, but no one had come knocking on her door. Since then, there'd been newspaper reports of people getting prosecuted for looting and she'd been more wary of stealing on her shifts, but that didn't mean she had to get rid of the things she'd already accumulated.

'Very cosy, beta,' her dad said, patting her shoulder.

'Oh, this is pretty,' said Mum. She reached for something behind the vase with the dried lavender sprigs.

Ruby froze. Her mum was holding a gold brooch inlaid with blue enamel.

How had she missed it? This was the thing about your own room, your own belongings. Things became so familiar that you could ignore them entirely.

Ruby smiled. 'Picked it up at a market.'

'Did you?' said Mum, surprise in her voice. 'Feels heavy. Here, look at this, Amrit.'

'Hmm, good quality,' Dad nodded, hands clasped behind his back.

Ruby went to open the window in the bedroom, settling her breath as she remembered the exact moment she'd snatched the brooch from one of the nice houses in the southern stretch of Bloomsbury.

'Well, I got lucky, didn't I?' She managed a smile. 'Now, why don't I make you a cuppa?'

'It's nice to finally see the place,' said Mum, after Ruby had poured the hot water into the teapot. She'd have loved to be able to offer them some cake, or even a biscuit. Things they'd all taken for granted once.

'How have you been keeping, manika?' Dad asked as she put the cups and saucers on the table.

Ruby gave him the latest on her warden work. There was still plenty to do despite the end of the raids: helping people in and out of shelters and checking the blackout precautions were being followed, but it was nowhere near as nerve-racking. It was just as well. She had barely been able to sleep since the night she pulled Archie from the rubble. She'd dreamt of being buried down there, of not being able to reach him in time, of losing him entirely. Ruby had heard he'd been evacuated to some farming family in Wales. Which was fine while the war lasted, but with no other known relatives, who knew where he'd end up after that?

It was why Ruby did her best to keep busy with work and found herself going to more Forum meetings: always better to fill your head with revolution than loss.

'Here, Dad . . .' Ruby shifted in her seat, 'have you heard about the India Forum?'

He shook his head. As far as Ruby knew, her dad didn't have a single Indian friend, not since they'd left Stepney, and even then it had only been a younger man he worked with at the factory that he said hello to in the street. Mandalji had been mentioned in the *Holloway Press* a couple of times for speaking at local meetings, but the chances of her parents seeing those news reports were slim.

'It's a group that lobbies the government, here in England. They're demanding Independence for India.'

'Oh, yes?' he said, brows wrinkling, clearly confused as to what it could possibly have to do with Ruby.

'I've been going to their meetings.' It sounded so strange

to say it out loud. That she would be involved with something so political.

'Are they freedom fighters?' he said, a look of concern on his face. 'What do you do exactly?'

She explained that, for now, all she did was attend the meetings and rallies but that she was thinking about volunteering. 'Handing out pamphlets, helping at the events, that kind of thing.'

He gave a laugh. 'I came to London so I could leave all that behind.' He slurped the last of his tea from his saucer, as he always did.

Ruby glanced at her mum, who was too busy swirling the last of the tea in her cup, and then looked back at him. 'What do you mean?'

'My family, they were always talking about it. My father went on protest marches.' He paused, leaning back in his chair. 'But I saw the darker side of it too.'

'Like what?'

'Arrests. Harassment. Violence,' he said, then quieter, 'I saw a man beaten to death in front of me. There was nothing we could do to stop it.'

Ruby swallowed. Her mum's eyes widened; maybe she hadn't known about this either.

'And it never got us anywhere.' He stared into his cup and her mum patted his arm gently. 'India's still fighting, isn't it?'

'You never told me any of this,' said Ruby. But then, of course, she'd never asked.

'Why would I want to think about that? I wanted to get away, live my life.' And not be crushed under the weight of all the things I wasn't allowed to do, she thought.

'But they're making a difference now, Dad,' she said, leaning forward.

'That's what they all used to say, beta, thirty years ago.' He waved his hand dismissively. 'Do they tell you that change is just around the corner? Do they promise that life will be different when India is free?'

Ruby looked down at the table.

'Exactly. I could have wasted an entire life waiting for freedom. Instead, I built something of my own.' His voice almost faltered at the end. He must have been thinking about Freddie.

Dad carried on, a softer tone now. 'I'm proud of you, manika. What you're doing with the ARP. Your mum is, too.' He glanced across at her. 'But you should forget all this India business. Waste of everyone's time.'

Ruby sipped her drink. Who could say whether the India Forum was really making a change? Her dad's words had echoed Jit's. *All these decades people have been fighting . . .*

Still, Jit seemed to think there was a chance, a way to break through. And it had to be better than sitting in the flat night after night, waiting for a bomb with your name on it.

'Why don't we go for a walk?' said Mum, getting up from the table. 'It's a lovely day. Not a cloud in the sky.' She looked out of the small window.

'You and Ruby go, my back's been hurting since we got here.' Her dad shifted in his seat.

'We can stay here,' Ruby said, quickly.

'No, you go out with your mum for a while.' His tone was sombre, he'd retreated into himself. She wondered what memories she'd summoned by bringing up India.

Outside, the afternoon sun was in full glory. 'Is Dad all right?' asked Ruby, as she headed down the street with her mum.

'He doesn't like to talk about all that. You shouldn't prod him with your questions,' said Mum. A rag-and-bone man clipped past on his horse and cart.

Was it so bad, wanting to know her Dad in his own right?

Her childhood had been so different to his, but they could find common ground, if only he'd tell her about it.

She'd seen that lost look in his eyes before. He had struggled for months after Freddie died, had to take time off from work at the factory for a while. Somehow they still kept going, stretching out the pennies between pawnshops and payslips. Even once he'd got back on track Mum went on at him, about never bringing in enough money, nothing was good enough.

They carried on past Caledonian Road Tube station, with Mum sticking to the shade of the buildings to try and keep cool. Although Hitler seemed to have turned his attention elsewhere for now, the ruins his forces had left behind would not let anyone in London forget.

It had been a long while since she'd walked down the street with her mum. How different it was to being out with her dad. Or Jit. She remembered the looks they'd got round by Marylebone that day.

'Here, maybe we can go down to King's Cross,' said Mum. 'They've got a WH Smith there, haven't they?'

'Yes, what do you need?'

'They might have the latest copy of *Vogue*.'

'I didn't know you still bought those,' Ruby said.

'Well, of course.'

'Why do you bother with it, Mum?' She recalled all those times, her mum browsing the high-fashion magazines, then buying patterns and cloth to make pale imitations of the clothes on the pages. All those times Ruby had just gone along with it, letting her dress her up in clothes that didn't fit, in any sense of the word.

'Nothing wrong with them.'

'Even though we'd never be able to afford any of it?' Ruby couldn't hide the sadness in her voice. She'd have given anything to live her life as though no one was watching.

'It was good to forget for a while, to dream,' Mum said. 'To let yourself dream.'

'They weren't my dreams, though. All it did was make me feel I never measured up.'

'None of us measure up, love,' she shrugged.

Ruby carried on. 'All it showed us was more things we'd never have.' Things you couldn't lose because they'd never been yours in the first place.

Her mum looked at her, eyes glistening. 'It wasn't about that, Rube. It was to take us away from it all, for a bit.' She didn't need to explain what 'all' meant. Ruby could hear it in the fall of her voice. 'I was just trying my best to give us something else to focus on.' There she was, her mum, her heart opening up for a moment.

'And did it work?' asked Ruby.

'There's nothing wrong with a bit of make-believe,' said Mum, her tone hardening as she glared at her. 'Now you need to fix your lipstick; it's smudged in the corner.'

And just as quickly, her heart closed again.

They carried on, past the wide expanse of the old Caledonian Road Cattle Market, which had been partly taken over by the military. Ruby thought of all the times she'd seen Mum turn the pages of those magazines, gazing at velvet gowns and knee-length furs, as though she could pick out any one of those lives and claim them for herself. But no, Ruby realized now, it was up to her: the only person who could decide who she wanted to be.

16

Kitty

The letter was there on the mat, unopened. Staring at Kitty when she passed by. Waiting, as though it was red hot.

'We're going to be late, Kitabi,' Haseeb called out from the bedroom.

'Coming,' she replied, looking over to the chessboard in the living room. She'd accidentally knocked it earlier; the rook lay dying. Kitty bent down and picked up the envelope, paper creased in one corner, the black stamp on the front. Something so small and easy to throw away, yet it carried the heaviest words inside.

In the bedroom, Haseeb was putting on his linen jacket. 'You know we're expected at the cricket by eleven,' he said, with a good-natured smile.

Kitty couldn't bring herself to say anything, so instead she handed him the envelope along with the letter opener she'd taken from the hallway.

'What's . . .' Haseeb began, but trailed off when he saw the black Ministry of Labour and National Service stamp in the corner.

Haseeb read the letter to her. He had been called up to service and was required to present himself at the recruitment centre in two weeks' time.

'We'll start putting your tribunal case together tomorrow,'

she managed to say, the initial shock of the letter now giving way to anger. They'd find a way out of it. They had to.

'Let's talk about it later,' he said quietly, putting the envelope on the side table.

'But Haseeb—'

He came closer, holding her gently by the shoulders. 'We'll talk, I promise. But we're going to be late if we don't leave soon.' There was nothing else she could do but nod.

Kitty stood on the veranda, looking out across the lush green cricket pitch framed by oak trees. If it hadn't been for the letter that morning, she might almost have felt as if the exhaustion of war had been neatly tucked away for a short while.

'Well, this is lovely,' said Lettuce, sweeping a strand of honeyed hair from her face. Her full name was Lady Lettice Harcourt, but she was known to her friends, including Kitty, as Lettuce. 'I'm so glad you invited me.' She clinked her glass against Kitty's.

'I thought you'd like it,' she said. The people around them were mainly a mix of civil servants, councillors and other supporters; everyone laughed and chatted in anticipation of the players – including Haseeb – coming out.

'So how long has the club been here?' asked Lettuce. She and Kitty had met at Oxford, where Lettuce had had a room down the hall from her at Somerville College. They'd kept in touch by letter over the years, and when Kitty returned to London with Haseeb they had seen each other when they could. Though Lettuce was never particularly interested in hearing about the India Forum or any sort of politics, really, her ears had pricked up when Kitty had mentioned the charity cricket match at the Indian Gymkhana in West London.

Kitty explained how the Gymkhana had been built in 1917. It had been funded by the Maharaja of Patiala, along with various other maharajas from Jaipur to Cooch Behar to Indore, and a few wealthy Indians like Dorabji Tata, to provide a home for Indian cricket. 'And then they bought further ground for those two pitches on either side,' Kitty said.

Though the war still raged on across the world, the Blitz was well behind them. Spring had given way to summer. Usually Kitty would have relished the scent of jasmine and honeysuckle wafting through the nearby shrubs, but she couldn't help it, her mind kept going back to that letter. She took a deep breath. Now more than ever, wasn't every moment precious? She resolved to make the most of the beautiful day.

There was applause from the guests as the two teams walked out onto the pitch in their cricket whites, Haseeb among them. All the players were either India Forum regulars or British friends of the cause. Mandalji, who was over on the other side of the veranda, had barely noticed, too busy talking to an Englishman in a pale linen suit.

'This will be such a delight!' said Lettuce. Butterflies with canary-yellow wings flitted past, too busy having fun to settle. 'Is Haseeb a good player?' Lettuce always seemed to add an extra 'e', elongating Haseeb's name.

Kitty smiled. 'Well, he knows which end of the bat to use, at least.'

'Well, I'm *sure* he does.' Lettuce gave a laugh, eyes glittering. The first bowler bowled the ball and cheers rose from the crowd as the batsmen began to run.

On the surface, Kitty and her friend had little in common – at Somerville, Lettuce had taken Modern History and Kitty read Law and, of course, their respective backgrounds were worlds apart – yet Lettuce had easily welcomed her into her fold. In part, Kitty suspected it was the novelty of an Indian friend that Lettuce was drawn to, but she didn't delve too deep. Oxford was a lonely place – there were few fellow Indian women to make friends with, while most of the English girls tended to keep their distance.

There was a ripple of applause across the veranda as someone hit a six. A young man had already been dispatched to go and find the ball, which had disappeared behind the perimeter, while a new one was used in the meantime. Kitty looked for Haseeb out in the field, shielding her eyes from the sun with her hand.

'How's Alexander getting on?' she said. Lettuce had married her husband – now Captain Alexander Harcourt – straight after university.

Lettuce's voice was quieter now. 'He's still stationed in Egypt. It's been over a year since I last saw him.'

'And there's no chance of leave?' Kitty tried to focus on her friend but it was impossible not to be drawn into 'what ifs' in her mind. What would happen to Haseeb if he didn't win the tribunal?

'Who knows? They never seem to be able to tell us anything,' said Lettuce, staring out at the cricket pitch. But never one to dwell, she somehow managed to conjure some brightness back into her tone. 'So, who are all these people, then?' she said.

Kitty told her what she knew about the guests but when it became apparent there was very little scandal or infamy to devour, Lettuce turned her attention back to Kitty.

'And what mischief have you been up to recently?' She gave a playful tap on Kitty's shoulder. The cricket players had stopped for a break and were walking back up towards the pavilion.

'I've been helping with some tribunal work,' said Kitty.

'Oh?' Lettuce was gazing out at the match, Kitty wondered whether she had already lost interest.

'Yes. Helping Indian men who are called up for military service.'

Haseeb came over. His cricket whites remained remarkably pristine, save for a murky grass patch on his knee. 'So did you ladies actually watch any of the match, or were you too busy gossiping?'

'Haseeb!' said Kitty, giving him a good-natured swipe on the arm.

'We did actually watch the match, you'll be pleased to hear,' said Lettuce. 'And Kitty was just telling me about her tribunal work, weren't you?'

'Yes,' said Kitty, her voice quieter. 'I'm helping Indians to object on conscientious grounds.' She stared at her friend to see how she'd respond. Everyone knew how vilified 'conchies' were, no matter their reason for abstaining from battle.

'Oh, I see,' said Lettuce, tilting her head.

'Actually, Haseeb's been called up, too,' Kitty continued, tentatively.

'Lettuce doesn't want to hear about all that now,' said Haseeb, in a low voice. The veranda was filling up with people. Mandalji had been cornered by one of the cricket players.

'No, it's perfectly fine, Haseeb,' said Lettuce. 'So you'll have to attend a tribunal too?' she asked.

Haseeb opened his mouth to speak but didn't say anything.

'Yes,' said Kitty quietly. How would her friend feel about Haseeb abstaining, knowing her own husband had no choice but to fight?

Lettuce looked into her glass, then back up at Kitty. 'Well, it seems only fair, really. For Indians, I mean.'

'You think so?'

Lettuce sighed, eyes level with Kitty's. 'If I could have done anything to keep my darling Alexander with me, I wouldn't have hesitated.'

Kitty's heart tinged with relief.

'Now, you must be parched, Haseeb. Why don't I get us all some nice cordial?' Lettuce said, heading over to the refreshments table.

'I know you're still unsure,' said Kitty, gazing at Haseeb.

He sighed. 'Let's enjoy the day, Kitabi.'

'How am I supposed to enjoy anything with this hanging over you? You heard what Lettuce said about Alexander.'

'It's not that simple, though. They're saying the Japanese will invade India soon. The Nazis could land at Dover any day,' said Haseeb.

'They'll say you're betraying India,' said Kitty.

'Who cares what "they" say? The people who talk too much but never act for what's right?'

'But freedom is right, isn't it? That's what we came here for.'

'If we fight, the British government will have to listen to us,' said Haseeb.

'Listen? How do you listen to a dead man?' Luckily the chatter around them hid the sharpness in her tone. Kitty knew she should stop now but it was the last chance she had to hold onto him. 'We have to fight this.'

He gently stroked her shoulder. 'I know it's hard, but—'

'No! It's the only way. After everything else we've been through . . .' There was a tremor in her voice, enough to start an earthquake. 'I can't lose you.'

He stared at her. 'All right, I'll fight it,' he said finally.

'Promise me, Haseeb.'

He nodded. 'I promise.'

17

Ruby

'Come on,' said Jit, taking Ruby's hand. In the dark, she could just make out the unlit sign: *HAMMERSMITH PALAIS DE DANSE*.

Inside, Jit helped her take off her fur coat and handed it to the cloakroom assistant. 'You look beautiful,' he said. Ruby smoothed down her sea-green tea dress, suddenly a little shy. The feeling took her by surprise.

Out in the wood-panelled bar, they watched couples doing turns around the dance floor. It was already packed; with close to a hundred couples. The band was framed by a froth of curtains, while the light from the chandeliers winked at the dancers. Beautiful as the lighting was, she didn't care what anyone said; you could never be entirely sure that the weight of all that crystal wouldn't come crashing down on you at any moment.

Two servicemen stood next to Ruby drinking bitter. Young faces that looked as malleable as clay, wearing enough after-shave to knock out a horse.

Jit handed her a gin and lemon, putting his ale down on the bar top. She couldn't quite adjust to Jit in this new setting but when he'd asked her out after a meeting at the Forum the other day, she'd decided to try him on for size.

The music drew her back to the present. Cigarette smoke

cut through the cologne- and perfume-filled air. 'Have you been here before?' she said. The gin was predictably weak, just when she could do with a boost of confidence. It wasn't that she was nervous, exactly, but she never quite knew where she stood with him. Although perhaps that was part of the appeal.

He shook his head. 'I've never had anyone to bring before,' he smiled. Ruby wasn't sure she believed him. His finger brushed hers as he picked up his glass.

A man in uniform was standing at the other end of the bar with a young woman, staring at Ruby. No, in fact they were staring at her and Jit together.

Jit turned to follow Ruby's gaze. The couple were still looking at them, whispering together. 'Ignore them,' Jit said.

'Maybe they're just not used to seeing an Indian person,' she ventured, as much to reassure herself as Jit, though of course in London it was hardly the rarest sight.

'We both know what they're talking about,' he said in a low tone.

Old memories, of walking down the street with her dad and Freddie, came back to Ruby. She would have to face this, if she wanted to keep seeing Jit. No hiding now.

'Do you like to dance?' asked Jit, knocking back his drink.

'I can hold a turn or two, I suppose,' she said, holding his gaze. 'How about you?'

'I need more practice,' he grinned. 'Maybe you can show me how?'

He took her hand, leading her to the dance floor, and she enjoyed the pleasing warmth as their palms touched. They kept nudging other couples, the vast ballroom too small for so many people, the dance floor full of apologetic smiles and 'sorry's. Jit was a passable dancer. Ruby wondered where he'd picked it up from, but she was soon too swept up in the music to care about that, or about the couple who had stared at them. Let the whole world look.

The air fizzed with collective joy. With danger, too, but an entirely different kind from the dangers outside. The danger that anything could happen, if you wanted it to.

After a few songs, the beat slowed down and Jit pulled her closer. She was surprised by the firm press of his hand against her waist, the brief touch of his thigh against hers. Surprised at how much she liked it.

The music sped up again, and they gave each other coy smiles as they tried to keep in time. Ruby danced for an hour straight, jitterbug to Lindy hop, ignoring the blisters that pricked at her feet, until finally she had to stop a while. 'Give me a minute, would you?' she said.

She went into the toilets, where copious puffs of Soir de Paris perfume were becoming closely acquainted with the sharp smell of Jeyes floor cleaner.

There were a few women letting their hair out, taking off their khaki and blue service uniforms and revealing their pretty tea dresses underneath. There was free entry for anyone in military dress; they'd arrived decked out in their sackcloths but clearly had no intention of staying in them. 'Here,' said one, pulling out a canvas holdall for her friends to stuff their clothes into.

A huddle of nudging elbows at the sinks, the trill of their conversations punctuated with the click of lipstick cases and the snap of powder compacts.

Ruby reapplied her Victory Red in front of the mirror. Away from the India Forum, Jit was easy company. There was something about him: the fire in his eyes when he'd fought for his cause, never backing down despite the swell of arguments against him. His presence, especially here at the dance hall, swept away all the horrors she'd seen these past few months.

Jit had managed to find them a table on the mezzanine overlooking the dance floor. There were men and women in all kinds of uniforms and it was clearly an international crowd: along with the Europeans there were West Indians and Africans; a few Indians, too, people who had joined the war effort from all across the Commonwealth. Some of them were dancing with women who were white and Ruby wondered how they had all fared, whether they'd faced the same attention as her and Jit. Or worse.

'Do you think you'll be called up soon?' she found herself asking. She wished as soon as she'd said it that she'd not brought the conversation back to war and India.

'I already have been,' he said.

'Oh? Is Mrs Akhtar helping you with your case?' she said, leaning towards him. There was spilt liquid on the table and she felt it trickle down her elbow as she moved her arm.

'No need.' He took a sip of his drink.

'Didn't pass the medical?' Ruby felt a surprising flicker of relief as she wiped her arm clean.

'Something like that,' he said with a small smile.

She wondered how he'd managed to avoid it. Ruby had heard rumours of people who could help you fail your medical test and get you out of conscription. She'd been disgusted by it; she'd always felt you had to do your bit for your country. No excuse for shirking your responsibilities. And yet, of course, it was different for Jit.

'Where in India are you from, then?' Ruby asked, taking a sip of her drink.

'Would you know it if I told you?'

Ruby returned his smile. The truth was, she knew barely anything about the country, even Gujarat, where her dad was from. 'Well, if you tell me about it, I'll start to learn, won't I?' She tilted her head playfully.

'I'm from Bengal, in the east,' he said. He drew an imaginary outline of India on the table and then pointed. He told her more and Ruby was enthralled by his stories of terracotta temples and fishing ports, surprised to hear about the cooler hill station of Darjeeling – Ruby had always imagined India as a single, sweltering mass of heat. 'We grow many things there: sugar cane, rice, cotton, jute. All taxed by the British, of course,' he added, with more than a hint of contempt.

'And that's where your family are?'

He looked away, pulling out a cigarette box from his breast pocket. 'Some of them,' he said quietly, offering her a Player's and lighting it for her.

'It must be difficult, being away from them?' She knew he had friends at the Forum; she'd seen them huddled away in corners during meetings, but it was never the same as family.

'Everything I do is for them.' He met her gaze, serious now.

'Well, I'm sure they're very proud.'

'Perhaps,' he said, turning to look out at the dance floor. She could feel him closing off.

'Will you go back one day?'

'I want to,' he said, tapping his cigarette into the ashtray. 'But it's not that simple.'

'You don't want to see your family?'

His eyes darkened. There was an unfamiliar sadness under his usual tone of confidence. 'Maybe sometimes it's just too late.'

She felt a flicker of recognition then. Had he felt loss just as she had?

'You don't seem to like talking about yourself,' she said, giving a playful pat to his arm and trying to infuse the conversation with a bit more fun again.

'Oh, yes? Because I know so much about you,' he laughed.

She blew cigarette smoke out into the air. 'I'm not very interesting.'

'Well,' he said, 'I find you very interesting,' holding her gaze so long that she could feel herself blush.

They returned to the floor and danced for a while longer, but the room had grown so sweaty and crowded that it was difficult to hold a step, so they went outside.

It had started to rain. 'Maybe I can find you a taxi.' Jit pulled his suit jacket across to try and keep her dry. She liked feeling the warmth of him against her; how long it had been since anyone had got this close.

They took shelter under an awning that drooped with the weight of trapped rain. Ruby stared at him. She put a cigarette to her mouth, holding his gaze. Then she said with a smile, 'Light me up.'

He looked at her in surprise. 'My pleasure,' he whispered, delicately taking the cigarette out of her mouth and slipping it into his jacket pocket. His lips brushed hers and Ruby marvelled at his self-restraint. She wanted to get closer, to feel his body against hers. Just then, the drunken laughter of a group of revellers awakened them from their desire. In the glow of their torchlight, she saw that Jit was smiling, just as she was.

He put the cigarette back in her mouth, the edge of his finger tickling her lip. He brought his lit cigarette to her own, and the tips kissed, glowing amber.

18
Kitty

Kitty walked into the tribunal with Haseeb. With its semicircular oak seating, traditional stained-glass windows and maroon leather upholstery, the formal setting of the council chamber at Fulham Town Hall was not unlike a courtroom. In the six months since she'd fought her first case, Kitty had learnt not to be intimidated by her surroundings. She knew how to make a strong case, to answer the questions of the panel calmly and astutely, to foresee possible objections. Unlike many of the men she had helped in the tribunals, Haseeb was more than capable of arguing his own case and she had prepared him for all that would come his way. Still, that didn't stop the nerves swilling in her stomach now.

At the front of the room, five older gentlemen in dark suits were seated behind an oval table. Haseeb and Kitty were ushered to a smaller table in front of the panel with three plain wooden chairs set out. A few people, presumably members of the public, sat in the circular seating surrounding them.

'Come in, Mr Akhtar, sit down,' said the older man with tortoiseshell-framed glasses who was sitting in the middle of the group at the oval table. All around the room were ornately framed paintings of men who were presumably Town Hall councillors, complete with gold chains and robes.

'I am Judge Gastrell and I'm the chairman of this tribunal,' said the man with the glasses. He introduced the four other men, a mix of former mayors, council members and one chairman of a university.

Haseeb nodded. 'And this is my wife, Mrs Keerthana Akhtar,' he said.

The judge explained the process and Haseeb was asked to read out the statement that Kitty had written for him.

'I came to England with my wife in March 1939. We live in London and I work as a barrister at Inner Temple. While I wholly support Britain and her Allies in the current conflict, I wish to conscientiously object to military conscription on two grounds. Firstly, there is no legal or compulsory requirement for men in India to join the war and there should not, respectfully, be a different rule for Indians in the UK. In addition, I object on pacifist grounds and wish to abstain from armed combat that could kill and maim others.'

Kitty shifted in her seat. She knew from their various recent debates that Haseeb was not entirely against armed combat but she had led enough tribunals now to know they had to fight this with their strongest arguments.

The judge nodded, then opened up the floor for questions.

'I have a question,' said the man who Kitty had noted down as Mr Bailey, sitting to the right of Judge Gastrell. He had a salt-and-pepper moustache so thick that it hid most of his top lip. 'You stated you've been here for more than two years, Mr Akhtar?'

'Yes,' Haseeb said, glancing at Kitty. He had already clarified that in his statement, which the tribunal had received and read in advance. Where was this heading?

'You've already pointed out,' continued Mr Bailey, 'that men in India are not compelled to join the military. But you are an Indian man living in Britain.' Kitty took a deep breath, trying to ignore the patronizing tone in his voice.

Haseeb leant forward. 'Sir, I am a foreigner here. I cannot—'

'Foreigner?' Mr Bailey laughed, the top of his moustache creeping into his nostrils. 'Mr Akhtar, let us be perfectly clear, you live in Britain and you're a British subject.'

Kitty stifled an exasperated sigh. So now they were actually needed for something they were back to being British subjects.

Haseeb glanced at her. Though he hid it well, the comment had riled him. 'A British subject who does not have freedom in his own country,' he said.

Panic rose in Kitty's chest; she had tried so hard to avoid any mention of the freedom fight. This was far more volatile ground.

'Your argument here was about pacifism,' said Judge Gastrell. 'Are you now saying you're objecting for political reasons? This wasn't stated on your form.' He put down his pen and scanned through the papers.

Kitty jumped in before Haseeb had a chance to reply. She had to steer this back on course. 'This is a moral objection on the grounds of pacifism.' She had to focus on this argument now that their objection about men in India had failed.

'And your statement about India, Mr Akhtar?' asked Mr Bailey. Judge Gastrell gave him a frustrated look. They all knew that the judge, as chair, was supposed to lead and direct the discussion.

She subtly touched Haseeb's hand with her little finger, a sign to let her speak. 'Mr Akhtar's view is in line with the Indian Congress's position: he sympathizes with the British but requests freedom for India.' Kitty tried to keep her voice neutral, hiding her concern as best she could. 'But this is a separate point to the objections he's making today.'

'I'm sorry, but whose tribunal is this, exactly?' Mr Bailey laughed. 'We've heard more from your wife than from you, Mr Akhtar.'

Haseeb's fingers curled into a fist on the table but he kept his composure. 'My wife is simply here to support me,' he said.

'All right.' The judge put his hand up. 'Let's get back to the matter at hand, shall we?'

When he'd confirmed there were no further questions Haseeb and Kitty were asked to wait outside.

She swallowed, nausea rising in her chest now, not helped by the smell of wood oil and furniture polish lingering in the hallway. They had gone so far off course they were practically in Antarctica.

Haseeb sat down in an old mahogany chair, elbows on the armrests. Kitty sank into the seat next to him.

'What do you think?' he asked, his voice so quiet she had to strain to hear him.

'I don't know.' She lightly rested her hand on his arm. 'We were clear on the pacifism argument.'

He nodded. They both fell silent, the exhaustion of the tribunal wearing into her bones. Finally, after what felt like hours but was probably only a few minutes, the clerk opened the doors. 'Mr Akhtar, please come in.'

They stood up but Haseeb stopped in the hallway, taking her hand.

'I'm sorry,' he said. 'I can't do this.'

'What do you mean?' Kitty frowned.

'All this discussion, all of it,' he said, shaking his head. 'Today made me realize. Once and for all. I've got to join up. It's the right thing.'

'Haseeb . . .' But words failed her. How could he do this to her now? Her heart seized in her chest.

'Mr Akhtar!' the judge called out from the council chamber.

A tear had fallen, trailing all the way to her jaw, hanging precariously.

'I'm sorry, Kitabi.' He let go of her hand and stepped forward. 'We can get India back this way.' The hope in Haseeb's voice was almost too much to bear.

'What good is a free India without you?' she said, but her words were lost to the empty air.

PART TWO

19

Ruby

'Well?' The Indian woman was tiny and gap-toothed. Her hand rested on her hip, though in truth she was too busy glaring at the customers at the next table to pay Ruby and Jit much attention.

'*Do aloo paratha, doh chai,*' said Jit.

The woman reached out a hand and snatched the cardboard menu from him. 'Thirty minutes, we are busy,' said the woman. Half the tables were empty.

'So now you have met Ma Jalili,' Jit grinned.

Before they'd arrived at the tiny cafe, nestled between a fish-monger and a haberdashery on Commercial Road, Jit had told Ruby that customer service was not the reason you came to Ma Jalili's. Between her warden duties and his travelling with work, it had been tricky to find another time to meet after the Hammersmith Palais, and Jit had promised to show her real Indian life in London, so here they were.

'Can't say you didn't warn me,' Ruby said with a weary smile.

'I promise you, she makes the best aloo paratha this side of Delhi.'

Ruby wasn't exactly sure what aloo paratha were, or whether 'the best' was saying much given that the cafe seemed to be only one of a handful of places in the city that offered

Indian food, but she was willing to give it a try. One of the cafe staff hurried over to the glass door and propped it open, trying in vain to let in some cool air.

'So, you're really thinking about breaking away from the India Forum?' asked Ruby, continuing the conversation they'd started on the way to the cafe.

'I'll still go to the meetings,' Jit shrugged. 'But it will take more than words to get what we want.' He flipped the cigarette box round and round on the tired pine table and she had an urge to reach over and stop him.

'Like what?' she said.

The question was interrupted by Ma Jalili hurrying past to another table. 'Yes?' she snapped at two young men in turbans. They both looked at her, wide-eyed and open-mouthed.

Jit leant forward. Although he lowered his voice, there was an intensity in his tone. 'They've restricted our freedom of speech in India. It was hard enough before, but now they're using the war to stamp down on everything,' he said.

'So what does that—' Ruby began.

'We need to keep our voices down. I don't know who these people are,' he said, looking around. Apparently Indians were just as concerned about the 'loose-lipped' as everyone else. The cafe was filled with a mix of young men, probably students, and older men with leathery skin and gnarled hands, likely dock workers and seamen like the ones she'd seen at the India Forum. But she knew well enough now that not even Indians could agree on what was right for India.

'But if you don't want to work with the Forum, how will you fight the restrictions?' she asked quietly.

He glanced around him, then said, 'We're finding ways to get things to India.'

Ma Jalili hurried over with the paratha. The cups of chai shuddered in fright as she slammed them on the table.

Ruby waited for her to move away before she continued. 'What kind of things?'

'Here, try this,' he said, spooning some kind of quartered fruit that was covered in a thick, jam-like sauce. 'It's lemon pickle.'

She took it and followed what he did, dipping a little with a piece of the paratha. The pickle had a zingy sweetness to it, undercut with the heat of the spice. She nodded, impatient to hear more from Jit.

'We're encouraging ordinary people to rise up against the British, to stop them,' he said.

'What do you mean – rise up? Protests?'

'That's one way,' he said, fingers glistening. The only way Ma Jalili could have got that much butter was on the black market. 'There's lots of different means of slowing down the British authorities; we want to strike at the very heart.'

Ruby watched him. There was a fierce look in his eyes. An anger that seemed more familiar than it should. Perhaps Jit noticed her uncertainty, because his voice suddenly brightened. 'Anyway, we don't need to talk about all that on a nice Saturday afternoon.'

Though he had piqued her curiosity, she knew he was right. 'There's going to be some kind of celebration next month, did you see?' she said. 'Raksa—'

'Raksha Bandhan,' he said.

'Yes, that's it.' She had heard at the Forum that it was some kind of festival to do with sisters tying threads around their brothers' wrists as a symbol of protection.

'Do you celebrate that too?'

He shook his head, sweeping up the last of the crumbs with the final piece of paratha.

'You're not religious, then?' Ruby was hardly the churchgoing type. Though her mum would always go for Christmas and

Easter, that was about the extent of it. Her dad never mentioned religion, but from what she'd seen at the India Forum most Indians seemed to take their faith seriously. Now more than ever, everyone clung onto any hope they could find.

He shook his head. 'Without God, there's no one to fear, no one to judge,' he said. The ferocity of his gaze unsettled her. 'The only thing I believe in is a free India,' he said, getting up. And there he was, back to freedom above everything.

Outside the cafe, the sun was in full force and it was a welcome relief to walk under the shade of the shop awnings. Jit frowned as he looked across the road. 'Wait here a moment, will you?'

Ruby watched as he wandered over to a white man standing outside a bakery. He was dressed in a suit and trilby. Jit smiled jovially, talking away to him, but the man looked far from happy to see him. After a moment, Jit stepped back, tipping his hat with a flourish as he left him standing there.

'Is everything all right?' asked Ruby, as they carried on down the street.

'Oh yes,' he said, casually opening his cigarette packet and offering her one.

'That man didn't look too happy to see you.'

'He's a surveillance man.'

Panic rose in her chest. 'What do you mean?' she said, unable to hide the alarm in her voice.

'They follow me around,' he shrugged. 'I asked if he'd like me to go and get him a cup of tea, as it must be boring standing there,' he said, smiling as he blew smoke from his mouth. 'I said I could give him the bus fare so he could get back to his family and he wouldn't have to stand around waiting on street corners.'

'You never said that?' Ruby was horrified. The authorities

were on high alert. Everyone had to be careful, let alone Indians.

'I'm having lunch, they can't arrest for me for that.'

'But what *would* they arrest you for, Jit?'

'It's just something that makes them feel important and busy. They think keeping an eye on Indians will somehow help them win a war that has nothing to do with us.'

'And it doesn't bother you, them following you?'

'I must be doing something right if they're paying attention to me,' he grinned, taking Ruby's hand in his and picking up the pace.

'But why you? Is it the black-market business with Fleet?' Fear shot through her chest. Had they been watching her too? No, she'd stopped going to him when she'd first met Jit and she'd have been arrested by now.

He shook his head. 'I only go and see Fleet when I'm sure I'm alone.' Jit had told her he bought from the black market so he could sell more goods for peddling, but Ruby had wondered whether it was yet another way of sticking one to the government, just one more anti-British act.

'So is it about the India Forum?'

Ruby glanced back; the man was keeping pace with them, about 300 yards behind.

'Go home,' Jit said softly. 'They won't be interested in you. I'll find a way to lose him.'

She nodded and began walking away, but there was no leaving the worry behind.

20
Kitty

Kitty pushed the glass door of the bookshop open, the bell tinkling as she entered. She said hello to Bhupeshbhai, who had set up the Crescent Moon bookshop on Little Russell Street a few years before the war. A committed bibliophile, he focused his collection on rare and out-of-print books, particularly those about Asian history, politics and culture.

Though it was late afternoon, it had been raining earlier and the light was low, so Bhupeshbhai had turned on one of the lamps. The shop bell rang again, and more people came in, bringing in a cool air.

Books and journals were crammed into every last crevice, the wood of the shelves bowed under the weight. A lumpy, moth-eaten Persian rug was spread over crooked floorboards, and even the walls were not straight. Folding chairs had been set out in a circle in the middle of shop, the squeak of unoiled hinges now vying for attention with the creak of the wooden floor. And yet, for Kitty, there was something comforting about the shop, enveloped in millions of words, both familiar and undiscovered; in the toasted scent of ageing book pages and the smell of old leather covers.

Miss Thacker came in, still in her ARP uniform. She wasted no time in going over to Satyajit. Kitty thought back to the first time Miss Thacker had come to a Forum meeting. How suspicious Satyajit had been of her then. 'She might be useful,' he'd said. Kitty still wasn't sure what that had meant. Now they were laughing together like old friends. Or more? Miss Thacker leant against the shop counter; Satyajit's body aligned with hers. Was it a ploy on his part, Kitty wondered, or had attraction clouded both their judgements?

Haseeb would have loved to be surrounded by all these books. He had left a month ago. Kitty had barely been able to look at him when she said goodbye. She had made her peace with what had happened at the tribunal, no longer spending her time wondering whether they could have won the case. It didn't matter what the panel decided. Nothing could have changed Haseeb's mind. It had been there in the many months before; as much as she had tried to talk him out of it, it had always been inevitable. And wasn't it part of the reason she had fallen in love with him? His determination to do the right thing, to show it through actions, not just words. And Haseeb truly believed that it was the right path to freedom.

He'd decided to try for the RAF. Though the air force had been quite strict about who they admitted when the war began, they were now more in need of pilots than ever, and he had nearly completed his training. Kitty didn't dwell on why the constant need for fresh pilots might be. It was very difficult to pass the complicated pilot tests, though, and she found herself hoping that for once the ever-capable and smart Haseeb would be terrible at something.

People had begun to take their seats, so Kitty took off her coat and began the meeting. 'Namaste, everyone,' she said, introducing herself. 'Mandalji is away for a few days, meeting with some of our colleagues up in Manchester, so I will be leading the discussion today.' One man looked around the room as though searching for someone, probably wondering why a woman was the best they could come up with.

Kitty | 161

She didn't let it bother her. Kitty's experiences in the law had toughened her up. Hadn't other women stood where she had stood, reaching far greater heights? Like the women who were joining men in the military. Times were changing, even if they weren't moving as fast as she'd have liked.

Kitty kept the agenda going with news from India, the latest on the conscription cases, even swatting away a comment from a young Indian man who said he had a question, though none could be found within his tiresome monologue. 'Now, we have some time for any other business,' she said, opening the floor up for further discussion.

'I wanted to draw attention to the new selection of books and materials we have in the shop now,' ventured Bhupeshbhai, as he pushed his spectacles up his generous nose. He had a tentative manner, pausing between sentences. 'We have secured a whole new selection of books currently banned in British India.' He looked around the room, face full of pride, a glint of mischief in his eyes.

Kitty stared at him from across the circle of seats. 'How did you manage to find those, Bhupeshbhai?' Transporting them across India was one thing, shipping them abroad was another altogether.

Bhupeshbhai glanced at Satyajit, a moment longer than he should have, then back to Kitty. 'They're not banned in England,' he said quietly.

Kitty decided not to push the matter in front of others. It was clearly a sensitive subject.

'*Wah, wah!*' said one of the men in the audience, clapping in praise. 'We need to spread the word about the restrictions on Indian subjects and our freedom of speech. This is absolutely excellent, Bhupeshbhai!' There were murmurs of agreement.

'Well, unless there are any other matters,' Kitty said, taking off her glasses, disconcerted by the response, 'I suggest we draw the meeting to a close.'

Quite a few of the members stayed behind, keen to see the incendiary words inside Bhupeshbhai's new literature. As Kitty waited to get closer, she took in the books on the other shelves. There was no denying that they were selected to inspire people, rouse them to action, from Dostoevsky's *Crime and Punishment* to a translation of Hugo's *Les Misérables*. She couldn't help thinking of all the texts she'd studied at Oxford. How she had happily pored over Mill's *On Liberty*, so forthright on the right of the individual to live in a non-authoritarian state, without sensing any hint of irony about the reasons she was there in the first place.

But it was also at Oxford that she was finally woken from her slumber. All that time, she'd drifted along with the Independence movement because her family were so involved. But it was while mixing with fellow Indian students at the Oxford Majlis, a debating group that met every week, that she learnt for herself. She knew of the famous events, like the horrific Amritsar Massacre of 1919, but the Oxford Majlis drew Kitty's attention to lesser-known and little-reported incidents. She recalled it now, her fists clenching in anger as she heard the stories about the protesters in Gujranwala who had set fire to the railway station and other prominent buildings to make their feelings clear. In return, British Indian army planes had flown over the city and dropped bombs to disperse them.

Outside, dusk was ebbing away and Bhupeshbhai pulled down the blackout blinds.

Finally, after a few people had moved away from the collection of banned books, Kitty was able to take a closer look. Gandhi's *Hind Swaraj*; *Angarey*, a set of Urdu short stories and a play, some of which satirized colonial rule; as well as pamphlets that didn't shy away from the heart of the matter, one title translated as *Why Are We Tired and Hungry?*

Kitty flicked through them, books filled with words that could set fire to the very paper they were written on. It was only right that ordinary Indians should know the truth about their own country. But these books were dangerous for the Forum, and the war threw more scrutiny on them than ever.

Kitty went over to Bhupeshbhai, who was standing and speaking in low tones with Satyajit and Miss Thacker. They stopped as she approached them.

'How were you able to get hold of all this material, Bhupeshbhai?' said Kitty.

The bookseller pushed his spectacles back with his finger. If he pushed any further, the glasses would be up on his forehead.

'I don't want to get anyone into trouble.'

'We could *all* get in trouble,' she replied. He had created a link between the India Forum and his bookshop by offering to host the meeting there.

His spectacles made their ascent up his nose once again.

Kitty pressed on. 'The authorities might wonder why you're stocking this literature here.'

'They're banned in India, but there's no law against having them here,' said Satyajit, eyes lighting up with amusement.

'There's a reason they were banned in the first place.' Kitty couldn't be bothered to hide her irritation. 'And by having the India Forum meet here, it draws unnecessary attention to us.'

'I think this is exactly what we should be doing. Out into the real world. Into protest, into action,' said Satyajit.

'Exactly. If we're serious about securing swaraj,' said Miss Thacker, the Hindi word for self-rule flecked with that London accent of hers, 'we have to actually *do* something.'

Kitty glared at her. 'Oh really, and what exactly would you suggest?' She arched her eyebrow. The woman had only been coming to meetings for a few months and now she thought she knew it all.

'We call ourselves Indian and we can't even determine the future of our own country!' Satyajit gave a bitter laugh.

She glared at him. 'That's what the India Forum has been working for.'

Satyajit laughed, waving his hands around the room. 'And yet here we are. How free do you feel, exactly?'

A sharp crash of glass; a thud as something heavy hit the ground towards the front of the shop. Kitty turned, along with everyone else. Voices rose now; the scraping of chairs being set aside. She hurried over to see what was going on, Satyajit following close behind.

'Someone's thrown a brick!' a voice shouted. Bhupeshbhai moved forward and opened the door, peering out into the street, a look of deep concern on his face. 'I can't see anyone,' he said.

Satyajit ran outside.

'Jit!' Miss Thacker called out, grabbing her torch and hurrying behind.

'You should stay—' Kitty called out, but it was too late. They had both vanished into the night.

21

Ruby

Ruby tried to catch up with Jit, who was already turning the corner of the street. It was just as he was a few yards in front of her, in a narrow road flanked with Victorian town houses, when her torch caught the silhouettes of two figures nearby. There was a broad man in a pea coat, walking quickly away. The man next to him was taller, with a wisp of light hair, his torch beam gleaming erratically along the wet pavement.

'Why did you do that?' Jit shouted after them.

'Jit, maybe it wasn't them,' said Ruby, but as soon as the men turned towards them, the big grin on the broad man's face gave it all away. Her realization gave way to deep unease.

'Do what?' There was a goading in his voice.

'The brick,' Satyajit fired back.

'Brick?' The man turned to his tall friend, in mock confusion. 'Did you see any bricks?'

Ruby swallowed. They shouldn't be here. 'Jit—'

'You've got no right.' Jit's voice was sharp.

'Who are you, telling us what rights we have in our own country?' The man laughed. 'Bugger off back to where you came from.'

'I'm free to do whatever I want,' said Jit, facing him square.

'Yeah? And I'm free to do this,' said the man, his dark

shadow springing out in front of him. The punch landed hard on Jit's jaw.

There was blood on the side of his face; shock tore through Ruby's body. But before she had a chance to call out and stop them, Jit had straightened up, firing a hard punch straight at the man's belly. He stumbled backwards. It didn't take much more for Jit to shove him to the ground.

The man's tall friend raised his torch high into the air. 'Bloody bas—' he called out, arm outstretched as though he was about to use the torch as a weapon, but Jit managed to grab his wrist and throw it out of his hand. He swiftly followed up with a right hook.

Ruby tried to say something but no words would come. And beneath it all, a brief flash of joy. They deserved it, didn't they?

The man who'd held the torch fell backwards off the kerb onto the ground. She flashed her torch at the pair, trying to take it all in.

'Are you all right?' she asked Jit.

He stared at the two men, his body astoundingly still as he watched them, his hand still clenched into a fist. When he seemed sure they wouldn't get up, he grabbed her hand. 'Come on,' he said and now they rushed away, Jit leading, Ruby trying her best to keep up in her court shoes.

'Let's go back to the bookshop,' she gasped. 'We can get you cleaned up.' A car moved slowly past, lights off.

'No, we should go home,' said Jit, his voice brittle.

After a few minutes, when they were sure that they weren't being followed, they finally stopped in an alley opening.

'I can't believe it,' said Ruby, her breath coming hard and fast now. She leant against the wall, the faint glow of the torch casting shadows.

Jit lit a cigarette, the familiar click of the lighter and the soft flare of the flame soothing her a little.

'The way you just saw them off like that.' Ruby shook her head, incredulous. Despite herself, she had been glad. Sod those stupid men. Jit had showed them you couldn't just act like a bully and get away with it. All those times she'd had to hear the abuse, out with her dad or in the playground, and take it. And Jit hadn't given it a second thought.

She pulled out a handkerchief from her bag and dabbed it on his jaw. Fortunately there wasn't too much blood. 'Is it painful?' she said gently.

He stroked her hand then gave her a smile. 'I'm fine.'

But Ruby pulled away, as the reality of what could have happened dawned on her. 'What if the police had come?' She thought of the surveillance man following Jit. Though he'd have been careful to check he wasn't being followed to the bookshop, what if someone reported it now?

'I wasn't going to just stand there and take it,' he said, staring at her.

'They could have really hurt you, Jit. You were lucky they—'

'I wasn't lucky.' There was a jagged edge to his voice. 'That's just it. India teaches you things. Whether you want to learn them or not.'

22
Kitty

Kitty looked out across the room. The gramophone was on; music and chatter bounced across Lettuce's drawing room as young men and women dressed in their finest suits and cocktail dresses milled about, but the heady scent of alcohol mixed with the smell of fine tobacco just made her nauseous.

'Why are you standing over here looking so forlorn?' said Lettuce, giving a playful tug to a strand of Kitty's rolled hair.

'Just catching my breath.' Kitty gave a tired smile.

'All right, well, I'll come back over in a bit,' said Lettuce, heading to the back of the room towards her husband Alexander, who was home on leave. Kitty marvelled at the size of such a house in the middle of Mayfair. Now that the raids had been over for a few months, Lettuce was willing to venture back to her marital home, closer to the buzz of the city.

There were more women than men at the party, of course, as there were in most places filled with people Kitty's age. A couple of the men showed signs of the times, an eye patch or a walking stick hinting at what they'd left behind in France or North Africa. Some of the others were presumably in a reserved occupation – doctors or farm owners, perhaps.

It was stuffy in the room. The blackout meant making a choice between having your windows open and sitting in total darkness or keeping your windows closed so that you could have the lights on. Didn't dare risk a curtain flapping open and betraying the light.

She knew a few of Lettuce's friends but she was tired of making small talk. A few had asked her about India; by now, she was used to being the novelty in a room.

But often, once they spoke to her, Kitty was a disappointment; the fox furs and heels, the grammatically correct English, the law degree. They wanted saris and long plaits and broken language, when it suited them.

A mellow alchemy of notes from the sax, trumpet and double bass came together on the gramophone. Benny Goodman's 'Moonglow', a tune that always reminded Kitty of Haseeb. He was due his first leave soon and she was counting the days. They filled the gaps with letters, but it was never the same.

Kitty found herself with a lot more time to fill now. She had been invited to the home of one of the other Indian families from the Forum, but she found the conversation difficult. The women tended to be focused on housework and children; most hadn't had the education that she had. Those who did – teachers, nurses, a doctor – all had husbands to think about. And lately, it was difficult to be around families altogether. She and Haseeb had put off starting a family. They were alone in London, fighting for Independence in the middle of bombing raids. They'd both agreed that it was not the time to be thinking about bringing a baby into the world.

At weekends, after all her India Forum work was finished, Kitty would find herself travelling on the bus alone, boarding whichever one came first, simply to have some company from the passengers.

Other times, she went to the National Gallery. Most of the paintings had been evacuated but there was usually a small, temporary exhibition on. There in the galleries she felt invisible. When Kitty looked at the artworks, the soft brush-marks that came together to form faces, she saw no one who looked like her and she felt even more alone.

Kitty took a sip of her champagne, the chatter of those around her summoning her back to the present. This shadow life she'd been living here, what was it worth? She wondered who she would have been without the movement, without the British government to rail against. Would she have found her way to this same spot, in these same clothes, loving the same man, without the shadow of Empire cast upon him and looking towards the saffron light of freedom? Would any of this have happened without the shackles of the Raj?

'Come on,' said Lettuce, grabbing Kitty's arm and leading her out of the drawing room. They stole away to the back of the house.

She followed Lettuce through the French doors into the garden. The moon was a silver smudge, a thumbprint on the night sky. Kitty waited for her eyes to adjust to the dark. Though there were still searchlights, the sky was rarely disturbed by aeroplanes now.

Lettuce lit a cigarette, the flame creating an orb of light around her elfin features, then she kicked off her heels. 'God, they were killing me,' she laughed.

'Must be nice to have Alexander back for a while,' Kitty replied.

'Muddling along, darling.' She gave a weary smile, then paused a moment. 'You get a little used to it, you know? The not knowing. The worrying. And so many of us are in the same position; that makes it easier to bear, in a way.'

Kitty swallowed. 'I hope so.' It was all she could manage to say. The breeze lifted, the smell of the last days of summer, the leaves about to give way to the approaching autumn, the scent of jasmine plants that were beginning to wither.

Kitty | 171

'How long are you in London for?' Kitty asked.

'I'll go back to my parents' house in the country once Alexander finishes his leave.' It must be nice, Kitty thought, to be able to escape, to have parents to escape to.

Lettuce leant against the wall of the house. 'When will you next see Haseeb?'

'Soon, I hope, still waiting for his leave,' said Kitty, taking a sip of her drink. 'The India Forum keeps me busy, though.'

She looked out at the vast moon that held the stars in its thrall, and racked her brain for something else to say to Lettuce. At Oxford, despite their different backgrounds, they at least had their student experiences in common. Kitty recalled the day she'd first met her.

'Hello, I'm Lettice,' she'd said, holding out a lithe arm, 'but you can call me Lettuce.' Her freckled nose wrinkled as she smiled.

'I am Keerthana,' Kitty had replied, shaking her hand.

'Hmm, yes,' Lettuce replied, not even attempting to repeat her name.

Each time Kitty had run into Lettuce after that, she gave the name a try, but it never seemed to come off.

'Now,' Lettuce had eventually said, 'why don't we call you Kitty?' Though it sounded more like a decision than a question.

Kitty had let the name stick. Yet when she'd gone home to India after graduation and asked everyone to call her Kitty instead of Keerthana, her father had grown angry. 'A name is a gift, not something to be discarded on a whim!'

Kitty had thought that it was more than her name that would help her fit in. After all, she spoke fluent English, read Austen and Dickens as though they were travel guides (this, perhaps, was her first mistake), had learnt hymns and recited Shakespeare.

What she hadn't realized was that your skin colour meant

you were in constant dialogue with the world, whether you wanted to converse or not.

Aside from Lettuce, there was one other girl, Emily, who would come over to Kitty's room sometimes, or invite Kitty to her own. Emily never seemed to want to go out punting on the river, or out for a coffee. There would always be some reason: 'It's a bit chilly out', 'All my books are here and they're too heavy to carry.'

One day when Kitty had gone over to Emily's room, books piled high on every surface while they tried in vain to study, there had been a knock on the door.

Emily had turned to her quickly, putting a finger to her lips. 'Don't say anything, will you?'

Kitty didn't get a chance to ask what she meant.

Emily opened the door a fraction. Kitty could hear the voice of another student who had come to ask Emily if she wanted to go for a walk.

'Oh, not now, I'm studying,' she'd said in a firm tone. When the girl suggested she join her, Emily had closed the door on her with a hurried, 'Sorry, I really need to get back to it.'

Emily had barely been able to look Kitty in the eye after that. Kitty had accepted the reality. Friendship with an Indian was conditional, something that could affect your standing in the world.

And so Kitty had retreated to the relative safety of Lettuce, who, with her immense family wealth and connections, unlike Emily would never have to worry about what others thought of her.

Lettuce finished her cigarette, stubbing it out in the ashtray on the metal garden table. 'Shall we go back inside?' she suggested, perhaps noticing, just as Kitty had, that the conversation was lagging.

Inside, the gramophone had been turned up, and so had the voices.

'Oh Charles, you must meet Kitty,' said Lettuce, nudging Kitty towards a young man with cheeks the colour of a weathered cricket ball. 'You've always wanted to visit India, haven't you, darling?' she added, before flitting off.

'Kitty, is that an Indian name?' Charles asked, standing there awkwardly.

Normally, she would have said she preferred to be called Kitty, but today, as she looked around the room, full of people she'd tried so hard to dress and sound like, she couldn't do it any more. She was tired of taking part in her own erasure.

'Actually no, it's not,' she said. 'Call me Keerthana.'

Charles made a valiant attempt to pronounce it and got it right on the first go. As he told her about all the places in India he'd heard about and wanted to visit, he also displayed an impressive knowledge of her country. Over his shoulder Kitty watched her friend float around the room. Lettuce had always had the confidence that only came with fitting in and never having to question your place in the world.

As Kitty stood there, feeling a hollowing of her heart, the emptiness expanding, she now saw their friendship through clear eyes. It elevated the social standing of both parties. For Kitty, it meant that she was more acceptable in this new world – and for her friend, Kitty made Lettuce more interesting, even a little dangerous, perhaps.

Indian, but not too Indian.

23
Ruby

'I still can't get anything,' said Ruby, turning the dial again.

'This happened yesterday an' all,' said Errol, taking a sip of weak tea.

'Here, let me have a try,' said Stub. He came over and began turning the dial exactly the same way Ruby had. She got a whiff of his cigarette breath as he moved her out of the way.

There was still plenty of work to be done, making sure people were following the regulations, checking that shelters were safe – although it was mainly the elderly and infirm who bothered to go to the Underground now. The other warden, George, had been off for weeks and it wasn't the first time. If it wasn't his shingles, it was a stubborn cold. Most likely, he was spending time with his first love – the dog track – the place anyone would have found him before the war started.

Ruby was glad to have her warden work to keep her busy. After the fight with the two men in the street, Jit had told her he was going to lie low for a few days. He wanted to be sure that the authorities hadn't got wind of what had happened. Ruby had been checking the newspaper for reports every day, but luckily there'd been nothing. Unlikely that those two cowards would have wanted to go to the police anyway, reporting how they'd been beaten up by a lone Indian man, of all people.

She went over to her coat, which was hanging on a chair, and put it back on. An early autumn chill was closing in.

'It'll be back in a minute,' said Stub, giving the radio a frustrated thwack before going back to his chair defeated. He leant over towards Errol. 'Did you hear about that old Mr Yalden? Lives over on Ossulston Street,' he asked. Although it was important that they knew all the residents of the area so that they could account for them, Stub took this to mean that he should know every bit of gossip too. 'He got done for trading on the black market.'

Ruby kept her back to them, her eyes fixed on the logbook as if it held the secret to eternal life.

'Never!' said Errol. 'Always seemed straight as a die, that one.'

'I know,' said Stub, rocking on the back legs of his chairs. 'Thought it was the yids that ran the black market.'

Ruby turned to stare at him. Errol didn't say anything.

'Penny-pinching so-and-sos,' said Stub, warming to his theme as he took a swig of coffee.

Anger seared through her. Of the two of them, Errol was the one who usually irritated her, but here was Stub, showing himself for who he really was.

'Oh, do you know any, then, Stub?' Ruby turned towards him.

'What would I be doing with the likes of them?' He gave a laugh.

'Well, you seem to know a lot about them.' She walked over to the table.

Stub sighed. 'Well, you hear things.'

'Oh really. And how about Indians?'

He frowned at her.

'Do you know any Indians, then?' she asked. The way he'd spoken took her back to the night at the bookshop, the nasty way that man had spoken about her and Jit. Like they were beneath him. Like they were nothing.

'What's that got to do with anything?' said Stub.

'Would you know one if you met one?' She crossed her arms.

Stub looked over to Errol for clarification, but he was too busy taking in the entertainment.

'Course I would,' he said. 'It's all over their faces, for a start.' He gave a laugh.

'Did you know I'm Indian, Stub?'

'Leave it out.' He waved his hand in dismissal.

'My dad's Indian. I'm Indian.' It was as though there had been a hand pressed close to Ruby's throat all these years, and now the truth had been set free.

She enjoyed watching that look on his face. The shock first, then the search for something in her skin tone or features that should have given her away.

'You're not . . .' His voice was full of incredulity, but it faded as he realized she was telling the truth.

'What's the matter? Angry that one of us crept under your radar?' She glanced at Errol, who was smiling, apparently impressed with her for once.

In the past, she'd let comments like Stub's wash over her. Anything for an easy life.

Wasn't it why she'd left Mum and Dad's house in the first place? But it still meant hiding who she was. Just as her world was supposed to get bigger, it contracted.

Jit felt no shame for who he was, proud in a way that she had never been. She thought of her dad. She had to try harder, for all of them.

Ruby | 177

The shortwave radio sprang into life just as the sirens started.

'Better watch out, Stub, you never know where we're lurking.' Ruby grabbed her torch and hurried up the stairs.

'Here, Ruby.' Errol caught her up. They'd been told to look after the southern borders of Bloomsbury, but Ruby was in no mood to talk.

'Indian, hey?' said Errol.

'And what of it?' Ruby snapped.

'Oh, who cares about your dad, your mum or your great-great-grand-uncle for that matter?' Errol shook his head. 'Anyone who gives a fig about that when we've got this going on,' he said, pointing up at the searchlights, 'needs their head checked.'

Errol still managed to surprise her sometimes. 'Now,' he said, already moving the conversation on, 'Stub asked us to check the flats over on Bedford Place. The Thompsons sometimes need a bit of help,' he added, referring to an elderly couple who lived in one of the blocks of flats there.

'I can go and check on them,' she said. Errol agreed to visit the basement shelter around the corner. The sky was deepest indigo as she carefully made her way to Bedford Place.

Once Ruby got to the lobby of the building, she kept her torch on as there was no light here or in the stairwell. She made her way up the large wooden staircase lined with carpet that was still plush at the edges, but threadbare along the centre where hundreds of footsteps had climbed it. There was no one at the Thompsons' top-floor flat. As Ruby made her way back downstairs, she noticed that the door of the flat on the floor below was ajar.

'Hello,' she called out, pushing the door open.

She stepped inside the front room and found it frozen in

time: a blanket draped on an armchair; a book, spine up, on the antique desk; lives interrupted, to be picked up again tomorrow. If they were lucky. She didn't know the occupants; they had only moved in a little while ago.

Ruby carried on. The kitchen and bathroom empty. A huge, high Victorian bed dominated the main bedroom. She almost expected to see a little step on either side, so that the owners could climb up. Her torchlight tripped on sharp lines. A tiny marble-topped bedside table had been squeezed into the corner. She opened the drawer, feeling her way around: a velvet-lined spectacle case, letters wrapped in ribbon and, at the back of the drawer, a pocket watch. Ruby took it out. It was gold, with intricate engraving, some kind of motif that looked like a bird. She liked the feel of the pattern under her thumb, and how heavy the chain felt wrapped around her hand. She opened up the case, to reveal a white face with black dots to mark each number. Ruby shone her torch over the inscription on the inside of the case.

Love always, Eleanor

Ruby stared at the words a moment, then turned to look around the room. There were photographs on the other bedside table, though she couldn't make them out. She closed the watch, laying it carefully at the back of the drawer, over the bundle of letters.

She thought of Freddie. She thought of all that had been lost since the war began.

Her breath skittering, she rushed out of the room and down the stairs, undoing her jacket, unable to breathe. She had been intruding on a life that wasn't hers; she had always known it, but before she hadn't cared. At the bottom of the stairs she halted, steadying herself against the wall as she gasped between the tears, an ache that started at the bottom of her stomach and worked its way up to her chest.

Ruby stood there now at the bottom of the stairs, the engraving on the pocket watch still a ghost on her fingertips. And now, where once her tears had been unrelenting, even violent, now they came more softly. It was a letting go, rather than a holding on.

24

Kitty

Kitty smoothed the cotton sari into place beneath her coat as she walked past the high red-brick buildings along Montague Place. She looked up at the morning sky, rippled with grey clouds that threatened to burst open at any moment, and realized she'd left her umbrella at home.

The sari she wore was made from rough, hand-spun cotton – a *khadi* – a fabric that had a strong political significance. As an emblem of Indian industry and the *swadeshi* movement, people wore khadi across her home country as a visible boycott of British goods and services.

Kitty undid the coat. Though summer was long gone, it was unseasonably warm for October and walking had warmed her up. A couple of people glanced at her as she passed them. Curiosity, or annoyance, she couldn't be sure; perhaps bemusement at the strange mishmash of Indian and English clothes together. Besides, it was still somewhat unusual to see a sari-clad woman on her own.

It was strange to be wearing a sari again after all this time. There were only three pins that held the single piece of folded and wrapped fabric in place – two by her navel, attached to the petticoat underneath; one on her left shoulder attached to the blouse. Despite the fact that it was just as secure as a tea dress, she still found herself checking with her hand that the pins were in place.

Kitty had been wearing a sari since she was thirteen, although it was usually only for special events. Her dadi and her aunt had agreed that she had reached a suitable height to do the long fabric justice. Kitty had dreamt for years before then of beautiful silk and organza confections like the ones she'd seen her aunt wear to weddings and cocktail parties. But her papa, much to Kitty's annoyance, insisted she wear the plain, drab khadi saris instead.

Kitty's grandmother refused to wear swadeshi clothing entirely. She said the rough cotton made her skin itch, but as Kitty grew older, she suspected it was simply that Dadi thought it nonsense to insist on traditional clothing while Kitty's father happily read British books, partook in British education and, when the whim took him, had their cook prepare a roast dinner with gravy and mashed potato (although Dadi wouldn't touch the stuff, saying that the mash looked like something a stray cat had retched up in the street).

As she approached the church on Thornhaugh Street, a woman in a navy coat stopped her.

'Come church?' said the woman, cocking her head. 'You learn too. Christian?'

Kitty frowned. The woman then pointed at a bible she was holding in her hand, smiling at her as though she was a toddler.

'Bible – see?' She nodded her head, holding Kitty's gaze as though Kitty would nod along too.

There were plenty of British missionaries in India, but it was a first for Kitty in England: the assumption that the sari was a symbol of an uneducated heathen who needed to be converted.

The woman was still smiling at her, perhaps hoping that

the Good Book alone would help her communicate without the aid of words.

'I'm sorry,' Kitty said slowly. 'I'm in a bit of a hurry so I must get on. Do have a lovely day now.' Patronizing smiles were not solely the province of the religious spreading the good word. She left the woman open-mouthed behind her.

Kitty used her key in the front door of the India Forum. Mandalji was out on an errand and there was no one else staying upstairs for the time being, so she'd been asked to open up.

In the library, dust motes glimmered in the light. There was a faint trace of morning chai wafting in the air. She opened the window, letting out the musty air, then set out the papers for her cases.

Some men had escaped back to India, or at least that's what she assumed; it was harder to travel than ever with all the restrictions. Some, like Satyajit, had failed their medical, although in his case that had all seemed a bit convenient, she thought, remembering how he had been so utterly sure from the beginning that he wouldn't have to fight.

She found herself thinking of Haseeb, wondering what he would make of it all. He had passed his RAF tests and was a fully fledged pilot now. She had met up with him halfway between his RAF base and London on his last twenty-four-hour leave, though he'd been too exhausted to do anything except sleep for most of it.

He'd laid his head on Kitty's shoulder, holed up in their little bed and breakfast. 'The missions are relentless,' he'd said. 'When you're up there, you can't lose focus, not even for a second, otherwise you could get yourself—' He caught himself. The language of death must be so commonplace among the pilots.

Kitty had worked out a little for herself. Haseeb was stationed in Southern England, which meant that he was probably carrying out missions over the English Channel, perhaps even over France.

'I worry so much about you,' Kitty had whispered to him as they waited for his train, trailing the curve of his jaw with her hand.

'It's all right, Kitabi, they wouldn't have let me fly if they didn't think I was capable,' he said, wearily.

'It's not your flying ability I worry about,' she sighed. 'You could be the best pilot in the world—'

'I *am* the best pilot in the world,' he said with a grin.

'But what if there's a bomb with your name on it?' Kitty said, softly.

'I doubt it,' he laughed. 'They wouldn't be able to spell it, for a start.'

Kitty had smiled with him, but inside her heart, fear swelled greater than ever.

In the dark of night, her bedsheet cold beside her after he'd gone, she had found herself hoping he'd get injured: just something small, no permanent damage, just enough to get him out of the RAF until the war was over.

There seemed to be no escape from the battles of war. No matter where she went, what she was doing. She'd seen children playing in the ruins of old houses, looking for bits of shrapnel to collect as though they were marbles. The children showed no fear, making Everest out of debris, Amazon rivers out of water leaks.

That's how wars were fought, weren't they? On the blind hope of the young. But still they called it victory, called it triumph. A light lost in the sky, a life lost in the ocean, what did a few million matter, after all? Playing with lives as though they were free and unending, instead of the most precious things on earth.

Kitty tried to bring herself back to the present, finishing off her conscription work before she moved on to drafting some of Mandalji's speeches. He had told her that he wanted fresh words, new arguments, and she had offered to help. It wasn't such a leap, to go from pleading cases to rousing others to action through public speaking.

Yet sometimes it seemed so futile to write: such a small gesture, mere words instead of feet on soil, fighting for freedom. Kitty would sit, pen in hand, or fingers hovering over the old Remington typewriter at home, and it felt like someone had stolen the words from her mouth; they simply wouldn't come. Every sentence that she managed to summon had been said before, better than she could ever say it. The biggest challenge was making words that you had looked at over and over again, that you had crossed out and underlined and rewritten a dozen different ways, feel brand new; feel as though you were saying them for the first time to each and every person in the room, as though they were the only one sitting in front of you. To reach out from your heart to theirs, to grab hold of them and make them see. Eventually she'd find herself putting away her notebook, the typewriter abandoned to dust.

*

'Who says Subhas Bose doesn't have a chance with Hitler?' said Satyajit, pacing the room.

'I can't believe you're happy to say things like that out loud,' said Kitty. She had just started setting up for the meeting and Satyajit had arrived unusually early.

Kitty hadn't seen him or Miss Thacker since that day at the bookshop, when they'd disappeared to find the culprits, and she'd assumed they'd not been able to track them down. But the faint mark on Satyajit's jaw that looked as if it was still healing gave her pause for thought.

Somehow, she had found herself in yet another debate with

him. 'Your honourable Netaji is a traitor,' she said. The rumour was that Subhas Bose was now in Germany, working with the Nazis on a possible way forward for India. How could he possibly think that he would solve all India's problems?

Satyajit gave a rough laugh. 'At least he'll get us action. Better than standing here, still arguing over how we'll live when we're free.'

'And you're just going to ignore the things Hitler said about the Aryan race?' asked Kitty, shifting the last chair into place. It made her stomach twist every time she saw the Nazi swastika – a religious symbol of peace in India, seen in temples all over the country – appropriated by Hitler for his own evil gains.

Satyajit crossed his arms as he leant against the table. 'Netaji will use Hitler to get what we want.' Most people at the India Forum thought Bose's ridiculous venture didn't stand a chance. Besides, there were not many people at the Forum who would be brave enough to speak up in support of the Nazis. Yet it never seemed to bother Satyajit. Nothing seemed to bother him.

'What are you doing here, then? What's the point of coming to the India Forum and working with all of us?'

He pulled out a cigarette and lit it. Kitty could hear the pitter of rain against the window.

'Do you actually have any other suggestions?' Kitty laughed, incredulous. 'Or are you hoping Bose will come and save us all?'

'Well.' He blew out the match, eyes still on her. 'It has to be better than giving up, flying planes for the people that keep us in chains.'

Kitty had to steady herself, gripping the chair back so hard that the wood cut into her fingers. How dare he? 'Leave my husband out of this.'

'Well, if we're going to talk about traitors . . .'

'There's nothing wrong with fighting in the war.' Her voice began to waver, but she couldn't let Satyajit hear it.

'Accha. Nothing wrong when you're fighting for *your* own country, yes. But how is your husband doing that? Too busy up in the air risking his life for people who don't care whether he lives or dies.'

She swallowed hard, gathering herself before she said, 'I don't have time for this,' waving her hand by way of dismissal. 'I can't stand here arguing nonsense with someone who has no idea what he's talking about.'

'I couldn't agree more,' he said, stubbing out his cigarette then walking out of the room.

As she watched him go, she wasn't sure whether she was angrier at Satyajit for what he'd said, or at herself for wondering if it was true.

25

Ruby

Ruby was being followed.

She turned again, clutching the collar of her fur coat close to her. The man in the trilby and dark suit behind her could have been just another person out on a Sunday afternoon, back from church or visiting family, just as she was on her way back from lunch at Mum and Dad's house. But there was something a little forced about the man's apparently relaxed manner: hands in pockets, cigarette dangling from his mouth. This wasn't the kind of area where you took in the scenery.

She swiftly turned off the Caledonian Road into Wheelwright Street, a road that she ordinarily wouldn't go down. Some of the Pentonville prison warders lived in the little two-up, two-down cottages around here; you'd see them trudging back in their uniforms of an evening. Despite the cold, her neck bloomed with heat. She unbuttoned her coat, dizzy with exhaustion after all the late nights at the warden post. She quickened her step; he did the same.

She shouldn't have come down this road. There was no one around.

Ruby thought of Jit, the way he wouldn't have thought twice about confronting this man. Or worse. Jit had told her he was going up north for a couple of weeks with his work, but that had been over a month ago. She had started to wonder whether the authorities had taken him in, but one his friends at the Forum had said he'd heard from Jit the other day, just busy with work and nothing to worry about, apparently. Still, he could at least have told her.

Nothing else for it. Ruby turned around sharply, fixing her gaze on the man.

Blue eyes stared out at her from behind thick lenses. 'There's nothing to worry about, Miss Thacker,' he said casually, raising his hands in the air as though she had a gun pointed at him.

Her stomach plunged. 'How d'you know my name?' She hadn't stolen anything in weeks, not since she'd seen the pocket watch that night. If it had been the stealing, it would have been uniformed policemen, wouldn't it? Ruby tried to remember the faces of the men who were following Jit, but this one didn't look familiar.

The stranger didn't say anything for a moment. 'My name's Sergeant Langley. Do you live around here? Let's find some-where to sit down and I can explain.' The man was all charcoal voice and sawdust skin.

'I'm not in the habit of letting strangers into my home. Who are you?'

The man held her gaze, not blinking. 'I'd rather not do this here, but well . . . You attend meetings at the India Forum, over on Endsleigh Street.' He wasn't asking, he was telling her.

Was it about what happened outside the bookshop? 'I'm not saying a word until you tell me who you are.' Her voice was as taut as a rubber band.

'I work for the authorities that are keeping this country safe.'

'What's that got to do with me and the India Forum?' Ruby stepped back. They couldn't arrest her for going to meetings and handing out pamphlets, which was what she'd been doing since Jit had gone.

'We think you can help us.'

'I don't see how that's possible. Unless you're looking for tips on how to black out windows at the local police station.' She tweaked the corners of her mouth into what she hoped was a placid smile.

'Oh yes, you're a warden,' he said, fixing her with a long stare. Ruby's throat went dry. Her hand felt for the metal railing but there was nothing there, of course; they'd all been taken.

'That's right,' she said quietly, glancing around. Along the pavement, the winter trees stood naked and shorn of leaves. The street was quiet, but she could see someone across the way pulling their curtains closed, preparing for the blackout.

'We want information. What's being discussed outside the meetings, anyone of interest, that kind of thing.'

'You want me to spy on them?' She shook her head. 'They're ordinary people.'

'You can do your turn as a good citizen.'

Before Ruby could respond, they had to step aside as an older woman came past, dragging a shopping bag behind her. She gave them a flustered look.

'But why, the Forum aren't a threat?' said Ruby. Mandalji, for all that fire in his speeches, seemed harmless enough and there was no doubt that Mrs Akhtar was always on the right side of the law. Unless it was Jit and his friends they were thinking about? 'You must have better things to worry about,' she said, her voice sharper than her mum's lemon curd.

He glanced down the street, checking there was no one around, then said, quieter now, 'We understand they may be collaborating with possible communists.' So that was it. Fascists were the obvious enemy, but plenty thought the communists were just as big a threat to the future of the country.

'I'm not aware of anything like that.'

'But we can't be sure. Some of the people who attend the Forum have socialist leanings, at the very least. And you can find out more for us.'

She wondered if the man knew that her dad was Indian. Or did he simply believe that the English side of her would trump the Indian and betray her Forum friends?

He continued, 'Unless you're saying you don't want to help your country?' His tone was hard and urgent now.

'I'm sorry, I don't think I'd be much use to you,' she said, about to turn.

'Oh, of course, I haven't mentioned, have I?' He patted his forehead with his hand, as though he'd just remembered something. 'You'll be paid for whatever you send our way.'

Ruby stared at him.

'Now, shall I tell you how this all works?'

26
Kitty

In solitude everything lay still exactly where it had been left: lifeless, with no surprise.

Kitty looked around the room, the chill of the outside still clinging to her skin. The only sound was the faint tick of the clock, the occasional creak of a floorboard elsewhere in the building.

The rest of the country had been buoyed with a renewed optimism that she couldn't quite bring herself to feel. The bombing of Pearl Harbor had changed things. The United States' hand had been forced by the Japanese, and GIs had begun to appear on British shores every day. The world was truly at war now.

She hadn't touched the chessboard in days. She played against herself these days, white pieces in the morning, black in the evening, trying to outfox herself with each new move. When Haseeb had been around, he'd sometimes leave a playful note for her: *Good move, but this one is better!* She had kept all the notes he'd written her, locked away in the same drawer where she kept the letters she never sent home to her family.

She played with the edge of the wool blanket she'd draped across her lap, the rain outside growing louder. When she and Haseeb had first come to London, they had somehow been cocooned from their loneliness, brought closer together than ever because they had no one else to rely on.

In loneliness you become a hollow, a negative space around which other people move. Kitty had never been the sort to visit the temple every week. Some of the Sikhs at the India Forum went to a gurdwara in Shepherd's Bush; Haseeb had gone to a mosque in Southfields once or twice. Last week, she had visited the home of one of the people from the Forum, who had held a *pooja* event for a few people in their living room. But somehow, sitting there singing and clapping just made her miss her family even more.

She roused herself from the armchair, remembering the unopened letter she had left in the hall that morning. It was from her old friend Devika, one of the handful of people she still kept in touch with in Bombay. She hadn't been able to bring herself to read it, knowing it would leave her longing for home again. Usually, the letter would be filled with the latest news about Devika's family, or hints that some of the Hindi, Marathi and Urdu newspapers seemed to take a more sympathetic view of the German fight.

Kitty thought of Subhas Chandra Bose, still languishing in Berlin, waiting for his audience with Hitler. Her chest prickled with worry as she remembered her argument with Satyajit. He was so convinced about Netaji. The last thing they needed was more division, but he seemed set on this dangerous path. Why did the fight for Independence have to be so hard, so insurmountable?

She was tired of thinking about it. Kitty dragged her attention back to Devika's letter, keen to hear of her friend's latest adventures. But instead the letter began with news for Kitty. Her dadi was ill, Devika had written; she wasn't exactly sure what it was, but she'd been ordered to bed rest for the past two weeks. The letter would have taken weeks to reach England,

and then Kitty had simply tossed it aside. How was Dadi now? She felt her throat swell at the thought of it.

Kitty knew that her family had turned their backs on her years before, but it was hard not to worry for the people who had raised her.

She quickly took out her letter-writing set and began to write to her father. She asked him if Dadi was all right and told him that he could write to her anytime, even call her at the India Forum if he wanted. She told him she was sorry for everything that had happened. Sorry: a word she had refused to say all this time, because why should she be sorry about who she loved? But the regret came from being apart so long and the fact that it might be too late now.

She went into her bedroom and edged her way past the double bed – there was barely enough space to move. She wished Haseeb could give her a hug, tell her that Dadi would be fine.

On his last forty-eight-hour leave a month ago, he'd seemed smaller, somehow. Certainly, he'd lost weight; despite the good rations provided for RAF pilots, and though they were given ample breakfasts of bacon and egg, he could only eat the latter, for a start.

And now the unwanted thoughts came. Where was Haseeb? What if she never saw him again? She sometimes wondered what would happen when their religions dictated different paths for them, even at the end: her body burnt to ash, his returned to the soil, never truly together, in death nor in life.

Kitty opened the wardrobe, putting her bleak thoughts away. She pulled out the package from the top shelf, wrapped in a shawl to keep it safe, and peeled away the fabric.

The *charkha* box was made of teak and it had been carved to look exactly like a book. There was the curve of a spine, and it opened up like one too – with the top revealing the spinning wheel inside – like the beginning of a story.

Madhubai, an activist friend of her father's, had given the charkha to her back home. One evening, her family had invited Madhubai, as well as various other freedom-fighting colleagues of theirs, to their house. Kitty was only twelve at the time, longing to be somewhere more interesting, anywhere but in a room with people droning on about Indian politics.

That day, they had gathered in the sitting room, with the loom-woven *asan* scattered around the edges of the room. The tea-and-aniseed scent of the *daunaa* leaves outside in the garden wafted through the open window. Kitty folded her feet under her and took a place in the corner next to her dadi.

There was an array of good food, at least. They had feasted on *aloo chaat* sprinkled with pomegranates; *salli murgh*, the chicken scattered with thin potato crisps which her father had specially ordered from the Irani cafe on Jagannath Shankar Seth Road; and Kitty's favourite, *falooda*, the neon-pink rose syrup at the bottom of the glass, which turned the milk to a baby pink, and was filled with translucent sago balls. It was so sweet that your teeth could have fallen out right there and then. Her father had asked Madhubai to do the spinning wheel demonstration at their home. The older woman had also lost all her teeth, which hollowed out her face, the skin sunken beneath her cheekbones.

'We are so honoured today to welcome Madhubai!' Kitty's father said, clapping his hands together. 'She is an inspiration to us all. When we falter or fatigue, we should look to you, Madhubai, to strengthen our resolve. You have marched with Gandhiji at Dandi,' he went on, referring to the protest against the oppressive British salt tax which meant that salt was too expensive for many ordinary Indians. Women had been told not to march alongside Gandhi, but a few, such as Madhubai, had joined anyway. 'You witnessed dear Gandhiji taking a fist-ful of the clay mud, studded with salt crystals, that marked the beginning of the march. And today, you will show us just how important cotton spinning is to our fight for Independence.'

Madhubai was an unassuming woman; she simply smiled and raised a hand briefly by way of thanks, before beginning her task. She opened up the large metre-long box which housed the charkha. With her wispy finger, Madhubai wrapped a cord around a smaller wheel, then twisted the unspun cotton over the spindle. She held the handle on the larger wheel and turned, while holding the spinning cotton in the other hand. The wheel made a clicking sound as it turned.

Kitty had sat there, bored, in a corner, staring out of the window. How was this helping their cause?

Madhubai spoke as she spun. 'Cotton is as Indian as we are. The roots grow strong in Mother India's earth, nourished by her monsoon rains, pulled up with Indian hands, to be spun on teak looms just like this.'

'What self-important rubbish is this?' Dadi muttered under her breath, then crossed her arms with a gruff sigh. 'This silly woman really thinks spinning a wheel will save her,' Dadi whispered fiercely.

Kitty stifled a smile.

'I have lived for sixty years and still the British man rules us,' Madhubai continued. 'Wasting our lives on fighting for something that will never be ours.'

She looked at Dadi now, and what their guest said next made Kitty wonder if she'd overheard her grandmother. 'We can think to ourselves, "It is just some cotton, it is hardly going to help us win Independence." But we would be wrong.'

Kitty glanced to her left. Dadi's cheeks were flushed as she glared at Madhubai.

'Cotton is not something to be ripped from our land and

shipped away,' said Madhubai. 'It clothes our people, protects them, so all our roots can grow strong.'

Kitty sipped her tea as she thought back to that night, running her hand over the charkha that Madhubai had given her. The old woman had pulled it out of her bag as the evening drew to a close and said, 'You must carry on the fight when we no longer can, beta.' The charkha was smaller than the one Madhubai had spun on and Kitty had put it away in a drawer straight afterwards, barely paid it any attention. It was only once she came back to Bombay from university, fired up by revolutionary talk of change from the Indian students who attended the Oxford Majlis meetings, that she took it out again and thought about the significance. A simple piece of wood, a basic tool, but she realized that she held her history in her hands, and the fate of her country. That something so mundane could hold so much emblematic power, and that she had nearly missed it entirely.

It didn't matter what people like Satyajit did, nor Netaji. She could still make a difference, the right way, the honourable way, and she would stop anyone who tried to sully the India Forum's name. Didn't she owe it to all the people who had gone before her?

Kitty put down her chai cup, bundled herself up in her coat and scarf and ventured back out. Clutching the letter to her father in her hand, she walked down the street to the postbox at the end of the road, painted white to stand out in the darkness. Though it was the colour of death for Hindus, on this rainy afternoon it was a beacon of light.

27

Ruby

'We'll see you next week, Miss Thacker?' called out Mandalji.

'Oh yes, hopefully,' said Ruby, before hurrying out of the India Forum to the street.

Outside, the sky was a sheet of pale grey; sunlight had no chance of breaking through today. Ruby quickened her pace, not wanting to get caught up in a conversation with anyone as they were leaving the Forum.

This was life now, keeping an eye out for the authorities half the time, and curious fellow Forum-goers the rest. Still no sign of Jit. If his friends at the Forum hadn't kept insisting that he had just gone away up north with his peddling work, she would have been sure that he'd been taken in by the surveillance men. She should stop wondering about him at all. Ruby hadn't even meant enough to him to be told his proper plans.

She carried on north up Camden Road, where the old tram tracks still cut through the street. The pavement here was mottled with greying blossom, ground in by a million footsteps.

The Black Horse was a scrappy pub, with black-framed windows and patchy brickwork. The inside was not much better, with tartan carpet that might once have been red and green, and a sooty fireplace that probably hadn't been cleaned since Queen Victoria's coronation. Ruby scanned the pub. There he was. Langley – though he had told Ruby to call him

Sergeant Langley, she never did in her head – was sitting in the corner, with his crossword and an ale. Ruby went and sat opposite.

'So what have you got for me?' He stared at her through his glasses. There was something particularly unnerving about the way he rarely blinked.

Ruby clutched her handbag in her lap. 'I've not had much of a chance to go to the India Forum recently, but there's a man called Jagadish—'

'Spell that for me?' he said, pulling out a pen and notebook from his breast pocket.

Ruby spelt out the full name, Jagadish Ghose. 'I think he works for an insurance company. At the Forum, he keeps going on about whether civil disobedience is the right way forward. Whether Gandhi and Nehru should be ousted. This and that,' she said.

'I see,' said Langley, writing it all down. 'And how long's he been coming to the meetings?'

'Oh, he's new. Maybe a couple of months,' she said, thinking on the spot. She'd conjured up this Jagadish Ghose from nowhere, and when Langley inevitably couldn't find any record of the man, she would have to say that he must have given a false name.

Over the past few months since Langley had first approached her, Ruby had been careful to pepper her information with things that were true as well. There was just enough there to keep them trusting her, things that could easily be discovered if anyone bothered to pay enough attention. It had to be enough to keep them off the scent.

Sometimes Ruby had also given the names of real people, Indian and British, the sorts that were clearly harmless. One man only came to the India Forum because he lived on his own and there were sometimes Indian snacks laid on after the meeting. Ruby knew there was a chance they might even stake his house out for a while, but eventually they'd lose interest.

She carried on, giving Langley a bit more to chew over, running through meeting agendas, which were usually the same old things about conscription and news from India that were widely reported anyway.

Either way, the money they were paying her came in handy. Most of Ruby's clothes no longer fitted, what with the rationing. She'd tried to take some in, but with her hapless sewing skills it hadn't quite worked out, and the money would mean she could afford a new dress and a smaller pair of ARP trousers instead.

'And have you heard of a man called . . .' Langley paused to look at his notebook, 'Satyajit Deol?'

Ruby's heart was in her throat. Though her mouth was dry, she managed to say, 'No, doesn't ring a bell. Why?' Jit had disappeared before Langley had first approached Ruby. Was he back in London, was he one of the reasons the authorities had been keeping tabs on the Forum in the first place, or was this why Jit had run off after all?

'And there's nothing else?' asked Langley, sipping the last of his ale and ignoring her question.

Ruby paused then shook her head. She couldn't push it with questions about Jit or it would make Langley suspicious. Surely if they'd made the connection between Jit and Ruby, Langley would have mentioned it already? Even before, Jit had told her that the surveillance men never took photographs of him – probably too conspicuous with the war going on, and liable to get them mistaken for a fifth columnist or some such. Jit said there was never as much money to go around for Indian surveillance, not when they had to keep the fascists at bay; she'd only seen them following him that one time at the cafe. So it was unlikely there'd be much, if anything, to connect them. 'I think that's it,' she said. She was going to get up and leave, hoping that what she'd given him was enough, but instead she found herself asking, 'Do you really think they're dangerous?'

'Well, that's what we're trying to find out,' he said. His eyes narrowed. 'Why, do you feel unsafe in any way?'

'Oh no,' she said quickly. 'Nothing like that.'

'Good. But you still need to be a bit careful. I know you think these are just harmless people trying to do right by their country but like I told you, we're keeping an eye on them for a reason.'

Ruby nodded. The way he talked about 'these people' and 'their country', she was fairly sure he hadn't cottoned on to her own background yet. In the meantime, she'd been careful to avoid her mum and dad, until she knew for sure just how closely Langley and his friends were actually watching her.

'But just imagine,' he added, warming to his theme, 'if you help us catch them?'

Ruby's eyes narrowed. 'Yes, imagine.'

28

Kitty

She was going to be late. Kitty looked at her watch as she approached Drummond Street. It was almost twelve o'clock and she still needed to cook lunch before Haseeb came home. He'd been given a forty-eight-hour leave, the first in forever, and everything had to be perfect.

At the corner of the road, she stopped in her tracks.

Along the street, Miss Thacker was in her ARP uniform, talking to a man in a trench coat and trilby. Kitty clutched her cloth bag of rations, wondering whether she could go down to the next street, to avoid having to say an awkward hello. Though the women often saw each other at the India Forum meetings and were civil enough, she had no desire to speak to her more than she had to.

Just as Kitty had decided it would be quicker to give a brief hello to Miss Thacker and carry on her way, the man she was talking to took out a notebook. Kitty stepped back, hidden behind the building on the corner. Miss Thacker glanced around her nervously but didn't appear to have seen Kitty. She looked annoyed with the man and started to move away from him, back towards her warden post. The man called out to her, but Kitty couldn't catch what he said.

Kitty tried to take in what she'd just witnessed. The man in the trilby looked official. And Miss Thacker had looked concerned about being seen. But why, exactly?

*

'The smell from the petrol bowsers on the aerodrome never seems to leave you, I swear I can still smell it in my hair,' said Haseeb, wearily. He and Kitty had been able to walk straight into Tavistock Square, now that the railings and gates had been removed. Most of the green space had been given over to growing vegetables, with rows of floppy carrot tops sprouting out of the fresh earth, but there were still a few patches of grass.

'Well, I hadn't noticed.' Kitty squeezed his hand and gave him a sly smile. 'You smell lovely to me.' They sat on one of the benches, looking out across the open square, framed by tall Georgian buildings. The last of the spring blossom had fallen now, giving way to bright-green leaves.

Haseeb stared into the distance. He'd been quiet since his return.

'Perhaps we could go and see a film later?' Kitty ventured. An older couple – the man with a walking stick, the woman clutching a fine leather handbag – were making their way up the path.

'Yes, maybe,' he murmured, still gazing across the square.

'What's the matter?' She placed her hand on his arm, drawing him back to the present.

'Nothing, Kitabi.' He mustered a smile.

'Are you still flying with that Bowers man?' Kitty knew from his letters that there had been a lot of flying and little sleep, but as with all the censored letters, there was little space for the reality. Perhaps she could prise it from him now.

'Yes.' Haseeb rubbed the back of his neck. 'Still as annoying as ever.'

Haseeb had explained that Flight Officer Richard Bowers was born in Rawalpindi, following a long line of British military men in his family, and liked nothing more than to show off his fluent Urdu and talk about feasting on *murgh cholay* and *meethi kheer* like a true Punjabi. 'Thinks he's above us all.' Haseeb rolled his eyes.

Kitty remembered Haseeb's talk of the RAF when he'd first joined. It had felt wrong, he said, 'like putting your left shoe on your right foot', to fight alongside British pilots. The enemy was no longer the enemy, at least for now. At the base, Haseeb mixed with pilots from the UK, America, the Commonwealth nations. All of them on the same side, fighting for the same thing. Yet on leave, off the battlefield, he took off his Sidcot and spit-and-polish boots and still fought for a free India.

'What's it like, near the base? Can you go out at all?'

Haseeb turned to her, shadows beneath his eyes. 'Why don't we talk about something more interesting?'

'I want to know how you are, Haseeb.' She stroked his hand.

'Tell me what's been going on at the India Forum,' he said.

Kitty knew there was no point in pushing Haseeb. She knew from the raids just how vicious enemy bombers could be. 'It's fine. The tribunals are keeping me occupied,' she said, although in truth there were far fewer than before. The rules stated that Indian men had to have been in England for at least two years before they were called up, and not many had come to the country after the war had started. Those who'd arrived before, like Haseeb, had already been called up.

'Let's walk a while.' she suggested. They made their way out of the square.

'I saw that Miss Thacker today, do you remember her?' said Kitty.

Haseeb nodded.

'I was over by her warden post on Chalton Street. She was talking to an Englishman.' She linked arms with Haseeb as they carried on past the high apartment blocks of Woburn Place. She described how she'd seen Miss Thacker talking to the man in the street, how he'd been writing notes, the way she had looked so anxious about being seen.

'Perhaps he was a council official, needing to get some information on bomb damage or warden protocol,' Haseeb shrugged.

'Why was she looking around like that, then? She seemed worried and angry, like she wanted to get away.'

'Maybe she was running late, just like you were, running home to your *jaan*.' He playfully tapped her arm.

'I don't think so.' Kitty smiled despite herself. 'You've heard Mandalji yourself, he's always concerned about who's keeping tabs on us.'

'Is that what you think it is?'

'I don't know,' said Kitty. She was so glad to have Haseeb to talk to. Despite a distance in him that was unmistakable since he'd come home, at least on these matters she could still confide in him.

'But didn't you say Miss Thacker's been supporting the India Forum recently, volunteering?'

'Yes, she has. It's just that she never really seemed the typical sort to ally with us.' Kitty remembered the way that Miss Thacker had become so close to Satyajit in the months after she first came to the India Forum. And yet Satyajit hadn't been to the India Forum in a long time, and still Miss Thacker came on her own.

'We have all kinds at the Forum, I suppose,' said Haseeb.

She nodded, thinking of the writers and poets rubbing

shoulders with the staid politicians in their grey suits and the worn-out dock workers.

'It's probably nothing,' said Haseeb. 'But you could ask her about it?'

'Yes, perhaps I will,' she replied, giving his hand a squeeze.

*

'*Nahin*, I can't! I can't do it!'

Kitty opened her eyes. She could just about make out Haseeb's silhouette; he must have cried out during a nightmare and jolted upright in bed.

'What is it?' she asked, reaching out her hand. His skin was hot and damp. Faint light filtered through the weave of the blackout curtains, signalling early morning.

His breathing was shallow. 'Nothing,' he said.

She sat up, stroking his chest. 'A nightmare?'

'I'm fine, Kitabi.'

'No, you're not. You act as though we barely know each other. I can see you haven't been yourself since you got home.' She edged closer to him. 'Please tell me, what's going on?'

'I—' he began. 'I don't know where to start.'

She waited for him to continue, not wanting to disturb this fragile glimpse of his real feelings.

'We were on a flight. Last week. It was a terrible . . .' He seemed to struggle to find the right words. Her eyes had adjusted to the light now and she could see his ruffled brow. Haseeb sighed. 'I shouldn't really be telling you . . .'

'Who am I going to tell, Haseeb?' Of course, some things were classified, she knew that as well as anyone, but all she needed to hear was what had happened to him. She pulled him close, resting her head on his shoulder.

'Last Thursday.' He stared out across the room towards the dark shadow of the wardrobe. 'The conditions weren't great, for a start. We were waiting in the dispersal hut. Bowers had already said it was –' he switched to English – '"looking a bit grubby out west."'

'Grubby?' asked Kitty.

He switched back to Hindi. 'The British boys say it, it just means cloudy. Harinder brushed them off as "a few cirrus clouds", but we all knew the visibility wouldn't be good.' Harinder was one of the younger members of Haseeb's squadron. He told Kitty that Harinder had come over with the Indian Air Force, selected from the very best. 'Swears more than he blinks.' His mouth curved up into a small smile.

Kitty was glad he had a countryman alongside him, someone who understood what it was like to be an outsider, but Haseeb was old compared to most of the fighter pilots at base. Early on in the war, the RAF was mainly full of young recruits. Youthful minds, too immature and full of testosterone to realize that, inside a cockpit, everyone was just as vulnerable to death. In pilot years Haseeb was practically middle-aged, but the RAF needed everyone they could get now. Young or older, British or Indian.

'Eventually we headed out to the planes from the dispersal unit. It was especially dark that night; the clouds hid the moon. We all prayed for safe flights, as usual. I could hear some of the others through my earphones.' Haseeb glanced at Kitty. The hope of staying alive. A sky full of prayers.

She imagined Haseeb, his plane ascending through ink-stained skies, the beams of the searchlights cutting and carving up the black.

'Once we were in the sky, I could see the silver of the Thames below. No sign of a horizon, though; all I had was the slight glow of the exhausts from the Spitfires either side of me.

'There were three Heinkel bombers in formation. And then the Messerschmitt 109s, a group of them to cover the

Heinkels.' He paused, glancing at her. 'The drone of them is enough to strike fear into you. Then there was chaos,' he said. 'A dogfight.'

Kitty had seen the dots and dashes of artillery fire in the sky above her during the Blitz, had smelled the cordite vapours in the air. She wished she didn't know, wished she couldn't imagine so clearly.

'I was so close to the enemy planes that I could see the faint glow from the cockpit lights, reflecting on one of the German pilots' helmets.' He took a deep breath. 'I could almost see his face.'

A part of Kitty wanted him to stop telling the story, couldn't bear the idea of how close he came to death every time he went into the air. But she also had to know, wanted to feel closer through his experiences. She stroked his back, waiting for him to continue.

'But I had no time to think. Another of the 109s had me in his sights. I made a break downwards to steal out of his way. I could see the flashes of red slashing through the dark sky. I tried to look either side to see what was happening behind me, but my Mae West – life jacket – was restricting my movements. And then I heard a hiss, this kind of boom.'

His voice was breathless, as though he was there all over again. Kitty braced herself as Haseeb continued. 'I'd been hit.'

His voice rose. 'Anger tore through me but I put it aside. If you're angry, you can't think clearly and that can be just as deadly. My engine cut and my fuel tank was out. I couldn't see now. The smoke fumes were black.'

'*Haseeb, mere jaan*,' whispered Kitty.

'I called out through the radio to the other planes, but there was nothing. I'd fallen out of range from them.' He took a gulp of air. 'I made a sharp turn. I was falling too fast and I knew I had to get closer to base. I tried to make out where I was but with the engine now flaming it was hard to see further afield. My propeller shuddered to a halt. I pulled the stick back hard to shave off some speed.'

Kitty wondered if there had been time for him to worry about what would happen if he came down in the sea, or behind enemy lines. The thought gripped her heart. He certainly wouldn't have the option of passing for a French farmer. His skin would betray him immediately.

'Somehow, the flare path appeared beneath me.' Brightness in his voice now, and Kitty's heart rose with it. 'I still wasn't sure if I'd make it, but I had to try. I got the flaps down, then there was a loud clank. The plane slammed down and the wheels rattled along the runway. I was bumping along, and the engine was still on fire.

'The smoke had cleared and I heard the thud of someone climbing onto the wing. It was Ted, one of the ground crew, and he helped me get out of the cockpit.'

'Haseeb, I can't believe . . .' Kitty didn't know what to say. How to comprehend the significance of it – how many other flights had there been, how many other times had he come so close to dying?

'I'm sorry,' he said quietly. 'I shouldn't let this all get to me when we have so little time together.'

'I want you to tell me. You can't just keep it all to yourself.' She held him close to her, resting her cheek against his chest. 'You've been through so much.' And then she thought, but how much more lay ahead?

29

Ruby

Jit was back.

After all these months, he had turned up at the India Forum and cornered Ruby before the meeting. 'I'm sorry,' said Jit, as they stood at the bottom of the staircase.

'Oh, are you really?' She gave him a bored look, then turned her gaze away and started to pick bits of lint off her cotton tea dress.

'I couldn't say anything about leaving.' His suit jacket seemed to hang off him and there were dark circles around his eyes. Mrs Akhtar walked past, frowning as she glanced at them.

'You don't owe me anything, Jit, it's fine.' Of course, it wasn't fine, it was about common courtesy. He should have told her. They'd begun courting, or at least she'd thought they had.

'Look, I had to go away. It was important. I am sorry.' The grandfather clock in the hall chimed four o'clock. Despite the rain outside, it was a warm and muggy day. Her skin felt sticky and uncomfortable.

'Were the authorities on to you?' She thought of the time that Langley had asked her about Jit.

'Oh, they're always sniffing around,' he said, waving his hand. 'I had to make some plans. There's some people I needed to speak to.'

'What people?'

There were more attendees coming into the hallway now, shaking off the rain from their coats and umbrellas, and it was hard to hear over the chatter. Jit gestured for Ruby to follow him to the back of the house. They stood by the garden door, the rain rattling on the windowpane.

'There are some people who can help us. They have money. Take proper action.'

'What does that mean?'

'Look, I can show you if you want. How we can finally make the British listen. Let me explain properly what we want to do.'

'You disappeared, Jit, and now we're supposed to just pick up where we left off?' Her tone was spiked with frustration.

'I understand you're annoyed. But we can really help the cause now.'

'I *am* helping the cause. People are listening to us.'

Jit gave her a wry smile. 'Do you really think handing out folded pieces of paper filled with polite words to a group of bored middle-class people is helping?'

'Then why do you keeping come here, Jit?' She struggled to keep her voice down now.

'So I can learn from their mistakes.' He gave a cold smile. 'Good luck with all your hard work, though, Ruby. See how far it gets you,' he said, then walked away.

30
Kitty

Even in the lamplight, there was no hiding the fact that the walls of the Forum were cracked, the oiled floorboards looked dull and worn. But the war had dragged on and Kitty knew there were always far bigger priorities than the maintenance of this old building.

As Mandalji finished the meeting, Kitty rested her pen and notebook in her lap and looked across the room. Miss Thacker had taken a seat further along her row, while Satyajit sat near the back as usual. Curious that they hadn't sat together this time. Kitty had seen the way they were talking out in the hallway earlier. There'd been a falling out, perhaps? Months had passed since Satyajit had been at the Forum. She remembered how she'd seen Miss Thacker talking to a man in the street. She wondered if Satyajit knew anything about it.

Everyone started to get up, with most eager to hurry home, armed with umbrellas. Across the room, Mandalji was talking to a young Englishman. He reminded Kitty of a wooden pencil with his pinstriped suit, the block of neatly pomaded hair. He seemed permanently startled; the clink of a cup on a saucer seemed to surprise him, laughter stunned him. Kitty wondered whether he had always been like that, long before the bombing began.

Miss Thacker gathered her things and hurried out as quickly as she could, but Satyajit hovered near the fresh chai that had been put out.

Kitty walked over to him. 'We thought you'd given up on the Forum,' she said, pouring herself a cup of tea.

'I didn't know you paid so much attention to my whereabouts.' He gave a sly grin.

Her cheeks flushed. 'Actually, it's part of my job to know who's attending our meetings,' she said. 'But speaking of people keeping an eye on you, perhaps you should pay attention closer to home.'

'Oh really?' He didn't look fazed, with his usual overconfident smirk on his face.

After Kitty had confided in Haseeb about seeing Miss Thacker talking to that stranger, she had mulled over all the options. In the end, she'd decided not to confront Miss Thacker directly, at least for now; far too easy for her to deny everything and cover her tracks. Kitty had been prepared to keep an eye on her, see if she could find out more for herself, but now that Satyajit was back, perhaps there was another course. 'How much do you know about Miss Thacker?'

He shrugged, then took a swig of chai. The room had emptied out, except for an older Indian couple who appeared to have scared off the young man in the pinstripe and were now talking to Mandalji themselves. 'What do you mean?' said Satyajit.

'I saw her talking to an Englishman, over by her warden post.'

He laughed. 'Is that a crime now?'

'He was making notes of some kind. She seemed to be very wary of being seen by anyone and kept looking around.'

Uncertainty flickered across Satyajit's face. 'She's a warden. Probably speaks to a lot of people.' And that was all Kitty needed to confirm that he didn't know anything about the man or who he was.

'And it's not strange that she seemed annoyed by him, wanted to get away?'

He tutted, but Kitty could see she'd begun to chip away at his bravado. 'You seem to spend a lot of time worrying about everyone else,' he said.

'So you're not worried at all?' She raised an eyebrow.

'She can do what she wants,' he said firmly, but there was no mistaking the doubt that lingered in his eyes.

31

Ruby

Ruby took in the grand hallway of Montague Villa, otherwise known as Moti Mahal, which someone at the India Forum had explained meant 'big palace'. Home to Sukhamar Chatterjee, a wealthy Bengali lawyer who had grown his already considerable family wealth further by speculating on the stock market and buying cheap in the years after the Black Tuesday stock market crash.

'Come in, please, join us,' said an older woman, presumably Sukhamar's wife, who was dressed in a delicate pink silk sari, finished with a long necklace of pearls. Given the surroundings, there was no doubt that they were real. 'You can go through and help yourself to a drink in the dining room. The garden is that way,' she said. Ruby smiled and nodded, making her way into the room.

When Sukhamar Chatterjee had offered up the house to Mandalji for a fundraising event, Croydon had seemed an incredibly long way to travel. Now that she was here in its plush surroundings, though, Ruby was glad she'd made the effort.

Glasses of water and rosehip cordial were neatly laid out on the dining table, sunlight glinting against them. Ruby took some cordial and walked around the room.

'You know,' whispered a grey-haired Englishwoman to the

Indian man next to her, 'it's got a drawing room, morning room, library and eight bedrooms. And they also have servants' quarters, a pantry *and* a wine cellar,' she said, raising her eyebrows. The man nodded wearily.

Ruby looked around. There was a family portrait over the mantelpiece, with all the Chatterjee family dressed in English evening wear. She had heard that Mr Chatterjee had been very keen on assimilation after he'd come to England. The contrast intrigued her, an Anglophile who was also entirely committed to the Indian cause. On the far wall, there was a dark wood and glass cabinet filled with silverware and ornaments. Ruby stepped closer, taking in a small grey mother-of-pearl inlay box. A pretty flourish of leaves and flowers decorated the exterior. Ruby flushed, as though she'd suddenly been found out. It was just the sort of thing she might once have taken during a raid.

She went out into the hallway and headed to the back of the house. Outside, there was a walled garden with an arch of climbing roses, a small wooden pavilion for resting and an old oak tree at the end which provided shade. A few people were gathered beneath it, including Mandalji, and Mrs Akhtar, who was in a bold floral sari. There was a short man with heavy black glasses talking to them, whom she recognized from the family portrait as Mr Chatterjee. Ruby decided to go and take a closer look at the walled garden.

'Enjoying yourself?'

Ruby turned to see Jit, a slight sheen of sweat across his forehead, clutching a glass of water.

'Hello,' she said flatly.

'Well, *are* you enjoying yourself?' The snap in his tone surprised her.

'I suppose so,' she shrugged.

'And will you be telling everyone else about it afterwards?'

'What d'you mean?' Ruby frowned. More people came out into the garden, admiring the tissue-thin poppy petals aflame in the sunlight.

'Who have you been talking to, Ruby?' He came closer, lowering his voice. 'You were seen with some Englishman near your warden post.'

Ruby's body went rigid. How did Jit know?

'Have you been following me?' Her throat had gone dry. She took a gulp of cordial.

'Who is he?' Jit fixed her with a stare.

There was no point denying it now. 'He's with the authorities –'

Jit's face flashed with anger.

'– but it's not what it looks like.'

'Oh really? So you're not sharing information about me and the India Forum and all these people?' He flicked his head towards the crowd.

Just as she was about to respond, Mandalji clapped his hands. 'Please, everyone, do gather around,' he said, drawing people closer.

Ruby sighed. 'No, not exactly. They think I'm an informant. But I've been giving them false information.'

'That's exactly what an informant would say,' he said, voice taut.

Mandalji began his speech. 'Thank you all for coming.'

'Look,' Ruby stepped a little further away from the crowd so it would be easier to talk, standing near the garden gate that led to the front of the house. 'For a start, what's there to tell about the India Forum? Mandalji's as straight as a die. And what could I tell them about you anyway? You dis-appeared, remember.'

Jit looked at her.

'I've been making things up and giving them false leads.

That's all. I'm trying to help, Jit.' Ruby wasn't sure why it was so important, but of everyone at the India Forum, she needed him to know that she was loyal to the cause. *Their* cause.

He stared at her, apparently deciding whether she was telling the truth. 'How long have you been speaking to them?'

Ruby explained how Langley had approached her and where they'd met.

'And they believe you?'

'They seem to. Why else would they keep coming back?'

'So this is what you've been doing between all your helping out at the Forum with the work that never goes anywhere?' He grinned.

'It's important work, Jit,' said Ruby quietly.

He bowed his head closer. 'If you really want to do important work, Ruby, then you need to forget all this and see what I've been planning.'

*

Ruby stood on the corner of Bethnal Green Road, taking in the bustle and noise. A young woman tugging a crying toddler along by his arm, a man walking a reluctant whippet, two old women tottering along with their shopping trolleys, past the baker's with the three sad-looking buns and a loaf of bread that looked as if it had made from sawdust, past the pawnbroker and its treasures.

'Ruby.' She turned to see Jit smiling at her.

'Hello,' she said.

'This way,' he said. It had been a week since the charity event at the Chatterjees'. Jit had told her it was better not to travel together, still being careful to make sure they weren't followed. Luckily Langley still seemed happy enough with the titbits of information she sent his way to trust her to report back to him without anyone needing to check up on her. He'd made no further mention of Jit and, for the time being, they didn't seem to be following him either – no steely-looking men hanging around street corners waiting for him now. Perhaps they hadn't even cottoned on that he was back in London yet. Still, she was always careful not to be seen, checking the road through the window before she went out, tentatively looking around her now and then.

They passed cramped Victorian terraces, the bay windows framed with once-white borders and arched porches covering ornate front doors. The low buzz of a wireless carried through a nearby open window.

Eventually they stopped at a scruffy-looking house and rang the bell.

A stocky young Indian man answered the door. He had a thick moustache and bristling brown hair that reminded her of a doormat. He glanced wearily at Ruby a moment. Jit exchanged some words with the man in Hindi, the rapid rise and fall of his words brisker than his slower, more cautious English. In his own language, of course, Jit didn't have to wait for his mouth to catch up with his thoughts. When he spoke English, though fluent, his every word seemed guarded, but in Hindi he appeared more relaxed than she'd ever seen him. The young man gave a curt nod and let them in.

Ruby found herself hitching the waistband of her skirt up again, the way she often had to do now. The rationing was whittling her away to nothing.

The hallway smelt of cooking oil. She followed Jit up the stairs and into a room to their right. On the windowsill, there was a thin six-inch stick that looked like a reed, propped inside a small metal pot, with smoke floating out from the top of it. The room was filled with a woody and herbal scent.

On the bed stood a crate full of leatherbound English books.

Jit took one out and opened a page, pulling out a black-and-white pamphlet that was tucked inside. It was written in what was presumably Hindi script.

Jit showed it to her. 'They print them outside London, and then we pack them up.'

'What are they?' Though she'd tried to get more answers from Jit that day at Mr Chatterjee's house in Croydon, he had told her that he wanted to show her for himself what he had in mind, that it would be easier to explain that way.

'Pamphlets written in different Indian languages,' he said. 'Calling for people to take direct action and fight back against our oppressors.'

'What kind of direct action?'

He stared at her. 'The kind that doesn't involve sitting around drinking tea with politicians and talking for hours.'

Ruby knew from the dark look in his eyes that he didn't just mean protests. She could ask him to elaborate, but she wasn't yet sure she wanted to know the answer. She ran her hand along the spines of the books; they were mainly British classics: *A Tale of Two Cities, Robinson Crusoe, The Moonstone, The Secret Garden.*

'It's a kind of joke we like to play,' said Jit. 'Some of the books mention India, others are about revolution.'

'And they have to be smuggled into India?'

'Yes.' He met her gaze with a look of pride.

Ruby flicked through the pamphlet. One of the pages was written in some kind of four-line verse.

'That one's written in rhyme. Not everyone can read, so poems are easier to remember and repeat to others.'

Just then the young man with the moustache came into the room. He said something in Hindi to Jit, and in turn, Jit replied quietly.

'My name is Rana.' The man switched to English. Ruby

wondered if Jit had said something to him about involving her in their conversation.

'Ruby,' she nodded.

'We have a new delivery of pamphlets,' he said curtly. She noticed a small scar that cut across his right cheek; it crumpled as he spoke. Rana opened up the triple wardrobe. There was another crate filled with smaller cardboard boxes. Jit pulled one out. Taking a letter opener from the bedside table, he sliced open the large package, then Jit and Rana began taking out pamphlets and sliding them into the books. Ruby stood near the window, placing her handbag on the sill.

'We need to get these out this week,' said Jit.

Rana looked up, then said something to Jit in an urgent tone. Rana seemed very wary of Ruby, but then she remembered what her dad had told her. Arrests, violence, for the smallest of acts. Everyone had to be careful.

Jit replied to his friend in a calming tone and, although Rana still looked agitated, he carried on with the packing.

She watched as they continued making piles of books on the bed. It was extraordinary, the idea that words could have such power that they were banned. After a while, Jit started repacking the crate and Rana left the room.

There was an address label in English on the side of the crate, along with 'Surat' stamped in black capital letters, a place her dad had mentioned to her. Though he still avoided talking about the Independence movement, he was more open to sharing memories of his earlier years. He'd told Ruby it was a historic port city, a place he'd found work in for a short while before leaving for England.

'You'll ship these to Gujarat?' she said.

Jit stared at her, eyes narrowing. 'Yes. How do you know that?' He glanced at the address label. There was no reference to Gujarat on it.

'Oh, I think I heard someone talking about it at the Forum.' Ruby could tell him right now that she was Indian too, couldn't she? She no longer felt shame about who she was, and yet she wasn't sure Jit would understand. Jit, who was so proud of who he was, who would fight for his country no matter the consequences, without fear. Would he ever be able to understand why she'd hidden the truth?

Jit looked at her a moment, as though weighing something up in his mind. 'Ruby—'

Just then Rana called from downstairs, an urgency in his voice.

'I've got to get going,' said Jit. He put the crate away in the wardrobe. 'Do you see why we need your help? We need to buy more second-hand books and to pack the pamphlets.'

Ruby took a breath. 'What if we're caught, isn't it seen as sedition? Didn't you say people were hanged in India?'

'Not for smuggling.'

'But we could still be arrested.'

'We haven't been so far, even when those men were following me about like stray dogs.'

Ruby looked at him. He made it sound so easy.

'Besides,' he said, regarding her with a playful look on his face, 'you seem quite comfortable with breaking the rules.'

32
Kitty

'Do or Die.'

Kitty watched Mandalji as he echoed the words of Mahatma Gandhi, a rising call from India, speaking to the audience in the India Forum garden.

Although they'd started the meeting in the library as usual, it had become apparent very quickly that it would be far too hot for thirty people to sit inside on a day like this. They had clumsily laid out the chairs across the parched grass and Mandalji's lectern was set up near the back door of the building.

Mandalji repeated the words for emphasis. 'Do or Die. Those were Gandhiji's words. "We shall either free India or die in the attempt, we shall not live to see the perpetuation of our slavery."' Mandalji looked up at his audience, his urgent tone far more forceful than Gandhi's soft voice had ever been. 'We must Do or Die, just as our brothers and sisters in India will. The Viceroy of India can keep Gandhiji, Nehru and the entire Indian Congress imprisoned if he wants to. But we must not weaken *our* resolve just because we are thousands of miles away.' Applause rippled through the audience. They all knew of the underhand tactics of the Viceroy, how he'd surprised Congress and imprisoned them under the Defence of India rules, exploiting laws that were supposed to be used to secure the country during the war. It had led to widespread protests and inevitable riots.

British newspapers had been swiftly bombarded with letters from India Forum members, a rapid response to hostile reporting. Kitty had helped Mandalji draft articles for liberal newspapers and journals such as the *Manchester Guardian*, giving the alternative view: that it was wrong to stop the democratic process, even in wartime – especially in wartime.

Kitty rested her pen in the spine of her notebook. In the garden, a small area in the corner sheltered by patchily painted brick walls had been given over to growing carrots, onions and radishes. Wispy echoes of dandelions were clustered around the tree.

The evening shade was at least starting to descend. Mahesh, one of the young men Kitty had helped at a tribunal, was in a row towards the back of the garden. Satyajit was sitting nearby, close to the high brick wall. Surprisingly, Miss Thacker was nowhere to be seen. Kitty couldn't keep up with those two; half the time they wouldn't go anywhere near each other, the rest they could be found huddled together in conspiracy, just as they had been the other day in Sukhamar Chatterjee's garden.

Kitty had briefly pulled Satyajit aside that day, when Miss Thacker had gone inside the house for a drink. 'Did you ask her about that man?'

Satyajit looked at Kitty with dark eyes. 'It's nothing. You made a mistake.'

Kitty frowned. 'Really? And how did she explain it to you?'

'It's just some council man. Nothing for you to worry about,' he said.

She looked for signs of concern on Satyajit's face but he seemed completely at ease.

'I'm glad you can be so trusting,' she said, glancing back

towards the house in case Miss Thacker was nearby. 'But I'll be keeping a very close eye on her.'

Satyajit didn't even bother to reply; he just looked at her with an indifferent gaze on his face.

As she walked off, Kitty tried to tell herself that Satyajit wasn't the kind of man to let things go; perhaps if he wasn't concerned, she shouldn't be either? After all, the India Forum had nothing to hide.

Mandalji's updates on Rangoon brought Kitty back into the present. The Indian emigrants there, along with the Anglo-Indians and Anglo-Burmese, had been caught in the crossfire between the Allies and the Axis powers. Kitty had seen the newspapers – the refugees had escaped and marched as far as they could before collapsing, a gruesome trail of bodies leading the way for the few survivors, reminding the 'lucky ones' that followed of the penalties of seeking safer ground.

But now there were further pressures on East India. Growing hordes were starving, both refugees and locals. Rangoon – now under Japanese control – had also been a key supplier of rice.

'The Japanese still have their sights on India,' explained Mandalji, brows furrowing, a grave look on his face. 'And our friends in Congress have confirmed that the British authorities are holding surplus rice stocks in East India. We have heard that they are also destroying any transportation deemed help-ful to the Japanese should they actually invade.'

'So what are the local Indians supposed to do in the mean-time? Is there no way to help them?' one man called from the front row.

'Congress have made their feelings very clear to the British Indian authorities. We will do the same here,' Mandalji said firmly.

Kitty sighed, her heart tired of all the sorrow, not only for the refugees, but also her own constant worry. She hadn't heard back from her father after she'd written to him asking about her dadi. Kitty had contacted her friend Devika again, who had told her that although her dadi was still not able to get out of bed, her condition hadn't grown any worse. The patchy news only served to twist Kitty's heart further.

If she wasn't waiting for letters from India, she was waiting for news from Haseeb. Everyone with family in the military feared the letters that arrived days or weeks after they'd been written by people they loved. The letters that could arrive long after they were dead. Ghost letters.

It'll be over in a year, they'd all said back in 1939, like a broken record. And here they were, still fighting, still praying for miracles. But at least Indians knew how to be patient.

Mandalji finished his updates and opened the floor to questions from the Forum members.

An Indian man with skin as leathery as an elephant stood up. 'Mandalji, why do you not say what no one else here will?' he said in Hindi.

'And what might that be, *bhai*?' Mandalji's voice softened, intrigued by the man. He translated the rest of the man's words into English so that the British people in the audience could also understand.

'It is only a matter of time before India is granted Independence. But what then? All these other cultures and religions together, it will never work. Let Jinnah and the Muslim League have their own country and leave us alone.' He became more animated now, raising a wiry hand as he spoke. 'The great Golwalkar praised the Germans . . .' he said, referring to the man who led the right-wing RSS party in India. 'He said that purging the Jews from Germany, as Hitler had done, is something we in India can learn from.' There were murmurs in the audience. The man's words sent a chill through Kitty's heart.

She shifted in her seat, glad to see that most people were as concerned as she was by the turn of the conversation.

'We don't need that kind of politics in our country,' came a voice from the back, also speaking in Hindi.

'You think that I am foolish?' The older man smirked. 'One nation can only thrive with one religion. We have seen that for the past two hundred years, with the Angrez trying to impose their British ways.'

'Come, my friend, we are all here together: Muslim, Sikh, Christian, Parsi, Jain, Buddhist,' said Mandalji. 'All for the same reason, a free and *united* India.'

'Hindustan should be for the Hindus!' The man became more animated, his hand flying about the air to emphasize his point. You almost had to admire the persistence of a bigot.

Kitty surveyed the crowd, many of whom were waiting for the translation. Some looked dismayed, but there were a few who nodded their heads in agreement. Nationalism had been the collective sword to unite Indians against British rule, but like any weapon, it was dangerous in the wrong hands. Kitty was a little surprised to see Satyajit glaring at the man, clearly displeased too.

'Bhai, Hindustan is taken from a Persian word.' Mandalji paused a moment. 'Did you know that?' It was derived from the Persians who had come to India centuries before. It was clear from the gormless look on the man's face that he didn't know. 'India is great because of our many faiths and cultures. Surely two million square miles is enough for all of us?' Mandalji smiled and a few people laughed along.

The older man's face hardened. 'You can all laugh, but once the Angrez go home, we will simply be with left another enemy on our doorstep.'

Kitty's stomach crackled with anger. *This isn't what we fought for.* What would happen to her and Haseeb if the country was carved up like a piece of mutton, one part for the Muslims, another for the Hindus? And Haseeb was as Indian as Kitty was; how could anyone say differently?

Her heart was heavy as she thought of her father and dadi now. Because she loved the 'wrong person'. As though love was a choice.

Mandalji leant forward at his podium now. Kitty could tell from the set of his jaw that the man in the audience had annoyed him, but Mandalji knew better than to reveal himself. Anger blunted rather than sharpened debate, he often told her. 'The British government's spell has not worked on all of us,' he said placidly, meeting the man's gaze. 'They have been trying to divide us and to make us hate each other for centuries.'

As Mandalji was about to say something else, Mahesh stood up, chair screeching behind him. 'Please, Mandalji, Hindus and Muslims had problems in India long before a white man ever set foot in our land, you must admit that?'

'No, India is strongest with all of us together,' said another voice.

Kitty turned in her seat, surprised to find that it was Satyajit who had spoken. He sat forward in his chair. 'You really want to uproot millions?'

Mahesh ignored Satyajit and addressed Mandalji. 'Give the Muslims their own country so that they can get out of ours.'

'It's not just your country, though,' Kitty called out, a jagged note in her voice. She was the one who had made sure Mahesh stayed out of the military, and this was how he had felt all along? He knew Kitty was married to Haseeb, but it hadn't seemed to bother him then. 'And you're just replacing one hostility with another.'

'You think all your troubles lie at your Muslim brothers' feet, when we should be standing stronger than ever.' Satyajit stood up. 'Look at your real enemies!' Kitty couldn't quite believe that, for once, they were fighting for the same thing.

But no one could hear him, as others joined in, standing up and all firing words at each other, while Satyajit was caught in an argument with Mahesh. Of course people didn't always agree on the best way to fight for freedom, but Kitty had never seen it escalate like this before. She caught the gaze of Iqbal Hussain, one of the young Muslim men who had only recently joined the India Forum. His eyes looked so sorrowful that Kitty had to turn away, knowing it was exactly the way Haseeb would have felt.

'Stop, please.' Mandalji raised his voice but no one listened.

Kitty wondered what the neighbours would make of this. They were playing straight into the stereotype of 'unruly foreigners'. After a moment Mandalji tried again, hammering on the lectern. 'Silence. Stop this!' Quiet descended as people stopped shouting, some falling back into their chairs. Mandalji looked every single person in the eye in turn as he spoke. 'This is what the Viceroy wants, to divide us in our thoughts, our words and our actions. You've already let him and his cronies win.' A note of something in Mandalji's voice that Kitty had never heard before. Despair.

Kitty sank back into her chair. It seemed that some people just wanted to restrict and isolate themselves. Split by nationality, by religion, by caste. They chose to squeeze themselves into ever smaller boxes, and to what end? More rules. The rules of the British were one thing, but when they were gone, hundreds of other rules would still remain.

Where would it all lead for Haseeb and her?

She turned towards the back of the garden a moment and glanced at Satyajit, a shared look of recognition at just how serious this was.

Mandalji continued, a ferocity of defiance in his voice now.

'Will we keep looking backwards at what didn't work, at the ways we were harmed, at the wrongs that were done?' Though he might often spend hours on his speeches, Mandalji could be just as eloquent in the heat of the moment. 'Or will we break free from the chains of our past to focus on our future, free to make our own laws, stronger together, in a united India?'

33

Ruby

'It's a nice little place,' said Jit, taking in Ruby's flat, scanning the small sitting room and the kitchenette. He was being polite, of course.

She went over to the window and opened it a fraction. Alma had gone away to see her parents in Kent that morning and the air had grown stuffy.

Ruby and Jit had been to the pictures that evening and, for once, they hadn't spoken about Independence or the war, but simply talked about ordinary things: whether Katharine Hepburn should have chosen James Stewart or Cary Grant, how they'd go up to Primrose Hill the next Sunday they both had free. Perhaps it was all that talk of easy things, or perhaps it was standing here now, holding hands with Jit, the warmth of his palm on hers; how good it felt to let someone into her life.

Usually, he'd have seen her to her door and been on his way, but this time Ruby hadn't wanted the evening to end.

'How long have you been here?' asked Jit.

'Coming up to three years now.' How much had changed in that time.

She went into her bedroom and took out some rose-scented candles – a black-market find, of course. After putting them on the mantelpiece, she lit them and turned off the wall lights.

The candles cast three glowing orbs of light, reflecting in the mirror over the fireplace.

She had never brought a man home before. Lucky Alma was away. Ruby could just imagine her prim face reproving her with a single look, about bringing home strange men and how it would reflect on her own reputation. Let alone an Indian man.

Ruby went over to the gramophone and put the needle on the record that was already in place. Benny Goodman's meandering clarinet accompanied Peggy Lee's melancholy refrain on 'Where or When', singing of how some things were familiar yet unknown.

Ruby asked Jit if he wanted a drink and he nodded. She poured him some whisky and mixed some gin and cordial for herself, enjoying the fuzzy warmth of the alcohol as it made its way down to her tummy. Jit stepped towards her, pulling her close, and they moved together with a lazy kind of lilt as Peggy sang in the background. Ruby smiled at him and Jit kissed her neck, a trail across her skin, all the way up to her lips. A flame of whisky on his tongue.

Ruby put her glass down and he followed suit, taking her hand in his.

In the bedroom, she closed the door behind them. Jit walked over to her, drawing her towards him, his chest pressed hard against her, and they fell back onto the bed. She pulled at his shirt but halfway through undoing his buttons, she stopped.

Scars all the way across his torso, lightning flashes across his skin. A gasp escaped her.

He gently put her hand to her cheek. 'It's all right, Ruby. They don't hurt any more.'

'What happened?' she whispered.

'We don't have to talk about that now,' he said, stroking her hair. Then, with a tinge of pain in his voice, 'I want to leave India behind for once.'

She paused, then nodded, moving towards him as he caressed her. He delicately slipped off her dress, kissing her shoulders. Her hands gripped his back, her thigh hooked tight around his hip; as they pressed into one another, nothing was enough. She wanted more and she took more still.

*

They woke early the next morning, although in truth she and Jit had found each other all through the night, lazy fingers trailing limbs, kisses finding bare skin.

'Morning,' she said, her voice hazy with sleep. Though the blackout curtains were drawn, a crosshatch of muted sunlight glowed through the fabric.

'Good morning,' he said, brushing her cheek with his thumb. The skin on the inside of his wrist was as fine as tissue paper, a blue vein running beneath it. She moved closer, their fingers interlacing. His hand was soft; the skin had not yet worked long enough to grow rough.

'Do you have to work today?' she whispered.

'No, but I have some errands to do later.' His cologne mingled with the faintest trace of sweat on her sheets. 'But I should be catching up with my sleep. You have worn me out,' he laughed.

She was glad they could stay where they were for a little longer, away from the world, away from the stares or the muttered comments, from constantly having to be on guard. She stroked his stomach, fingers catching on the bumps of his scars.

'What did they do to you?' she said, her voice low.

He looked at her, surprised at the change in her tone. He opened his mouth but hesitated. He played with a strand of her hair. 'Remember I told you about those bamboo sticks, the lathi, that the police use?'

She nodded.

'Well, they sometimes put brass tips onto the ends of them.'

Ruby raised her head. 'So they cause more pain?'

'Exactly.'

'Oh, Jit, I'm so sorry,' she said, stroking his cheek. 'When did they do it?'

'At a protest, a few years ago. And then this . . .' he said, pointing at another scar on his stomach. 'There were protests in our town once, when I was young. They turned violent and two policemen were killed. Afterwards, they cordoned off the roads. Said it was to make the area safe again. For three days and nights, if you lived there, they made the men crawl on their bellies to get underneath the barriers. I was only fourteen, but I was tall enough to pass for a fully grown man.' His hands tightened, fingers curling into balls. 'I still remember the way the stones cut into my chest. Breathing in that dirt. One Indian was as good as another for punishing,' he said, staring at her. 'Women were harassed, too.' He took a deep breath, trying to steady himself.

'I'm so sorry.'

He seemed to pull himself back into the present then. 'No need to dwell on that now.'

'No,' she said, not wanting to linger on bad memories, but how could you forget when the memory was there forever, etched across your body?

She moved closer to him, curling her arm across his chest. 'But I do understand, Jit. Really. I understand exactly why this is all so important to you. Why shouldn't all Indians live as freely as I do?' said Ruby, though she nearly stumbled upon the words. Had she ever really been free, hiding who she was all this time?

Jit turned his head and stared at her a moment, a questioning look in his eyes. 'Do you have family in India, Ruby?'

'Why do you ask that?'

'When you mentioned Gujarat the other day. At Rana's house.'

Would he think she was a coward? She traced his features in the grey-blue light of the room, the wayward strand of hair that always fell onto his forehead when it hadn't been carefully smoothed into place. The one thing she knew for certain was that she couldn't hide any more.

'My Dad,' she said quietly. 'He's Indian.'

When Jit turned to her, he didn't look surprised.

She lifted her head, propping herself up as she fixed her gaze on him. 'Did you suspect something?'

He shrugged. 'I couldn't be sure, but . . . most of the people who come to the India Forum fit into neat groups. Socialists, politicians, writers, the middle class, the dock workers. You weren't any of those things, but you were happy to listen to Mandalji and his friends droning on about their weak plans.' He gave an exasperated smile. 'And then there's your surname, Thacker.'

It was a well-known Indian surname, as well as an English one. Ruby rested her head on his chest, felt the rise and fall of his breath.

'You could have told me, Ruby.'

'I thought you'd think I was weak. Hiding who I was.'

'Can't have been easy growing up here.' He took her hand, wrapping his fingers between hers. 'We all do what we must to survive.'

Later, they went into the kitchen. Ruby peeled back the blackout paper at the window. They sat at the table, morning sunlight cutting across the room. She had told him everything, about her dad, about Freddie, about all the things that she'd kept locked up in her heart. She felt lighter somehow, that unfamiliar closeness with someone else. Grief had made itself at home in her ribcage, there so long it became a part of her.

Jit came into the kitchen, tie hanging loose from his shirt.

'Here,' he said, holding out a postcard.

Ruby put the kettle onto the stove and turned. 'What is it?'

The postcard had an ink drawing, a map of Bengal.

'I want you to have it,' he said, giving her a soft kiss on the cheek.

She traced her finger over the lines.

'A gift, from one Indian to another,' he smiled.

Ruby squeezed his hand, cheeks flushing. She thanked him and went and propped it up on her bedside cabinet. Once the tea was made, they sat at the table and she passed him the toast, spread with the thinnest sliver of butter. 'What are you doing today?' she asked.

'I need to make some preparations with Rana. We're getting more pamphlets soon. It's just difficult buying up the second-hand books. We can't buy too many in bulk or it will look suspicious.'

She sipped her weak tea, looking down at the table. 'What would the authorities do if they found out?'

'Even if they found out what *we* were doing, they wouldn't trace it back to you.' He took a bite of his toast.

She gave a shocked laugh. 'I'm in direct contact with the authorities.'

'Well then, you need to distract them as much as you can, don't you? The more information you give, the less likely they are to suspect.'

Ruby thought of the scars on Jit's body, of how her dad thought the fight for India was all futile, of the endless hours of meetings at the India Forum. This was doing something real to help ordinary Indians, wasn't it?

'I suppose buying some books is harmless enough,' she said, running her thumb along her plate.

Jit's ears practically pricked up. 'Really?'

'But we need to be very careful, Jit. Especially with those men following you about.'

He squeezed her hand. 'We're always one step ahead of them, don't worry. Now we can move,' he said. 'Really change things for good.' Ruby looked down at the table. The optimism in his eyes should have buoyed her, but she couldn't ignore the flicker of doubt in her heart.

34
Kitty

Kitty stepped from the cool of the ticket hall into the light and her heart leapt for joy. Haseeb sat astride a motorcycle, a huge grin on his face. The golden eagle of the Pathfinder badge on his jacket glimmered at her in the late August sunshine.

People poured out of the railway station with her, service-men and women in a mix of navy and khaki and grey-blue uniforms, an array of accents and languages from all over the world.

Kitty liked the way she had to stand on tiptoe in her court shoes to kiss him. She breathed in his starch and motor-oil scent, taking in his face, even more beautiful than she remem-bered, despite the dark circles under his eyes. She stroked the back of his neck. He was real, he was right there in front of her, after all these weeks apart.

The war was dragging on. The queues dragged on, the rationing and the shortages too, but some lives didn't get a chance to be boring or endlessly wait. She hugged Haseeb tight, flesh and bones in her arms, as though she could hold onto him forever.

'You look smashing,' he beamed. Another one of those words Haseeb had told her about in his letters. Kitty had laughed to herself when she'd read that, knowing that the RAF boys would have taught him all sorts of far more colourful phrases that couldn't be repeated in censored correspondence. 'Meet Bertie,' he said, stretching his arm out towards the motorcycle. 'Climb aboard.'

Kitty looked at him, then down at the hem of her skirt. Oh, who cares, she thought. She climbed on and did her best to hold the skirt down as far as it would go.

'I won't go too fast, I promise,' he said. She wrapped her arms around his waist, her chin resting in the curve of his shoulder. The engine revved and they were off.

They might almost have been on holiday. Apart from a requisitioned lorry and one army truck, all they saw in the country lanes were fields of barley, verges trimmed with buttercups and dandelions that nodded at them in the breeze. The blue sky shimmered in the heat like silk, a ribbon of starlings on a slipstream following behind them. The scent of fresh-cut grass was sharp in the air. As though there was no war, and they were back to peacetime, to innocence.

Haseeb had booked a night in a bed and breakfast with a cabbage-faced landlady who gave them disapproving looks when they arrived. The carpet smelt like wet dog and there were cracks in the window, but at least it was clean.

The room felt smaller than it was, the two of them together after almost two months apart. Kitty wanted to ask him so many questions to fill in the weeks they'd missed from each other's lives, but there were better things to do right now.

They tumbled onto the bed, trying to wriggle out of their clothes. He kissed her shoulders, along the track lines left by Kitty's bra straps. She undid his belt. Haseeb tried to help her with her clothes, but the bed was so soft that his body seemed to smother Kitty's. He took out a johnny from his shirt pocket. And now here was the familiar: the rock of the bed, the slip of their skin against rough cotton sheets. And yet making love to him was still warped with worry.

It was over too quickly, awkward even at the end. 'Maybe I should have slowed down, I'm sorry,' he said. Kitty didn't answer him. Let it be, let it fall where it likes, she thought. Though they lay next to each other, they were further apart than ever.

Everything felt wrong, nothing was as she'd imagined it would be. Was it the surroundings? The time apart?

'Why don't we go and find something to eat?' he said, his voice filled with a joviality that neither of them truly felt.

*

Later that evening she dabbed on her perfume, a rhythm and flow to the way she moved, a syncopation and beat, once on each wrist and then behind her right ear, the last thing she did before she went out, like a full stop.

Haseeb had explained earlier that the dance was being held in a disused aircraft hangar at the local army base. A nearby US Air Force squadron had set up a swing band and there would be plenty of food. The Yanks, as he called them, never let their own go hungry.

Sure enough, when they arrived there was ample beer, macaroni salad, chocolate cake, fresh butter and bread rolls that were soft, not hard as bricks.

There were quite a few white GIs at the event, of course. The black military men stayed away; 'separate but equal' was the motto in the US. Kitty had noticed the cold, sometimes nasty way they were treated by some of their fellow American servicemen. Of course, she knew all too well that bigotry didn't simply disappear with the start of a war and a trip across an ocean. But she was both surprised and pleased to hear that a fair few of the locals had come out in support of the black military men, making sure pubs were open to all – even after some landlords had banned them for fear of 'putting off' the white GIs – and giving them a warm welcome when they appeared.

'We should probably eat some food soon,' said Haseeb, glancing over at the troops and their female companions busy filling their plates. Perhaps it was the stiff uniform, or Haseeb's colleagues all around him providing constant reminders of flying, but he seemed ill at ease.

'*Bapu!*' came a shout, followed by a slap on Haseeb's back from a young Indian man.

'I told you not to call me that,' said Haseeb good-naturedly. She guessed that this was Harinder, with whom Haseeb shared a room. Kitty had heard all about him from Haseeb's letters, including how he liked to call Haseeb 'Bapu' – or Grandfather – to rub in their age difference, all five years of it.

'This is—' Haseeb began.

'The famous and esteemed wife, Kitty!' Harinder said, putting his palms together in salaam and bowing his head.

She did the same, then said, 'Hello. I've heard a lot about you.'

'Well, the good parts are true,' he grinned. 'Ignore the rest.' Haseeb had told her that while Harinder might have looked like he was made out of a slab of granite, he could fly a plane as though it was as light as paper. Haseeb and Harinder were unlikely friends, but thrown together in a foreign country, you found your allies where you could.

At first, the three of them made polite small talk, but after a short while (and two whiskies for Harinder), things became a lot more relaxed.

'Have you heard, Bapu, they're saying there's an Indian Legion fighting against the British, alongside the Germans?' Harinder pulled out some paper, rolling a few strands of loose tobacco into a stingy cigarette. Although they were talking in Hindi, Kitty wished Harinder would speak a little more quietly.

'*Bakwas*,' Haseeb said, leaning against the makeshift bar, 'the Germans are just trying to divide us with propaganda.'

Kitty agreed. 'The Nazis would tell you they were going to give everyone gold bullion if they thought it would help win the war.'

'No, really. There was a man brought back here from North Africa and he told a friend of mine,' said Harinder. All those months back Kitty had thought it unlikely that Bose's plans to ally with Hitler would work, but perhaps he had actually had some sway with the Führer after all.

'Maybe they've been forced into fighting with the Nazis,' said Haseeb.

'In exchange for freedom?' suggested Kitty, thinking of the Indian troops who were in the prisoner-of-war camps alongside their Allied counterparts.

Harinder raised a thick eyebrow. 'I would have thought living off a diet of gruel in a camp was better than getting your balls blown off.' He gave a loud laugh.

'Harinder!' Haseeb said, glancing at Kitty.

'Sorry,' said Harinder, raising his hand by way of apology. 'Let's face it, though, you'd have to be stupid to fight on Hitler's side.'

'But what if Indians end up fighting on both sides?' Haseeb asked. He didn't have to say the rest. Then Indians would be in combat against each other.

Harinder had simply shrugged and the conversation moved on to other things, though Kitty couldn't let the thought go. What if Haseeb was captured? Would they really offer people like him a way out by taking up arms against their British 'oppressors'?

Harinder went off to try his luck with some of the local ladies, while Kitty and Haseeb sipped their drinks. The two of them stepped over certain topics of conversation as though they were landmines; she didn't want to bring his mood down by asking about his RAF missions, or the terrible accounts of food shortages in Bengal. Instead, they stuck to safer ground: how the Forum was faring, the films they'd most enjoyed, though everything felt as though they'd been apart for years, not weeks.

The music changed tempo to 'Dream a Little Dream of Me'.

'We could go and dance?' Kitty ventured. Normally Haseeb would have gently led her to the dance floor without waiting for her to ask, but today he seemed so subdued that she wasn't even sure he'd say yes. He gave a small nod and took her hand. As they swayed together, his soft stubble brushing her cheek, his hand smooth against her cobalt-blue dress, each knowing the way the other's body moved, there still seemed to be a disconnect, a border they couldn't cross.

'I think I need some fresh air,' he said, not meeting her eye. 'Come on.' Kitty followed him outside the hangar and took the torch from her handbag. The fields all around were pitch black, only the silhouettes of the trees in the distance breaking the horizon. A few servicemen were outside smoking and, once her eyes had adjusted, she could just make out a young couple hurrying off into the darkness. The girl had removed her shoes, giggling as she went.

Haseeb lit a cigarette, another new thing he'd picked up in the RAF. They didn't speak for a while; the only sounds were the thump of the big band and the laughter inside.

'Is there something wrong, Haseeb?'

He didn't say anything for a moment, picking a speck of tobacco from his tongue. He looked out into the black. 'Do you ever wonder when this will all end?'

Kitty laughed, unable to hide her disbelief. 'Of course, all the time.'

He turned to her. 'I don't know, some people, I think they've forgotten why we're even fighting.'

His cigarette smouldered as he inhaled. The drink had softened her vision, everything thick like honey, and yet the way Haseeb was talking also made things somehow more visceral, like the moments before an air raid, nerve endings alert, waiting for danger.

He continued, 'We're fighting for freedom? For equality, even, yes?'

Kitty nodded. Haseeb came closer, speaking in a hushed tone. 'So tell me why I'm here in the middle of nowhere, while thousands, maybe millions of Indians are dying?'

She knew instantly what he was talking about: the fallout from Rangoon, the siphoning off of rice by the British, all while drought added to the damage in Bengal.

Though he still spoke quietly, his voice was strained with frustration. 'People are starting to starve.' In the distance, searchlight beams cut up the night sky.

'I know, Haseeb. We're doing what we can at the Forum to lobby the government and send aid, but—'

'Is this what I'm fighting for?' His words twisted with anger.

'You're fighting for the good of everyone, Haseeb. It doesn't change that,' she said, putting her hand on his arm.

'There you are!' A voice came from behind them.

Kitty turned. Harinder's tall silhouette emerged from the darkness. 'You're missing all the fun.'

Kitty gave a polite smile, not sure what to say.

'We were just talking about what's happening in Bengal,' said Haseeb.

'Bengal?' Harinder's smiled faded as he realized what Haseeb meant.

'I betrayed my country for what?' Haseeb threw his cigarette on the floor and stubbed it out.

'Don't, Haseeb,' she said. 'You said yourself; if you fight in the war, the British will have to listen when the time comes.'

'We could all be dead by then.' He laughed bitterly. 'I'm already beating the odds.'

And now her anger cut right through her. *You think I don't know that?* she wanted to shout, but Harinder's presence stopped her. She felt her breath catch in her throat.

'We don't talk about whether we'll die, do we?' he said, turning to Harinder, who looked on awkwardly; his youthful bravado had vanished.

Haseeb carried on now, an anguish in his voice she hadn't heard since the time he'd been forced to say goodbye to his parents in Delhi. 'In the anteroom it's all about good deaths and bad deaths. Will we suffer in our last moments, will it be merciful?'

'Come now, Bapu,' Harinder said, mustering a smile. 'We don't need to talk about that now. Why don't we go and get a drink? *Chalo.*'

Haseeb looked down at the ground.

'Why don't you go inside?' Kitty said quietly to Harinder. 'We'll be in shortly.'

Harinder gave a hesitant nod, then went inside. Two pilots tumbled out as he reached the door, singing and laughing.

What words were there now, Kitty thought. Instead, she and Haseeb stood there for a long while, both looking out into the dark barley fields.

35

Ruby

Ruby stepped inside Jit's flat, quickly slipping off her courts, the maroon-checked linoleum sticky and warm beneath her feet.

'Come in,' he said.

The flat was built into the eaves of a Victorian house, the ceiling cutting into the walls of the main room. There were two armchairs squeezed into one corner, with a low bookcase standing against the far wall. She scanned the spines, surprised at how varied the titles were, from Nehru's autobiography to John Stuart Mill's *On Liberty*.

She looked over to Jit, as he tended to some food on the stovetop. When did he even find the time for reading?

Through the open window, Ruby could hear a bus driving along the wide sprawl of Green Lanes, a man calling out to his friend, followed by laughter. It wasn't even dark outside yet; thankfully, summer kept the blackout at bay.

'Dinner won't be long,' he said, taking something out from the kitchen cupboard. The door hinge was loose and it hung crookedly from the frame.

'How long have you lived here?'

'Just a couple of months,' he said, back still turned towards her. In the time that Ruby had known Jit, he'd had three different addresses. He told her he had to move to keep the authorities off his scent.

Ruby knew she was playing a dangerous game with Langley, still handing over false information on a regular basis, but the longer she did it, the more of a thrill she got from getting one over on them.

Jit handed her a plate. 'Come,' he said. To her surprise, she didn't mind joining him on the floor to eat dinner.

'What do you think?' he asked. The potatoes were definitely overcooked but considering the poor ingredients on hand, he could be proud of his efforts.

'Unusual,' she said, nibbling at it with her slice of bread. 'I'm not sure yet.'

Jit laughed. 'This isn't really how they make it at home; it's all right if you don't like it.'

'No. It's nice to try something new,' she smiled. She had never eaten home-cooked Indian food before; her dad certainly never learnt how to make it.

Ruby sat with her back against the armchair, legs out straight, the plate on her lap. She ate heartily, tearing off bits of bread and scooping up the curry, the scent of ginger filling the air. Out there in the world, she always carried herself with elegance and poise, with careful control. But here with Jit she felt freer, as though she'd stopped holding her breath and allowed herself to take in big gulps of life.

'Do you remember that man I told you about? Subhas Chandra Bose,' said Jit.

Ruby nodded, recalling the Indian Independence leader who had escaped to Germany.

'He's finally working with Hitler and his friends to gain support for freedom, in return for joining the German fight.'

She gave a hard laugh. 'What happened to all that "Aryan" purity?'

'The Japanese already fight on the German side,' he shrugged.

'Sounds idiotic to me.'

He looked at her, leaning back in his chair. 'But what if it works?'

She laughed, making no attempt to hide her ridicule. 'Jit, come on. Allying with that Nazi sewage . . .'

'It's a means to an end.'

'A dangerous one.' She looked at him, brow furrowing. 'You don't think it's a good idea, do you?'

'I don't know. But if the Germans invade, perhaps with Bose's support, they'll treat Indian people, how do you say it in English, more gently . . .?'

'Leniently?'

'Yes, more leniently than we think.'

Ruby looked down at her hands. She thought about the news that trickled in from Jewish refugees, highlighting just how seriously the Nazis took 'Aryan purity'. Skin colour, birth certificate, a loose mouth; there were all sorts of ways you could be betrayed.

'Hitler can never be the answer.' Ruby shook her head. 'Never.'

'Perhaps you're right,' said Jit, quietly. 'Better to control your own destiny, I suppose.'

They ate in silence for a while, though Ruby had to force herself to finish. Outside it had started to rain. The faint crackle of raindrops on the windowpane. Ruby's earlier buoyance began to fade. That Jit would even consider the Bose–German allyship as a possibility? Fear stirred in her chest. Had he become so blinkered by his singular focus on Independence?

She was very tired. When would they be able to go back to some kind of normal? Where the most difficult decision was deciding what to watch at the pictures. Where you could walk around safely, where you could have an ordinary job?

'What is it?' asked Jit, softly.

'It's just the Independence movement . . .' She trailed off.

'Go on.'

She realized she'd been pursing her lips, the way she did when she was deep in thought. 'Don't you ever feel robbed of your youth?'

'If you mean a youth in a free country, yes, I do.'

'And you don't ever want more?'

'Like peace? Of course.'

She shook her head. 'No, I mean beyond the freedom fight.'

'Like what?' He gave a dismissive laugh.

'What are you going to do once India gets Independence?'

Jit didn't say anything. She saw it then; he had no idea what to do with freedom when it came, he was so focused on becoming free.

'See?' she said gently.

'There'll be plenty of time to worry about that later,' he shrugged.

'But later might be a long way away, Jit. Everyone's focused on the war—'

'You think I just sit around with vague dreams, is that it?' he said, standing up, a hard tone in his voice. He hurried over to the sink and washed his hands. 'Come with me, I'll show you what I'm really working for.'

Ruby followed him.

They went into the bedroom, where he opened up a three-legged wardrobe propped up with books and took out a large suitcase from the bottom.

He cracked open the metal clasp. There were papers inside, but these weren't pamphlets. They were some kind of instructions in Hindi, along with hand drawings in ink.

'What are they?' she asked.

'They're instructions,' he said, 'for making bombs.'

She dropped the paper as though it would somehow burn her hand. 'What?'

'We don't want to hurt anyone, Ruby, it's all right,' he said, putting his hands on her shoulders.

She gave a hard laugh. 'Oh really. Were you not here when the Nazis tried to blast us all to hell?'

'We just want to make a statement. Scare people, not hurt them.'

'With bombs, Jit? Where are you planning to use them?' The dull, endless meetings at the India Forum were suddenly very appealing.

'In the courts, in India.'

Ruby calmed her breath as best she could, trying to take it all in. 'What are you talking about? Do you understand—'

Now his face flashed with anger. 'Do *you* understand? We have the right to be paid back for everything we've been through.'

'A minute ago you said it was a scare tactic, now it's some kind of, what, revenge?'

His voice hard as granite now. 'Why can't it be both?'

'It's not right,' she said, hurrying out towards the front door and putting on her shoes. 'I can't help you any more, not after this.'

'Let me just explain,' he said, following her.

'Bombs. Listen to yourself. What if it goes wrong?'

'Just wait,' he said, voice quieter. 'I know I talk about how difficult it is in India, but really, you can't imagine. At least give me one minute to explain. Please, Ruby. Just listen to me.'

She paused. What could he possibly say to justify it? But she saw the anguish on his face. 'Fine,' she sighed. 'Five minutes and then I'm leaving.'

Jit leant against the wall, his voice low. 'I never told you about my father,' he said. He had never told her anything about his family.

'He was a freedom fighter. During the day, my father worked for a printing press.' Jit's gaze hardened, lost in memory. 'He used to take me to work sometimes when I was a young boy. He made me stand right back against the wall when the printing press was running. He'd take my hand and say, "You don't want your hand to be eaten up, do you?"' Jit smiled as he continued.

'I'd laugh as he tickled me. For years I was terrified of those machines, all that noise. The press looked like a monster with a big mouth, throwing out all that paper. But still, I loved going there with him.

'Then when he wasn't working,' Jit said, eyes fixed on a point across the room, 'he'd organize protests. Lead them. He had gone to a protest in Bishnupur, near our home. The police were there, the military too. The protest started peacefully enough, but . . .'

He looked over at Ruby, as though suddenly remembering she was there. 'Do you know how the police charge in India?'

Ruby shook her head, moving to the armchair and sitting down. Jit stayed where he was.

'They have horses, for a start. And they carry those lathi, the long sticks made of bamboo I told you about,' he said. 'No one's sure how it got out of hand, but suddenly the police and military were using them on the crowd.' Jit sighed. 'Somehow, my father and his friends managed to get away.'

Ruby let out her breath, feeling the knot in her stomach unravel a little.

'They came home. My father had some heavy cuts, which my mother had to clean up. I had crept into the hallway to listen to him. He said the whole area had been deserted before the protest, people had tried to find shelter in nearby homes and shops, even the washing that had been hung out to dry had been taken inside to safety.' He swallowed. 'He told my mother he could smell metal in the air and then he realized it was all the blood, on the ground, on the walls of the buildings. And he told her how confused he'd been by something else too. It was the sugary scent of fried *jalebi*. They are a kind of sweet we have in India.'

Jit's eyes darkened, holding her gaze. 'My father heard afterwards that some of the demonstrators had used the boiling sugar syrup from the jalebi shop to try and burn the policemen.'

Ruby's eyes widened in shock. 'But your dad was all right?'

Jit looked away, staring at the books on the shelf. 'My father rested and went back to work in the morning. But each night when he came home, he would to go to bed earlier and earlier, saying he was tired. He said his head was hurting, and he'd sleep for hours in his room.

'And then one day, when we were just about to go to school, he collapsed onto the floor.' Jit's voice fell. 'He was dead even before my mother had reached him.'

'I'm so sorry,' said Ruby, her voice barely a whisper. She wanted to go over and comfort him, but the thought of the bombs wouldn't leave her. Nothing could justify that.

'He must have hit his head at some point during the pro-test . . .' he said, looking down at the floor. 'My older brother had to leave school after that. We went to live with our uncle in Calcutta.'

They didn't speak for a while. Ruby perched on the arm-chair, looking down at the floor.

'Do you understand now?' he asked, pouring himself a glass of water and taking a gulp.

'Jit, what happened to your dad is terrible, but that doesn't make what you're doing right.'

'You still don't understand,' Jit said, incredulous. 'I've lived the rest of my life without my father. Because of one peace-ful protest and an order from a military man. The number of people that have been killed and maimed. What happened there in Bishnupur was just one part of it. You saw my scars. We're in the right and we're still treated like criminals.'

'But if you do this – the bombs, I mean – you *will* be a crim-inal.' Hanged for treason.

'I should have known you'd never understand. Living here, protected from it all,' he said with a sneer.

'Of course I understand. You think I would have helped you otherwise? Risked everything by talking to the authorities?'

'You just wanted a bit of fun.'

'Don't, Jit—'

'A bit of adventure, was it?' He moved across the room, standing over her now, so close she could feel his breath.

'Oh, now we hear what he really thinks.' She gave a cold laugh as she stood up and headed towards the door.

He raised his voice, a look in his eyes she'd never seen before, full of venom. 'You're happy to play at being a freedom fighter, but when it really comes down to it—'

'If that's what it takes,' she said, pointing towards the bomb drawings in the bedroom, 'you can keep it all, Jit.' She opened the door, grabbing her things as he rushed over to her.

Her heart pounded as Jit carried on, 'We don't need you helping us to feel good about ourselves!' He rammed his hand against the wall.

'Oh, no? See how good you feel about yourself if you go ahead with your stupid bloody plans!' she said, slamming the door behind her.

36

Kitty

There was little time left to prepare for the Houses of Parliament. Kitty leant forward in her seat, looking at the women assembled at the large table in the library. 'Then once the speeches are done, we should have time to speak to the MPs one-on-one,' she said.

It was Mandalji who had suggested an all-woman delegation to advocate on behalf of India. Most of the men at the India Forum had heartily agreed when it was proposed. One of them had even clapped his hands as he said, 'It will make the politicians think we Indians are progressive, like them.'

In any case, Kitty was hardly going to pass up the chance to speak to the British government in the most important building in the country.

Bunting had been put up at the Forum, someone had made fresh roti and another had conjured up carrot pickle to eat with them, all intended to give the delegation a proper send-off for Parliament. Foods from home had tended to be a comfort for Kitty, a connection to India when all else was missing. Today, they just made her long for Haseeb more than ever.

'And Albert Ashbourne will definitely attend?' said Savitribai, resting her arm on the table. Despite her accolades, she was still introduced by most people as 'Dr Chopra's wife'. People tended to forget that Savitribai had carved out her own space as a broadcaster on BBC radio, hosting shows in her native Marathi about Indians in London, while also fitting in part-time work as an ARP warden.

'That's right. He's the MP for Suffolk,' said Mrs Westlebury, the wife of one of their Labour councillor allies. 'He's always taken a keen interest in Indian affairs but he just won't give up the ghost on free rule,' she said, patting her grey hair into place. Mrs Westlebury was the sort who would search out indignation wherever it could be found, whether it was a badly made pot of tea (which was most, given the rationing), or the injustice of India. In a social setting she might otherwise have been insufferable, but her sense of justice was an asset and she had quite a line in bawdy jokes when it suited her.

Kitty looked over to Miss Thacker, who was fiddling with her pen instead of making notes as they'd agreed. 'Did you get that, Miss Thacker?' Kitty couldn't decide if it was the black suit she was wearing or something else, but Miss Thacker's skin looked unusually pallid today. She hadn't been to the Forum meetings in weeks.

'Hmm?' She looked up. 'MP for Suffolk,' she repeated, writing in her notebook.

'Good, so we'll meet at Westminster station at one o'clock tomorrow.' Kitty gave a nod. 'I think that's everything.' Murmurs of agreement.

'Let's have some chai before we head home.' Savritibai jumped up, clapping her hands together. Mrs Westlebury and the other two women who would be joining the delegation stood up as well.

Miss Thacker tore the pages from her notebook and passed them to Kitty, who sat to her right. 'All done,' she said, quietly.

'I'll take a quick look through them now,' Kitty said, not wanting to find that half the information was missing. Kitty had been reluctant to include Miss Thacker in the preparations but Mandalji had encouraged her to let all enthusiastic volunteers get involved.

'It's all there, you know!' said Miss Thacker.

Kitty was taken aback. 'It's best to look through it all now, rather than get to Parliament and find we don't have some key information about the people we're lobbying.'

'Fine.' Miss Thacker stood up, chair screeching across the floor.

'If you don't want to work here, you don't have to, you know?' Why was the woman acting as though she was doing everyone else a favour?

Miss Thacker muttered something under her breath as she picked up her handbag.

'Is there something wrong?' said Kitty, trying to keep her tone steady. She could feel her neck flushing now.

'No, you carry on, you know what you're doing, don't you?' Miss Thacker gave a tight smile.

Kitty found the words bubbling up before she could stop them. 'I'm surprised you're still here. I thought Satyajit had all the answers for India's future?'

Now Miss Thacker's smile fell.

Kitty knew she should stop but all her frustrations – the way she'd sat so smugly together with Satyajit at the Forum meetings, so sure that there was a better way – now they all came out. 'Didn't Satyajit say the India Forum work was pointless? I would have thought you agreed with him.'

'You don't know what you're talking about.'

'It's just you seemed happy to go along with him before.'

'I thought I was doing the right thing!' Her eyes darkened.

'What was it?' Kitty fired out the words now. 'Finally realized it was all empty talk?'

'It's not empty talk! That's just it!' Miss Thacker slammed her hands onto the back of the chair.

Kitty's breath seized in her throat.

Miss Thacker became still, a rare caution in her eyes that had replaced the usual bravado. She looked down, apparently trying to calm herself. 'If you only knew,' she whispered.

'What is it?' Kitty said, her earlier annoyance deflated by how fragile the woman in front of her looked. A faint ring of laughter came from the kitchen as something clanged to the floor.

'Jit's been smuggling things into India,' Miss Thacker said quietly.

'What do you mean?'

'Pamphlets.' Miss Thacker wouldn't meet her gaze. 'Calling for direct action. For a lot more than just protests.'

Kitty thought of the banned books her own aunt had kept in the house, remembered Bhupeshbhai's bookshop and its radical literature. Words were weapons too, after all.

'Well, that's not so unusual,' Kitty reasoned.

Miss Thacker's voice was low. 'But then I saw a plan for a bomb.'

A chill came over Kitty. 'What did you say?' She must have misheard.

Miss Thacker looked up at her now, despair in her voice. 'Jit said they were just to scare people, in the official buildings back in India, courts and so on. I don't think he'd actually . . .' Neither of them needed her to finish that sentence.

'People could get hurt, and if he gets caught—' Kitty's head swarmed with thoughts now; he'd be connected to the India Forum. 'When did you last see him?'

'It's been weeks. He might have left London, I don't know.' Miss Thacker sank back down into her chair. 'I didn't know what to do.'

A thought came coldly into Kitty's mind. 'Or he's been arrested.'

'No, I'd probably have heard about it,' Miss Thacker said.

'Heard from who?' Kitty stared at her.

Miss Thacker looked down at the floor, then up at her. 'I've been in contact with the authorities. They've been keeping tabs on the India Forum.'

'But I thought that was a mistake?' Had Satyajit lied to her after all? Kitty could barely keep up with all the new information.

'What d'you mean?' said Miss Thacker.

Kitty explained how she'd gone to Satyajit after she'd seen Miss Thacker talking to a man in the street, and he had said there was nothing to worry about.

'I never told them anything.' Miss Thacker shook her head. 'I fed them false information to keep them busy. Do you think Satyajit would have kept on talking to me if I had? You'd have had the authorities on you like a rash.'

Kitty put her hands to her face. 'This is an utter mess. Do you know how dangerous this is for all of us? If the Forum—'

'I know,' said Miss Thacker, clutching her hands together and rubbing her finger back and forth over her thumb.

'Have you spoken to your surveillance contact recently?'

'I try to have as little as possible to do with them.'

'What if you told them? Just about Satyajit, made it clear that no one else was involved?'

'I don't know,' said Ruby, putting a hand to her forehead. 'I know what he's doing isn't right, but if they caught him? They could hang him for treason.' Kitty could see the look in her eyes, heard a wavering in her tone. This wasn't so simple for her.

Kitty took a deep breath, pacing the room. She tried to approach the problem as she would a law case. Looking at the facts, working out the correct way forward. At least if Satyajit had gone to another city then he was no longer the Forum's problem. As long as the bombs really were scare tactics.

'Well, there's nothing else we can do right now. As long as he stays away,' said Kitty. Some part of her hoped that Satyajit's disappearance meant he'd decided against it entirely. Perhaps it was wishful thinking, but what other hope did they have right now?

'Yes, I suppose . . .' said Miss Thacker tentatively.

'What is it?'

'It's just, he's always talked that way. How the time had come for action, not words. Something that no one would be able to ignore.'

'Do you think he'll do something stupid?'

'I don't know.' Miss Thacker's shoulders fell. 'Maybe I should have done something to stop him.'

'I don't know Satyajit well, but the one thing I can say with certainty is that he listens to no one.'

Just then Mrs Westlebury came back in the room, a look of profound concentration on her face as she carried a precarious tray of steaming chai. 'Right, well, we've done our best with whatever we could find in the kitchen and at least it's hot!' she said. The other women followed behind her.

Kitty went over to Miss Thacker's chair, bending down as she whispered, 'There's nothing we can do now. But if you see Satyajit again, you must come to me at once.'

Miss Thacker was breathing hard but even as she nodded, Kitty wasn't quite sure whether she believed her.

37

Ruby

It was a cool but bright day and the beech trees had begun to shed their flames in Lyal Road. Along the street, low cloud shrouded the rooftops. Ruby passed two raucous kids, playing swords with some tree branches they'd found in the street.

She stopped in front of Rana's house. The garden was over-grown, the weeds were knee-high and the corners of the brittle house bricks were crumbled.

Ruby took a deep breath, then rang the doorbell. A little of the black paint flaked off as the front door rattled open. Rana looked more than a little surprised to see her, coming to the house on her own like this.

She hadn't meant to blurt out what Jit was planning to Mrs Akhtar, and while it had been a relief to tell someone else, why even now did it feel like a betrayal? She'd barely been able to sleep, unable to break free of her thoughts, as sticky as spiderwebs. She had to try and make Jit see sense before something awful happened.

'Hello, Rana,' said Ruby.

'Ruby?' He was barefoot; thick dark hairs were sprouting from his toes.

'I was looking for Jit,' she said, hesitantly.

He stared at her. 'He is not here.'

'When did you see him last?'

He frowned, more guarded now. 'When did *you* last see him?'

Rana had never been the friendliest but now there was no mistaking the ice in his voice.

'I haven't seen him in weeks,' she told him. 'I really need to speak to him.' She wondered then how much Rana knew himself. Was he in on the plans too?

'Satyajit will find you if he wants you,' he said, looking down at his fingernails as though bored of talking to her.

'He showed me his . . . plans,' she said carefully, waiting to see his expression. Was that a flash of recognition? 'If something goes wrong, then what he's doing—'

Rana's eyes darkened. 'What he's doing is for our country. They need to listen now. Time for talking is over.'

'Yes, but—' Ruby began.

'You going to tell the authorities?' His voice hardened. He moved towards her, leaning his hand up against the doorframe.

Ruby's body stiffened. She lightened her tone as best she could. 'I just want to speak to him, Rana, please,' she said, managing a small smile, as though it was simply a lover's tiff she needed to resolve with Jit. If she could just get him to see reason.

'No one gets in our way, understand?' She saw something of Jit in his eyes now. Stopping at nothing.

Her breath ran away with itself. 'Yes, of course,' she said quickly. She hurried back down the path, glancing back briefly, but he was still staring at her.

She had turned the corner of the street. The two children she'd seen playing earlier were still there, thwacking their sticks at each other.

'Ruby.'

She knew who it was even before she turned around.

'You were there all the time?'

'Come on, let's go inside.' Jit reached for her hand, but she pulled away.

'I don't know . . .' said Ruby. Even though she had chosen to find Jit, the way Rana spoke to her had left her feeling wary. And now that Jit was in front of her, the memory of the last time she'd seen him, banging his hand against the wall, came rushing back to her.

Jit glanced up the street, eyes narrowing as he watched a woman cross the road in the distance. 'I need to go inside. You can come with me if you want, Ruby.'

She watched him walk away. She had to try and change his mind. There was no getting around it.

She slowly followed him inside the house. Rana was at the end of the dark hallway, standing by the kitchen door. He spoke in an agitated tone to Jit, but Jit cut him off in that usual languid manner of his. For a moment, she wondered if she should turn around, hurry back down the street. But then Jit looked at her and said, 'This way.'

Instead of heading upstairs to the room with the books and pamphlets, they went into the front room. The red curtains were half drawn, casting the place in a maroon glow. There was a sofa against one wall, with a pillow and a crumpled old tartan blanket.

Ruby stayed by the door, still unsure of what she was getting herself into. Jit sat on the edge of the sofa, gesturing for her to take a seat in the battered velvet armchair in the corner, but she stayed where she was.

She noticed his leather pedlar bag by the mantelpiece, along with a small suitcase. 'Are you sleeping here now?'

'Just for a while.'

'What happened to your flat?'

'I might go away for a while,' he said, smoothing his hair back with his hand.

'Jit, are you still going ahead with the . . .' She could barely bring herself to say the words. 'What we talked about last time?'

He stared at her. 'Have you seen how the Viceroy, all the MPs who sit there at the Houses of Parliament smoking their pipes, make decisions about *my* country?' He pointed his finger at his chest, vehement. 'Letting people starve.'

'Not all of them. Some of the MPs are on our side, Jit. They're our allies.'

'No. They're all our enemies! My family are among those people in Bengal!'

Ruby blinked. 'Have you heard from them?'

'It doesn't matter now,' he sneered. 'They'll let all of Bengal die.' Ruby thought back, realizing that he never talked about his family in the present tense. Were they dead, like his father? Or had he lost contact with them during his many moves around the country?

'That's terrible,' said Ruby, quietly. 'And wrong. But it still doesn't mean you should be bombing people.'

'Bombing courts,' he corrected, 'for a start.'

She glared at him. 'What do you mean, "start"?'

'Look, it's clear whose side you're on, so it's probably time for you to leave.'

'Wait—' she said.

He went out to the hallway and held the front door open.

As she passed, he said. 'And Ruby . . .'

She paused. He regarded her with cold eyes. 'You're not going to say anything, are you?'

The way he looked at her then, she knew there was only one answer she could give him. She shook her head and turned.

*

'And you'll get your money next Saturday as usual,' said Lang-ley, peering at Ruby over his thick glasses.

Ruby nodded, pulling out a cigarette and lighting it. She looked around the New Crown pub. In the corner, two old men were sitting in silence, staring at the fire. A group of young servicemen played darts, their raucous laughter echoing along the bar.

Langley closed his notebook. 'So, if there's nothing else . . .'

'There is something, actually.' Ruby said it before she'd had a chance to think.

He looked up. 'Oh yes?'

Jit's voice ran through her mind. *They're our enemies.*

'Miss Thacker?'

A memory now: the feel of Jit's scars beneath her fingers, and then his voice. *This is just the start.*

'Yes, I found something out,' she said.

Langley looked at her expectantly.

Jit's face, standing in Rana's hallway, the cold look in his eyes. *You won't say anything, will you?*

She exhaled her cigarette smoke. 'There's a man connected with the Forum.'

Langley opened up his notebook.

Could they connect her back to Satyajit if they really started to dig?

Now Langley was staring at her, pen poised.

'His name's Bipin Rajendra,' she said, taking a sip of her cordial, retreating to safety. 'I think he's a doctor. He's only just started attending the meetings, but he doesn't seem to know anyone else there.'

Ruby looked down at her clasped hands, the lies tumbling out of her now. 'I think he lives somewhere in North London.'

She watched Langley make notes. 'Good, we'll check on that.'

Ruby took a breath. 'And actually, I meant to tell you, I won't be giving you any more information in future.'

Langley paused, pen held in the air. 'Sorry?'

'I need to focus on my warden work,' she said quickly. 'And it's very stressful, knowing that someone might find out I'm passing you information.'

'That's not really how it works.'

Ruby tapped her cigarette into the ashtray. 'Why not? You can't make me, can you?' She had to hold her nerve. If they had anything over her, now was the moment he'd tell her, to make her carry on.

'Don't you want to keep your country safe?'

'I've heard all that before and I am keeping the country safe, working as a warden,' she said, stubbing out her cigarette into the clear glass ashtray on the table. 'I'm sorry,' she lied, 'but it's too much for me now.' She got up from the table.

'Miss Thacker—'

Pulling her coat on, she hurried out. She took in big gulps of air as she came out of the pub.

She had to get herself out of it, Ruby thought as she did up her buttons and walked along Holloway Road. She was too caught up with Jit and the smuggling to risk telling Langley anything about the bomb drawings. What if she was arrested as an accessory? But as she carried on down the street, no relief came. All she could think about was that cold look Jit had given her the last time she had seen him.

38

Kitty

The Houses of Parliament loomed above Kitty. There was no doubt that the sand-coloured building was impressive, designed to inspire awe, though up close it was not quite as pristine as she had expected and the sandbags that had been piled against the walls gave it something of a dishevelled feel.

'They should give it a bit of a clean,' said Savitribai, scrunching up her face.

Once their delegation of five had completed the security checks at the entrance, they were greeted by Mr Ferguson, a white-haired man with a soft Scottish accent who ushered them inside. 'Welcome, ladies. Why, don't you look wonderful?'

Kitty had chosen to wear a sari, as had Mrs Westlebury, in a sign of solidarity.

They walked through corridors with high ceilings and arched stained-glass windows. The oak-panelled hallways were covered in vast paintings of death and destruction: the battle of Trafalgar; the battle of Waterloo; plinths topped with marble busts of great leaders and thinkers. Designed to make you feel the power of the place, thought Kitty. Or was it to make you feel less powerful?

'Now, we will hear your speeches in the central lobby,' said Mr Ferguson. 'Unfortunately, foreign dignitaries are not allowed to speak in the House of Commons. Although, of course, the Commons has moved to the House of Lords for the time being anyway, following the Blitz bombing.' He explained that after the Commons had been destroyed in 1940, it would be a long-term effort to rebuild it to its former glory.

Though the central lobby was apparently a vast thorough-fare with four hallways leading off to other parts of Parliament, it was beautifully ornate and intricately designed. Mr Fergu-son gave them a brief tour. There were mosaic ceilings made of Venetian glass, tiled patterned floors with Tudor roses and Latin inscriptions.

Kitty wondered what her father and her dadi would have made of all the pomp. The thought of them brought a lump to her throat. She heard from her friend Devika occasionally, and Dadi was still holding on somehow, but Kitty wondered for how much longer.

Light streamed through the stained-glass windows onto the rows of chairs that had been set up for the politicians who would be attending. 'So this is where all our money goes,' whispered Savitribai, rolling her kohl-lined eyes.

Kitty couldn't help but smile.

A few MPs began to come in. 'Apologies,' Mr Ferguson said to the women. 'The war has made the order of things quite erratic.'

He introduced Kitty to the honourable member for Suffolk, Albert Ashbourne. Kitty had caught a whiff of his cologne from afar a good thirty seconds before he'd come over.

'Welcome to the Palace of Westminster,' Ashbourne said. 'We're immensely looking forward to your speeches. *Aap kahaan se hain?*'

'I'm from Bombay,' she replied. 'Do you know it?'

'*Main saat saal tak Dillee mein raha,*' he said, explaining he'd been in Delhi for seven years. He had haphazard eyebrows that were at odds with his pristinely combed grey hair.

He carried on the conversation in Hindi, asking if she had visited various places in East India, and whether she had tried the Kashmiri fish curry served at Veeraswamy restaurant on Regent Street, which was better than the original version in Kashmir. Kitty had met his kind before. Language was not a way to bond or to connect for people like Albert Ashbourne, just yet another way to wield power. I know more than you, he was telling her.

She was saved by Mr Ferguson. 'Now, we'll be getting started in a minute.'

Fortunately, more MPs had arrived. They'd already been warned via Mandalji and his contact at Parliament that the prime minister would not attend and that it was unlikely any of the key Cabinet members would be able to take the time away from war matters, but Kitty hadn't been able to help herself, keeping an eye on the entrance just in case. Either way, there were people here who had the ear not only of the Cabinet, but of Churchill himself.

The speeches began, with Savitribai setting the agenda. They had come to discuss the imprisonment of Mahatma Gandhi following his Quit India speech. Almost the entire Indian Congress had been imprisoned for months, and there was no prospect of release. Yes, Britain was at war, Kitty thought, but such measures were totally out of proportion.

Savitribai's speech was diplomatic and full of platitudes, designed to appeal to hearts as much as minds. On the other hand, they had no idea what they were in for with Kitty's speech. She had written it only a few days ago, roused by the terrible stories she'd heard from back home, about the British bans on bicycles and river boats in the east, preventing Indians from going anywhere near the border in case the Japanese powers got hold of them. The Viceroy's mobs in the east torched anything worth saving, or stockpiled it away from

Indian hands; anything to stop the enemy seizing any kind of resource: transport, food, fuel. They appeared happy for the east of India to starve along with the enemy. Kitty had heard stories of mothers holding long-dead babies at their breasts, fathers killing their families so they wouldn't have to suffer the torturous slow death of hunger. East or west; on either side empires aimed to conquer, and India was squeezed like a lemon.

Kitty's heart fell at the thought of it.

There was applause as Savitribai finished her impassioned address. Nerves fizzed in Kitty's chest. This was the most difficult speech she'd ever written. For her, writing was like being on a road where you couldn't see what came after the bend, but you had to trust that the road would continue, the words laying themselves before you one by one, appearing just as you needed them to. Yet when she wrote in English, despite her many years of education, her many years of formal British Indian English, sometimes the words were somewhere else, far in the ether. A Gujarati verb or a Hindi noun came easily, one that would serve her purpose far better in meaning, because the English word was out of her grasp. Somehow, she had eventually found her way with this speech too. Kitty took a deep breath to calm herself, the musty scent of the hall filling her nostrils as she looked out to the audience and began.

'These British Isles are made in India. Its rivers of cotton, linen, silk, jute, muslin and wool, the church steeples of salt and rice, manor houses made with gold and silver, bridges with diamonds and pearls, terraced houses from tea and coffee. But we Indians were given the railways, so we must sit quietly in gratitude, even though those railways, too, were built with Indian hands. No, we Indians must not stop all those goods being carried out on the rail tracks, the ones that our own countrymen had laid with sweat and blood. We are told that we must let it all go, all the fabric and gemstones, the precious metals and coal, and finally the most precious thing of all. Food.'

She carried on, entreating the politicians to help the innocent Indians who were now without access to food. She knew that some weren't even willing to acknowledge the growing threat of widespread starvation. That somehow, because it was far away, and happening to people who looked nothing like them, it wasn't true. India only existed when it suited them.

When the speeches finished there was further discussion, some MPs passionately agreeing that more needed to be done, acknowledging that it was Parliament's responsibility on behalf of the British Empire, but others, including the undersecretary to Leo Amery, the Secretary of State for India, seemed less committed.

'My dear, you need to understand that the government takes this very seriously but it is a very complex situation.' Kitty knew the game was up and any positive discourse had been stopped dead as soon as he said, 'My dear'. What a waste of breath it had been, she thought, as he gave vague reassurances that they would look into it further.

Kitty watched the undersecretary walk off, his fists clasped tightly. How many more polite conversations would they have to endure before they finally saw freedom? Then again, perhaps she should be careful what she wished for, if Satyajit's kind of action was all that was on offer. Even if it was just to scare the British Indian government, how could he even consider jeopardizing innocent people's lives?

More than ever, she wished she could speak to Haseeb. There he was, risking his life every day for the Allies, while Satyajit played with the lives of others as though they were nothing.

Worry scratched at her stomach as she remembered the

look of fear on Miss Thacker's face when she'd told Kitty what he was planning. She thought of all she knew about Satyajit. Was he really the kind ever to stop, in India or in England? Was he so single-minded and focused on his cause that nothing else mattered? No one else mattered?

39
Ruby

Ruby looked out across Finsbury Park, framed by large Victorian houses. In the distance, the sun glimmered across the duck pond and the breeze weaved its way gently through the trees, which had just given up their blossom. She carried on up the path. In an opening shaded by sycamores, a small and low wooden platform had been set up. There were a fair few people there already to see the panel debate about the future of India, a mixture of Indians and English, suits and military uniforms, saris and dhotis – a word Ruby had learnt from Jit, to describe the white tunics some of the men liked to wear. There were quite a few people that Ruby recognized from the Forum, including Mrs Akhtar, who wore a navy cotton sari with a yellow embroidered border.

It had been many weeks since she had last seen her or Mandalji. Just being at the India Forum brought back bad memories – the place she had first met Jit.

He appeared to have left London, or at least that was what his acquaintances at the India Forum seemed to think. All she could do now was hope that somehow the time away might make him see sense about the bombs.

Mrs Akhtar was talking through the notes she had prepared for Mandalji. Once they'd finished, he went and took his place with the rest of the speakers on the platform. Mrs Akhtar stood in front, looking on.

More people had joined now, gathered in a group of fifty or so. Ruby stood on the fringes, where it was easier to see what was going on without trilbies or turbans getting in the way.

The panel chairman went and stood at the lectern. He introduced himself as Mr Geoffrey Rowland and the audience clapped. He was a tall man, ruddy-cheeked, with a thick, scruffy brush of a moustache. The distracting chirrup of two sparrows in a nearby tree cut through the hush.

Mr Rowland briefly introduced the panel. Mandalji and a Mr Harvey Montague – an ex-civil servant and ally of the India Forum who'd spent his early career in India – were arguing for an independent India. On the opposing side, a man in a grey pinstriped suit, Mr Jonathan Landsdowne, sat next to a man in military uniform, Colonel August Gladstone. His medals glinted in the sunlight.

As Mr Rowland went through the order of proceedings, Ruby caught a movement towards the back of the audience.

Her stomach fell. It was Jit. There was something about the way he held himself, not that casual manner that usually seemed to come so easily to him. Despite the spring weather, he was wearing a wool coat that hung awkwardly on his frame. He fixed his gaze on the stage, then dragged it away to briefly scan the audience. His eyes met Ruby's a moment, but he looked away just as quickly, back to the stage. Had he even seen her? She couldn't be sure, but it didn't matter because he was too busy concentrating on something by the platform.

Ruby carried on watching him, ignoring the man behind her who was glaring at her for not paying attention to the panel.

Why was he here when he thought the India Forum was useless? And where had he been all this time?

'And I would now like to introduce the esteemed Mr Jayant

Mandal,' said Mr Rowland, 'originally of Orissa, who now resides in London.' Mandalji looked impatient, itching to get on with it. 'Mr Mandal is the chair of the India Forum and works closely with the Indian National Congress. He will give the first argument in favour of Indian Independence.'

Mandalji stood up and took to the podium. Not a speck of nerves. He was born to it, the limelight, the persuasive speeches. He spoke with his usual wolfish stubbornness. No in-between. A free India or nothing.

She tried to focus on what he was saying, but knowing Jit was there distracted her. The splinter of fear she'd felt that last time they'd seen each other was still there, lodged in her chest, but there was something else too. Hope, that it wasn't too late.

'Thank you, Mr Mandal, for your persuasive and well-considered argument,' said Mr Rowland, trying to smooth his moustache into place – a pointless exercise as the hair clearly did what it wanted. Mandalji went back and joined his fellow speakers, who were standing in a row.

The next two speeches were a little dull, sticking to the well-trodden paths that Ruby had encountered a hundred times before: it was the Christian duty to guide and protect India (and of course India's riches, but no one mentioned that); or the familiar argument that now was not the right time for India to chart her own course.

Ruby glanced at the back of the crowd, standing on tiptoe. Jit's eyes were fixed on the stage and the next speaker.

'Finally, we will hear from Colonel August Gladstone,' said the chair. 'Now retired, previously of the British Indian Army, Colonel Gladstone spent much of his career stationed in East India, primarily Bengal. The colonel will argue against Indian Independence.' The colonel stood up uneasily. His hands shook a little as he flattened out his speech on the podium. He began by reiterating the time he had spent in India – complete with a tedious rundown of his military postings – and that he therefore knew it well enough to have an opinion on it. Then came the crux of his argument, that the only way India could thrive was under British guardianship. 'I have seen at first hand the importance of our involvement,' he said, 'of our ward, of the much-needed direction that India requires. She is not ready to stand on her own two feet and both Britain and India are stronger together, now more than ever.'

After the colonel had finished, Mr Rowland's summary of the four speeches stayed firmly on the fence, drawing together all the main arguments without coming to a final conclusion. After thanking everyone for their time, he quickly drew the meeting to a close.

On stage, the speakers shook hands, Mandalji giving a good-natured smile to the opposing side.

Some of the audience began to move away, while others milled about and chatted. Ruby stole a glance to the back of the gathering, but with all the people she couldn't see Jit any more. Just then, from behind her, someone seemed to be pushing past everyone, heading towards the platform.

It was Jit. He barely gave her a glance as he hurried past. Why was his hand raised?

'*Azad!*' he shouted, sweat dripping from his forehead. Eyes fixed ahead. A pistol in his hand, pointed at the platform. 'This is for Bishnupur.'

'No!' Ruby screamed, reaching forward to grab him, but there were too many people in her way and he was too fast. The gun fired.

Shouts and screams, the scuffle of hurried footsteps on grass. She couldn't see among all the moving bodies. The gun rang out again, echoing through the air. A volley of shots.

'Stop him!'

'Hold him down, damn it!'

'Call an ambulance!'

She managed to push through the people heading in the opposite direction. Above her, the colonel lay on the platform floor, the other speakers crouched around him, a grave look on Mandalji's face. Another man had joined them, perhaps a doctor, who was trying to stop the colonel bleeding out from his chest.

Nearby three other men were holding Jit down at the edge of the podium. The pistol lay on the stage, no one daring to pick it up and ruin the evidence. Ruby's head swam, a rush of breath.

She looked across to the other end of the platform, where Mrs Akhtar stood to the side, hand to her mouth, frozen in shock.

Ruby could just about see Jit, his head pushed against the ground. He stared at her, but there was no sorrow in his eyes, only victory.

40

Kitty

Kitty stood beneath the arched covering on the King's Cross platform, muted light coming in through the rectangular panes above. The platform thronged with people, a thrum of excitement as loved ones waited expectantly.

Down the way, platform 10 was closed, an empty shell after a bombing.

It had been two weeks since the shooting. All over the news. 'Assassination' was the word they used. A word loaded like a gun with meaning, far beyond a single murder. International, political. It didn't seem to matter that Jit had acted alone. Now the whole of India was involved.

Kitty remembered that day in Finsbury Park, after they'd watched Satyajit led away in handcuffs, his face fixed in a strange, nonchalant grin. An ambulancewoman had covered the colonel's body in a sheet, head to toe, confirming what Kitty already knew. The area had been cordoned off by the police, but a few groups of onlookers had gathered on the outskirts, talking in hushed whispers.

Miss Thacker sat on a chair by a tree, all the fire gone from her eyes.

'Did he . . .' Kitty had begun to say. 'He didn't say anything to you?'

Miss Thacker stared at her. 'Not this.'

Kitty sighed. 'I know you said he might be planning something, but I just never . . .' She trailed off. Neither of them could say the words outright. What Satyajit had done hung in the air between them.

'Did you hear what he said? This is for Bishnu . . . Where was it?' Ruby couldn't remember the word.

'Bishnupur?' said Kitty.

'Do you know anything about that?'

Kitty shook her head, with only the vaguest of recollections that there had been some violence there at some point. The panic in her body had fallen away, giving way to exhaustion.

Miss Thacker relayed what Satyajit had told her. How his father died. 'Jit said the military were involved. Maybe Colonel Gladstone?' Miss Thacker said, quietly.

'Maybe.' Kitty's voice was brittle. 'Or Jit was just looking for anyone to take his anger out on.'

'No,' she replied. 'He kept saying to me that they'd never paid for what they did. It must be connected.'

'Doesn't make it right.'

'I know that.' Miss Thacker's voice cracked as though broken by guilt.

At the station, the train seemed to pull in far too slowly, though Kitty knew it was just her impatience. Blue shadows beneath the carriages as they came closer. Now the click and squeak of train doors opening, and a rush of people, civilians and military, poured onto the platform.

Kitty stood on tiptoe, looking out across the sea of heads. Finally, she felt a warm hand on her shoulder. She turned, open-mouthed. She sank into Haseeb's shoulder and everything unravelled. Tears now, soaking the blue-grey wool of his RAF jacket. Once she began she couldn't stop: all the horror she had seen, the fierce look on Jit's face, the life ebbing from the colonel before he'd even hit the ground, the bloody footsteps across the wooden platform, the anguished cries. Haseeb let her sob, arms enfolding her. They stood there a while until Kitty finally caught her breath. She gently pulled away, taking in his face. A dark cloud of tears on his jacket.

'Meri Kitabi,' he said, brushing her wet cheek with his thumb.

That almost set her off again. How she had longed to hear his voice when she'd come home to the empty flat after the killing.

'Haseeb . . .' Kitty looked down. She didn't know where to start, overwhelmed by everything that had happened in the days since. Even now, when she closed her eyes at night, alone in bed, she could hear the shots. She'd reach out towards Haseeb's cold and empty pillow, searching for an impossible solace.

He stroked her hair. Usually, she wasn't keen on him doing that when they were out in public, not when it took so long to set, but today Kitty didn't care. The voices of the final few train passengers rang out around them.

'How have you been?' he said.

Too small a question for so big an answer.

'It was just so awful,' said Kitty, taking a handkerchief from her bag and dabbing beneath her eyes. Though he would have seen the news reports since, there was no room among the headlines for what it had really felt like to be there that day. She took him through the events, the amicable way Mandalji had spoken to the colonel before the speeches, the good turnout of the crowd. And then, more tentatively, how quickly it had all happened, between Satyajit raising the gun and the crowds running away.

'I just can't believe it, even now,' Haseeb said.

Kitty shook her head despondently. The platform was almost empty. Another train pulled into the next platform down. Haseeb was home; that should be a source of joy, not sorrow. 'Come on, you must be hungry?' she said.

As they walked over to the Lyons' Corner House by the station, Haseeb gave her his news about the RAF.

'And how are you feeling?' asked Kitty, gently. In the months since their conversation at the dance hall in the summer, the situation in Bengal had grown worse. 'About fighting?'

Haseeb took out a cigarette and lit it, sighing. 'I think a lot about it. But I said I wanted to join to help others and that hasn't changed. I believe more than ever that Hitler can't win.'

Kitty nodded in agreement as they weaved through the throngs of passengers in the station.

'And I know you and Mandalji, Congress too, you're all doing everything you can to make the government listen,' he said, briefly stroking her shoulder.

'We are,' she said, though she felt a pang of guilt. It never seemed to be enough. At least now, though, the India Forum felt less alone. The debates in Parliament showed there was concern among MPs on both sides of the divide, after entire families had been wiped out in East India. Even the British newspapers were open about it: 'man-made famine', caused by the 'lack of foresight and planning' and the exporting of rice while the region was in the 'grip of the epidemic'.

'But most of all,' he said, exhaling smoke into the air, 'after everything that's happened with Satyajit, it shows me that we have to finish this war so we can get on with building India the right way. Our way.'

At the Lyons' Corner House, they were ushered straight past the queue with little fuss. Haseeb's blue uniform with the golden wings was like a new face, a new skin that suddenly made him welcome everywhere. People would let them skip the queue at the cinema, give them free meals at restaurants; nothing was enough to show their gratitude now.

Usually, they both found it awkward to be given special service on account of Haseeb's uniform but today, Kitty was glad that they could quickly sit down. The 'nippy', as all the waitresses in their classic black uniforms with the white pinnies were known, came over and took their order.

Haseeb told her how his curious fellow pilots had been asking him and Harinder about what had happened with Satyajit, as though every Indian was some kind of personal news source. Haseeb had done his best to distance them from it all, stating that most Indians simply wanted peace, whether in India or Britain.

The nippy brought over a pot of tea, plus two iced buns.

Kitty looked down at her saucer. 'You know, Satyajit shouted something about Bishnupur.'

Haseeb paused a moment, thinking. 'I think there were some killings there once, during a protest. Long time ago now,' he said. 'Did he say anything about the famine?'

Kitty shook her head, but knew it was possible that had been a motivation too. She glanced at him as she held her cup in her hand. 'Mandalji's asked me to help with something, Haseeb,' she said. 'Satyajit's case.'

Haseeb's eyes narrowed as he waited for her to continue.

She had been out in the India Forum garden a week ago with Mandalji, as they surveyed all the work that needed to be done to the building, pointing at the brickwork and anything else that could no longer wait to be repaired.

The garden itself had seen better days. Kitty hated going out there, looking at all the signs of neglect. The leaves scratched underfoot; the greying, cracked earth and parched grass looked like a terrain, a mini map of the world. It would be gone soon, come stamping foot or heavy rain.

As they finished inspecting the neglect, Mandalji turned to

Kitty. 'Now, Keerthanaben,' he said, a grave look on his face. 'I wanted to talk to you.'

Kitty braced herself. He was unusually calm, less erratic than usual, but his tone was serious. In the days after the shooting, the police had wanted to know whether Satyajit had acted alone. They'd harassed his friends from the India Forum, even arrested another Indian man for having 'Azad' – free – written on the leather bag that he used for peddling.

'As you know, Satyajit is still on remand at Brixton prison,' said Mandalji, clasping his hands behind his back. 'And he has a good barrister, Mr Remington.'

Kitty nodded. He was a well-regarded barrister, educated at Cambridge, with over twenty years of prominent criminal cases under his belt.

'I think it would be good idea if you assist Mr Remington.'

Kitty stared at him. 'But I thought we'd agreed to distance ourselves from it all?' Back in India, Mahatma Gandhi had expressed an immediate and outright condemnation of the violence. Mandalji, guided by the response of the Indian Congress, had of course followed their lead, as horrified as Kitty was by what had happened.

'I think we have to be led by the mood of our fellow Indians, and the tide has turned.' He reminded her of the response, especially among younger Indians, in both India and Britain. Some of the new generation saw Satyajit as a hero who had made the ultimate stand against their oppressors. It was as though the youth of India carried the centuries of impatience in their blood and they wouldn't stand for injustice any longer. The way they saw it, Satyajit had sought justice for the many crimes that had never been paid for. 'And,' Mandalji added, 'there is a lot of publicity for the cause now.' There was no mistaking the steely undertone in his voice.

Haseeb took a sip of tea as she finished telling him the

story. 'So he sees it as a public relations exercise?' He gave a surprised laugh.

'I think he believes there's a better chance of us controlling the narrative if I'm involved,' she said quietly, staring into her cup.

'And how do you feel?'

Kitty looked across the teashop. The clatter of cutlery, conversations in full flow. 'Mandalji said that Satyajit deserves a fair trial. And I agree. But that doesn't mean I have to be the one who helps him.'

'Mandalji trusts you. You're a very good barrister, Kitabi.'

'I'm not a criminal barrister. Although it will be Mr Remington as the lead.' A white face played better to the jury than a brown one.

'You understand the Indian side of the argument better than Mr Remington would. And you have some knowledge of Satyajit already. How he thinks, how he behaves.'

'I wish I didn't.' Kitty sighed. 'Would you do it?'

Haseeb put down his fork and finished chewing while he considered it. 'Perhaps if it helped the India Forum and the cause, yes.'

'We're almost there, Haseeb.' She shook her head. 'And then he tries to ruin it for us.'

He looked at her. 'Then perhaps that's exactly why you should help him.'

*

'Now, Satyajit, it's very important that we all remain as calm as possible during the trial,' said Mr Remington, the lead barrister, using 'we' as though he or Kitty were just as likely to have an outburst as Satyajit was. The trial date had been expedited owing to the highly political nature of the killing, and they had less than two months left to prepare. The entire summer had been a whirlwind of gathering evidence and speaking to witnesses.

'I know,' said Satyajit, a dull, leaden look in his eyes. The meeting room at Brixton prison was cold and stark. Brick walls painted white, with indeterminate chips and stains across them. Kitty tried not to think about what the stains might be. The air smelt stale and musty, tainted with old sweat. In all her years of training and bar work, she had never had to visit a prison, used to smart law offices or the homes of wealthier clients.

Kitty glanced at Mr Remington and then switched to Hindi. 'Dekho,' she said, looking at Satyajit, 'I know it's tempting to make some kind of grand speech or statement in court, but if you don't want to be hanged, then you need at least to try to appear remorseful and humble.'

Satyajit gave her a mocking laugh.

Kitty swallowed, leaning forward. 'It's important that you keep the court on side. Let us do our jobs.'

He stared at her, eyes intense, but she couldn't hold his gaze. Kitty knew what he was thinking. Why should he be quiet? He had a right to speak just as anyone did, despite what he'd done. But Satyajit didn't seem to understand what those words could cost him. Or was it that he simply didn't care?

They began discussions about the latest witness statements, and Mr Remington asked Satyajit more questions to see if he could find any holes. After a short while, when he stood up to get a paper from his briefcase, Satyajit spoke quietly to Kitty in Hindi. 'All I have to do is hold on. When the British lose the war and the Germans take over, I'll be taken as a political prisoner.'

The words sent a chill through her. The idea that Jit placed more hope in the Nazis winning the war than in his own defence was absurd. She remembered that day long before at the India Forum, when he had talked about Bose making a pact with Hitler so that he could rule India after the war. But what was perhaps even more chilling was that Satyajit seemed so certain about the outcome.

He might have a point; perhaps Bose and his friends would hold Satyajit up as an example, a hero warrior against the British imperialists. There was no black or white, they were all operating in the grey.

'You need to face reality. Here, in this country, they will hang you because you killed a man,' she said firmly now. She needed him to understand, for the Forum's sake if nothing else. Didn't he realize that sacrifice could be selfish too?

Satyajit smiled, as though it was all so simple. Of course, he'd always been the kind that played on the edge, but now he'd tipped fully to the other side, not even trying to hide his contempt for the rules.

'I'm not going to live in the shackles of the British, pleading like a dog for them to give me freedom,' he said. 'Fighting their battles for them. Not like you and your husband.'

Kitty clutched the edge of the table but she knew she had to put her frustration aside. Indians still had to prove themselves in a way that many British people never did. They could act with impunity while every Indian in the world would be judged on the actions of one single Indian. She had a job to do, and that was all that mattered now.

41

Ruby

'Hello, Ruby.'

The air cut from Ruby's lungs.

It was Langley.

She glanced up and down the street. He must have been waiting there for her to come out of her warden post. A bus rumbled past, bringing a cold swoop of air and a flurry of autumn leaves. 'What do you want?'

'Charming.' He gave a little smirk.

'I told you I couldn't keep giving you information.' Although she had cut ties with Langley, she had wondered how far their investigations into the shooting would reach, waiting for the day they might knock on her door. Still, it had been months now since the killing and she almost thought she'd got away with it.

All this time, she'd wondered if she could have done anything differently. Had there been any sign? She remembered that day in Finsbury Park, the look in Jit's eye, the determination. Two shots at close range. No mistaking what he meant to do. It had continued playing in her mind in the hours afterwards, as the shadows grew long and the light left the day.

Langley stared at her. 'I asked you once about a man called Satyajit Deol.'

Ruby's mouth was too dry to speak.

'Do you remember?' he said, eyes fixed on her.

She swallowed, throat brittle. 'Yes, I think so.' There was no way she could deny knowing of him now, not with his name plastered all over the newspapers. All she could be glad of was that Langley hadn't formally asked her in to make a recorded statement at his offices, wherever they were.

A hearse rolled by. They both paused, with Langley taking off his trilby and waiting for it to pass.

'Why don't we take a walk?' said Langley, turning back to look at her. They headed down the street, Ruby stepping over a thick wad of tattered leaves that crunched beneath her shoes.

'You were there that day, weren't you? When Deol shot Colonel Gladstone?'

'Yes,' she said quietly.

'Did you speak to Deol at the park?'

Ruby knew that Langley must have read the ins and outs of what had happened. It would be in all the police reports. 'I called out, to stop him,' she said with emphasis. It was in her statement. But was it enough to get Langley off her back?

'Yes, that was very brave,' he said, staring at her. She couldn't tell from his dead tone whether he was being sarcastic.

She frowned, desperately wanting to loosen her scarf. An older man in a suit hurried past, clutching a long umbrella as though it was a sword.

'You must have seen him at the India Forum at some point.'

'If he was there, I don't really remember him, sorry,' she said, managing a vague tone. 'There were a lot of people coming and going at the Forum, you know that.' She and Jit had been extremely careful not to be seen together by the surveillance teams. If they knew anything she'd have been arrested already. Besides, she'd passed them plenty of other information, hadn't she? Time to divert attention. 'Have you spoken to Mr Mandal, he's the head of the India Forum?'

She did her best to hold his gaze now, resisting the urge to run. The look in his eyes suggested he didn't quite believe her. The question was whether he could find any evidence to the contrary.

He stopped on the pavement and she found herself pausing next to him a moment. 'We're speaking to a lot of people, Miss Thacker,' he said, eyes unusually large through the thick lenses of his glasses. 'We might be in touch again.'

42
Kitty

The courtroom at the Old Bailey was smaller than Kitty had imagined. It was wrapped in dark wood panelling, with alabaster ceilings above them, and smelt of furniture polish and old leather. The jury sat to one side of the judge, the barristers to the other.

Satyajit was brought in, handcuffed and flanked by two guards. The jury – made up of women and men, the latter mostly over the age of forty on account of the war – looked at him with a mixture of curiosity and revulsion. The fact that he was foreign must have played a part, at least for some of them. If Kitty hadn't known before what a task they were up against, she knew now.

She looked over to the gallery. Miss Thacker was there in a dark suit, a wary look on her face. Public attendance had been restricted due to the high-profile nature of the case, but Kitty had added Miss Thacker as one of her own attendees.

The press also sat up in the gallery, a dark sea of suits. Mr Remington had already told Kitty that they had effectively been gagged, agreeing not to report anything controversial or likely to cause unrest either in Britain or in India. Even in a court of law, propaganda had a part to play.

Satyajit stared with a neutral face at the wall opposite. His hair was uncharacteristically dishevelled and he had lost weight during the months he had awaited trial. Kitty willed him to make himself somehow more presentable, to at least look as though he cared about whether he lived or died.

The prosecution was led by Mr Rayner Slade, a spindly man whose underfed frame made him look twice as old as he probably was. His gown swamped him; his barrister's wig almost fell over his eyes. He wore his spectacles precariously perched on the end of his nose and peered at people over the top of them. But his eloquent voice could carry across the courtroom with a terrific baritone and an assertive note that resonated against the oak-panelled walls.

There were numerous witnesses on the prosecution side, people who had seen up close what had happened at Finsbury Park. They each took the stand and confirmed that Satyajit had definitely not aimed towards the trees behind Colonel Gladstone, as the defence were going to argue, but instead aimed deliberately at him at close range. A ballistics expert confirmed this view. Mandalji should have been called as a witness too, but the prosecution were perhaps worried that his account might be coloured by too sympathetic a view of Satyajit's actions.

Though no one from the intelligence services took the stand, Kitty and Mr Remington suspected that the MI5 surveillance teams had also fed information to the prosecution. There were references in the opening statement to 'an itinerant man with multiple names and addresses' – details that could only have been known by those who had been tailing Satyajit for a long time. They had interviewed Kitty and Mandalji, along with his various associates at the Forum, about the times that Satyajit had come to the meetings, but they seemed satisfied that he had been just an occasional attendee who had stopped going to the Forum many months before. Miss Thacker had told Kitty that the authorities had been in touch with her too but they seemed to see her as a dead end.

Finally, after a dozen witnesses had been called, it was the defence's turn. Kitty tried to ignore the itch of her wig as she handed Mr Remington his notes.

There was no one who could stand up for Satyajit. Even Miss Thacker's account to the police that day – which Kitty had access to during pre-trial preparation – had been clear. She had tried to call out to stop him. An indirect acknowledgement of Satyajit's guilt.

The defence's questions were easy. They had advised Satyajit to stick to the story he'd given ever since his first statement. It was a protest and he hadn't intended to kill anyone; it was a political statement that had gone wrong. Kitty couldn't help thinking it was lucky that his English was good and clear, as this would work in his favour. Had it come to this? Did the chance of victory lie in the proximity to England in some way or another?

The prosecution's cross-examination strategy was designed to lull Satyajit into a false sense of security. They used simple, disarming questions that also seemed to highlight that he was different, a foreigner, not 'one of them'. Where in India had he arrived from? How long had he been living in England? What was the nature of his apparent protest?

Kitty's heart raced as she waited for Jit to answer each question. He was cool in his delivery but to her relief he stayed on track. But then Mr Slade began his ascent to the summit.

'Is it not the case, Mr Deol, that you have long-standing connections to extremist organizations both in India and in England which have been linked to violent activities against the British authorities and leading figures?'

'I have the right to protest against imperial rule,' said Satyajit flatly, still staring at the wall.

Kitty held her breath, hoping that he wouldn't say any more, and was thankful that Mr Slade didn't want to stop the flow of his questions.

'And was there not another gun found at your stated residence in Mornington Crescent?'

During disclosure, Kitty had learnt that the police had found various things. Passports, all apparently validly obtained, but with an array of different Indian names. He refused to admit who he really was, so his most recent name was given for the sake of court records. She had always suspected that his name – a patchwork of India – wasn't real. There were address books filled with Paris and Berlin locations, maps marked with places across Western Europe. Were they places he planned to escape to? Places where he had allies and friends before the war? No one knew who he really was, perhaps not even Satyajit himself.

No matter, Kitty tried to hold onto her guiding beliefs. That everyone should have a fair trial, and that she had to play a part in ensuring that the Forum was kept separate from whatever a lone Indian man had decided to do.

'What were you intending to do with this second weapon, Mr Deol?' continued Mr Slade.

'It wasn't loaded,' said Satyajit. 'It was to aid protest against the British government and its actions in my homeland.'

'And yet bullets were stored with the gun, isn't that correct?'

Satyajit shrugged and Kitty willed him to show some respect in court.

'Please answer the question, Mr Deol,' said the judge sternly.

'They were planted there by the police,' Satyajit said, which Kitty doubted just as much as the rest of the court probably did.

Mr Slade continued. 'You also stated earlier that the incident on 17 April was simply a protest gone wrong. That you intended to aim the gun behind, not at, the victim, Colonel Gladstone, and fire. Is that correct?'

'Yes.' Satyajit looked mildly bored. 'Someone must have knocked it when it fired.'

'And yet we have no less than seven witnesses, one of whom is a ballistics expert who confirms that the weapon was pointed at such an angle and range that it could only have been intended to fire intentionally and deliberately at the victim.' Slade waited for him to respond but, to Satyajit's credit, he didn't answer. There was barely a question there. 'There is nothing to suggest that you pointed that gun at the trees, is there?' Slade added.

'Yes, there is,' Satyajit said, sitting forward in his seat. He was riled now. 'My statement.'

'But it is not backed by science or reputable third-party corroboration,' said Mr Slade, a hard edge in his voice now. 'Mr Deol, I put it to you that the only act that you were intending was one of murder. Pure and simple.' Now the fangs were out.

Satyajit glared at Mr Slade. 'This court made up its mind about me before I even set foot inside. It is a sham.' Kitty glanced at Mr Remington, seeing a matching look of concern. This was not good. Satyajit needed to stick to the facts of the case.

'Well, Mr Deol, you have the right to give the court your side of the story now, yet you seem reluctant to do so.'

'My story counts for nothing in an imperial court.'

Judge Abernathy interjected, 'That's quite enough, Mr Deol. Does Mr Slade have any further questions to put to the witness?'

'No, Your Honour,' said Slade, and Kitty could see from the ease with which he sat down that he thought the odds were in his favour.

Once the jury had retired, Kitty went outside to get some fresh air. She made her way across the impossibly grand marble floor of the entrance hall and out through the oiled wooden doors. Miss Thacker was already standing near the Old Bailey entrance, smoking a cigarette.

Kitty tied her coat belt tighter, though it was not much use; she could already feel the cold biting at her skin.

'Do you think he has a chance?' asked Miss Thacker, exhaling smoke into the air.

'I don't know,' Kitty said, looking out across the street towards the trees. It was strange, she thought, that though she and Miss Thacker had never been close in any way, they were somehow bonded now, after what Satyajit had done. 'We didn't exactly have a strong case.'

'How long do you think it will be before you're called back?'

'Could be an hour, could be days,' said Kitty. 'But I don't think it will be as long as that.'

'He's not helped himself,' Miss Thacker said quietly, peering down at her shoes.

'They still have to look at the facts of the case.'

She gave a dry laugh. 'Oh, that's reassuring, then.' Her eyes fell back into a melancholy gaze, out across the street.

A car rumbled past. The trial had worn Kitty out and she needed a moment to herself. All the poring over the forensic details had brought the vision of the event back to her: a trilby hat upturned on the grass, the colonel's lifeless body on the platform.

'Well, I better go back inside,' she said. Miss Thacker gave her a nod as Kitty went to find Mr Remington.

The jury returned two hours later.

'Mr Foreman,' said Judge Abernathy, turning to the jury, 'have you reached a verdict upon which you all agree?'

'We have, Your Honour,' said the foreman, his voice a little shaky. Kitty glanced at Satyajit, a cold look in his eyes. It was as though she cared more about the verdict than he did.

'Do you find the defendant guilty, or not guilty?'

The foreman cleared his throat and then looked at the judge. 'Guilty.'

Kitty took a deep breath. She knew it was the most likely outcome and yet it stung all the same. She looked across at Satyajit, expecting to see shock, perhaps even remorse, but still his eyes were blank.

'Before I pass sentence, do you have anything to say, Mr Deol?' asked the judge.

Kitty and Mr Remington had warned him not to say anything. Kitty didn't want to risk provoking further hostility towards Indians, back home or in Britain. The one saving grace was that the press reporting had been restricted, as any glory-seeking speech by the suspect could be seized upon by Indians on both sides of the ocean looking for a new martyr.

'Yes,' said Satyajit, unfolding a crumpled piece of paper. 'I am not afraid of death. I am dying for my homeland. My precious India which the dirty British imperialists have trampled over for centuries. This court, like the government, has forgotten the difference between right and wrong. Hundreds of thousands of Indians have died because of you. They are dying now, starving in Bengal because of your war policies. I go willingly to my death. Better to die with a free will than to live in subjugation. *Azad Hind!*' Free India, he said, over and over again. When he shouted the words Satyajit looked at Kitty, one of the few people likely to understand what they meant. There were disturbed mutters from the press and gallery. He spoke with the honesty of someone who had lost everything.

The judge placed the square of death-black silk on the top of his horsehair wig.

'You are sentenced to be taken hence to the prison in which

you were last confined and from there to a place of execution where you will be hanged by the neck until dead, and may the Lord have mercy upon your soul.'

Kitty glanced at Miss Thacker, seeing the look of horror on her face.

The judge ordered that the defendant be taken away.

Before the guards seized him, Satyajit tore the paper up. He laughed, a dark, hard laugh, then shouted, 'Traitors!' at the prosecution. 'Burn in hell!'

Kitty watched him as he was carried down from the dock. '*Azad! Azad! Azad!*' His voice faded to nothing in the court.

43

Ruby

Ruby sat in front of the clock on the mantelpiece, watching the minute hand ascend towards twelve. Eight o'clock in the morning. Outside, fault lines across the sky. The sun was trying in vain to break through grey clouds. The chill wouldn't leave her body.

She had gone to the India Forum the day before to say thank you to Mrs Akhtar, or Kitty, as she had now told Ruby to call her, given all that they had been through. Ruby wanted her to know that the outcome wasn't her fault, that it was an impossible task and that she had managed it gracefully. She thought of those last moments in court. Ruby had never expected Satyajit to bow out quietly, of course. He had fought until the very end.

'I'm sorry. They didn't make it easy for you,' said Ruby as she stood there in the library at the Forum. Then she smiled, 'Satyajit didn't make it easy either.'

'It was my choice. I did what I felt was right,' Kitty had replied, her voice firm.

Ruby had wanted to write to Jit after the trial, but she was worried that the censors would pick up her connection with him. There were a hundred questions she wanted to ask but they lay still in her heart.

Right up until the trial, Ruby had half expected another

knock on the door from Langley. But perhaps the various tit-bits of information she had passed on to him long before the shooting, that and her 'upstanding job' as an ARP warden, had convinced him that she really was just an ordinary girl who wouldn't recognize anything criminal, let alone get mixed up in it.

There were moments, in the razored edge before sleep, lying in her bed, gulping down sobs, when Jit's nettled words and furious face came back to her, 'This is for Bishnupur. *Azad!*' She would never condone what he'd done, it would never be right, but it was hard to ignore what had led him to that moment. Right up until the end of the court case, she'd thought there was a small chance that they might be lenient. But only fools hoped when death stared them in the face.

She knew she shouldn't think about it: the wooden plat-form, the prison guards around him, the noose around his neck. Wondering what he felt now. He'd shown no fear all this time, but was it all an act? Was the panic burrowing its way through his veins now?

The minute hand on the clock moved, hitting twelve.

How long before they took Satyajit to the mortuary, to be buried in the grounds of the prison, not cremated as he had asked?

How long would Ruby sit here, thinking about him, about what he'd done, about the way he'd chosen to live his life and the way she'd chosen to live hers?

EPILOGUE

1946

44
Ruby

The India Forum had made it through the war. Ruby stood across the street, taking it all in. The corner of the roof had been patched up following what looked like bomb damage and the plasterwork looked drab and grey. Of course, although the war had been over for a good year or so now, no one had had a chance to patch up London's scars.

She had stopped visiting the Forum after everything that had happened with Jit. Even before the war ended, Independence had become a matter of when, not if, and she felt that there was little she could contribute. Ruby wanted to feel as though she was making a difference, that her actions really mattered. She didn't have the way with words that people like Mandalji or Kitty did, and there were better things that she could be doing for the war effort than the ARP, so, like many other young women, she had signed up for the Auxiliary Territorial Service.

It was hard work, but more enjoyable than she'd expected. Although Ruby had paid little attention at school after her brother died, Maths had been her strongest subject. In the ATS she was on the ground while battles raged overhead. Ruby had stood in position with the women manning the height and range finder, who in turn gave her the correct information to operate her predictor. It was detailed work, turning the dials carefully to keep the enemy in sight and calculating the position for the gunners who worked nearby. It wasn't the calculations that were difficult, it was concentrating with all the tension and shouting going on around them.

They'd had weeks of training, but they all knew the stories of girls getting it wrong. Some had never recovered from watching a Spitfire or a Hurricane falling from the sky in flames instead of a Messerschmitt or a Heinkel. She'd once watched a Hurricane spiralling in slow motion, the plane taking an age to fall. Willing on the boys inside. *Come on, there must be someone in there.* She'd waited for the parachutes to appear, but the sky was empty.

Ruby had thought twice about coming to the Forum today, but there had been a lot of coverage about India in the news lately. Talk of a 'Direct Action Day' where the All-India Muslim League had called for direct action to secure a separate Muslim homeland following Independence. There had been violence across Calcutta, which had barely recovered from the famine. Countless riots leading to thousands of deaths and injuries. Reading yet another headline, she had found herself thinking about Jit and wondering how the India Forum was doing.

The front door of the Forum was ajar. She pushed it open. A hefty man in a blue turban was playing tabla, a woman in an embroidered sari was singing. Though Ruby didn't understand the words, she could tell it was a sad song from the melody and the slow rhythmic claps echoing down the hallway. There were people milling on the stairs and spilling out of the rooms. The scent of something spiced wafted through the house.

'Miss Thacker?' She turned around, not used to hearing her old civvy title now that she was a sergeant. It was Mandalji. His hair was now entirely grey, his skin dull from the years of poor sleep, but he still had that same fiery look in his eyes.

Ruby fought the sudden urge to hug him. He was alive, despite staying in that frail old building. Even the doodlebug raids that had stormed across the country hadn't stopped him. Far more vicious than those of the first Blitz, the V1 was the deadliest of all the bombs, its noise stopping just before impact, as though the entire world was holding its breath, and you wouldn't know whether it was coming for you until it was too late because death came in silence.

'Mr Mandal, how are you?' said Ruby, though the question didn't seem big enough for someone she hadn't seen in three years.

'All the happier for seeing you,' he smiled. 'And thank you for your war effort,' he added, looking at her uniform. Something in the way he smiled made her think of her dad, who had fortunately survived the war, along with her mum.

'I think a few of the old crowd are here. Keerthanaben is around here somewhere,' he said. Typical Mandalji: no interest in what was going on in the personal lives of those around him. He probably assumed Kitty and Ruby were friends.

Ruby walked through to the library, which was still more or less intact, except for a large crack that ran across one of the walls. She poured herself some cordial, looking for a familiar face. Her chest tightened as she remembered the first time she'd met Jit at the India Forum.

Wasn't this another reason she'd wanted to join the ATS? To get away from the memories? For the rest of the war, Ruby had been posted all over the country. She had snatched a little fun where she could, but never let anyone get too close. She met a Swedish man while on leave; she'd forgotten his name now, you met so many people who came and went – and died. He had a shock of white-blond hair that glittered in the light and they drank contraband Aquavit strong enough to light up the Houses of Parliament. He and his friends never mentioned the end of the war and Ruby never asked. What was the point in talking about something you might not live to see? Later still, she was posted in France, amid the terrors of Normandy.

There were good things about the ATS too, though. They were all equal. Ate the same dinners, wore the same clothes. Factory girls and debutantes, secretaries and housewives, with about as much in common as a duck to a broom. People couldn't look down on her. She'd started being honest about who she was: Indian and English, and she fought as hard as any man. She'd moved herself up, made herself better, just as Mum had always wanted her to, but it wasn't about knowing which fork went with the fish course, it was about what Ruby did with her own hands, her own mind. She'd fit in, as she'd done for all those years, before the war, during the Blitz; but this time, instead of pretending, she could be free.

'The uniform suits you,' said a familiar voice. She turned to see Kitty standing in the doorway of the Forum.

Ruby gave a laugh. 'No, it doesn't.' She'd seen herself plenty of times in the mirror. ARP warden uniforms were bad enough, but the ATS were even worse. Khaki jacket that was far too big; she tried to use the belt to pinch it into some sort of shape, but it tended to gather in a lumpy mess that just made her bottom look bigger.

'You manage to carry it well,' Kitty smiled. Ruby could see that she'd mellowed in the time since they'd last seen each other. For some, it was simply the exhaustion of the war, making them too tired to fight or prickle at the smallest of things; for others, it was seeing what really mattered. Life and love, more precious than ever.

'Well, I won't have to wear it much longer. I'm about to be demobbed.' Ruby had to wait her turn before returning to civvy street. The married ATS women got priority. She would miss the military, though she certainly wouldn't miss latrine duty or standing on cold, rain-sodden hills waiting for enemy planes.

'Where were you stationed?' Kitty asked, glancing at the scar, curved like an archer's bow, across Ruby's cheek. Shrapnel, after a bomber had exploded in the sky above her. She had learnt not to touch it and draw further attention to it.

'I was on the coast for most of it, some time in France as well. I retrained as a tank driver.'

'My husband was at Normandy too,' Kitty said quietly.

'Oh?' said Ruby, not wanting to actively ask about Kitty's husband, venturing into territory that might bring the worst possible news.

'He's waiting to be demobbed. He was decommissioned out of service as a pilot in 1943.' Kitty stroked the silk scarf around her neck, then, her voice tinged with sadness, said, 'He lost the hearing in his right ear and worked in the operations room after that.'

'I'm sorry.'

Kitty gave a tight smile, swiftly changing the subject. 'What will you do now?'

'Shopgirl, for now,' she said. There were bills to pay but she had her eye on something that would suit her far better. Still, she didn't want to jinx it until she knew it was certain. Some of the other girls couldn't wait to go back to their old selves, as if they could pick up where they'd left off, darning socks or washing clothes or popping out babies later. Ruby felt sorry for them, truth be told. Was that all? The powers that be had decided that the jobs that were 'fit for women' during the war were no longer suitable. For the time being, she'd taken a job in a department store, which she knew was going to require every inch of her willpower as customers came in clutching two bob and expected to walk out looking like Ginger Rogers.

'And what about you? Independence doesn't look far off

now?' They had finally done it. It was coming soon enough, although the growing violence in India was marring it all.

'There's still lots to do, agreeing exactly what will happen when they hand over power.'

Ruby had spoken to her dad about it the last time she'd visited.

'They're getting their freedom, Dad.'

'Yes,' he said, but where she had expected to see some hope, there was only tiredness in his eyes. 'But at what price?'

'They'll build a better country for themselves once things are settled.' She carried on with all the optimism she could muster.

'Perhaps, manika, perhaps.'

'You won't go back to India?' asked Ruby now, looking at Kitty.

'The India Forum is keeping me busy, but we'll see once Haseeb is demobbed,' said Kitty, a flash of a frown appearing on her forehead.

Ruby hesitated, wondering if she should broach the subject. 'I wonder what Jit would think of it all,' she said in a low voice.

Kitty glanced at Ruby. 'It's what he wanted all along. If only he'd had the patience to try it our way.'

Afterwards, Ruby had said hello to a few of the people she remembered from her old days at the Forum, but she didn't feel like dwelling. Kitty was standing across the hallway as she left. They looked at each other a moment, giving a nod goodbye, then Ruby opened the front door and walked down the steps of the India Forum.

45

Kitty

'It never seems to end,' said Kitty, her arms aching from holding up the broadsheets. She looked across to Haseeb, who was sitting at their table, making notes about a case.

Kitty shared the latest news from India, reading out the key lines from *The Times*. 'Some people just don't learn,' said Haseeb.

It had been almost a year since Haseeb had been demobbed, and things had grown increasingly unsettled in India. The months after the Muslim League's Direct Action Day had led to communal riots and further pockets of unrest had erupted across the country ever since.

It had been almost a year, too, since she'd last seen Ruby that day at the Forum, feeling that she had put that awful mess with Satyajit to bed once and for all. But Kitty had been wrong to think that every sadness could be put behind them.

Independence had arrived on 15 August 1947, yet now it brought with it the rupturing of the country. The Muslims in North India had packed up their homes and businesses, to go and live with 'their own kind'. Meanwhile Sikhs, Hindus and other minority religions whose homes were in the new state of Pakistan, had to leave for India.

Some people seemed to have lost all sense, regressed millions of years to when all they were was hunter and prey. Where once there'd been the crackle of fireworks across the country, now there was gunfire. Where once 'Om Jai Jagdish Hare' was sung in the street across the land, now it was replaced with patriotic songs and chants of *Jai Hind* or *Pakistan Zindabad*. And far worse. Babies dead by the roadside, women whose necks had been hacked with axes. They'd heard stories of people who had survived who were now nothing but emptied-out frames; people who'd not eaten or drunk anything for days, their flesh already yielding to death.

She had heard about a train that had arrived from Lahore, the top of it strewn with blood-red torsos and heads, a kind of human poppy field that had sprouted across the steel roof; the screech of the vultures above, ready for their gruesome feast. Entire families, entire generations reduced to lines in a news article and disappearing like dust in a fire.

'There must have been a better way than this,' she said, her heart swelling with sorrow at the thought of what her country had become.

She couldn't help thinking of an exchange with her father back in Bombay.

'Monsoon rains can only fall one way,' Papa would tell her.

'What does that mean?' she'd asked, trying to decipher yet another of his vague phrases that no one but he understood.

He peered at her over his glasses. 'That you can never underestimate humankind's capacity for ruining everything.'

In some ways, it was the same with the war. Kitty thought of the concentration camps, the films of poor haunted souls, life snatched from their eyes, naked and thin, as though they'd been skinned alive. Subhas Chandra Bose had also finally worked out that Hitler was not a man of his word, escaping to Singapore to build his own Indian army to fight alongside the Japanese. He'd died in a plane crash just before the war ended, though some people were still convinced he was simply in hiding.

Kitty put down the newspaper, no longer able to bear the horrors of her home country. 'Did you hear from your father?'

'My parents are still in Faisalbad, apparently.' Though there was relief in Haseeb's voice, there was no mistaking the sorrow in his eyes.

'That's good,' she said. Haseeb's parents had left Delhi, which had been apportioned to the Indian side, and gone to Haseeb's uncle in Faisalbad, now Pakistan. They would be much safer there, though for now they had nothing to live off except their savings.

'I suppose for once we are safer in London,' she said, her voice low.

Haseeb put down his pen and looked at her, resignation in his voice. 'But what's here for us now, Kitabi?'

'We could help with the handover. You know they want people to work with the British government?' The connections between their countries were as important as ever. Kitty stood up and went over to the window. It opened with a creak, letting in a surprising breeze for August.

'We got what we wanted. Freedom,' said Haseeb. 'And now we're just going to stay here?'

'Have you seen what they're doing to Muslims in India? What would they think of us, Haseeb?'

'The violence will die down. And some parts of the country haven't been so affected. Haven't we faced far worse, Kitabi?' he said.

She could hear the bomber planes rumbling in her ear once again. 'And we just start again with nothing? In a place where we don't know anyone?'

'Maybe. It's what we did when we came to London.'

'We knew people here, we knew the city.'

'And what has it given us?'

There was no denying it. Since Haseeb had been demobbed,

he had gone back to chambers but was struggling to secure cases. He was now competing with a far larger work pool of returned military men, and he and Kitty had to tighten their belts. They'd already talked about giving up their flat in Bloomsbury and moving somewhere cheaper.

Though Kitty was trying to talk him out of it, it was hard not to agree. They had fought for a free India and now they were going to turn their backs on her? They both had vital skills that could help create a brighter political future. And there were other stories: of Hindus helping Muslims, Muslims helping Hindus, neighbours and friends risking their lives for others, hiding them in basements, helping them to safe passage. Wasn't that what they were returning to as well?

She found her thoughts wandering to her father, back in Bombay. Her dadi had died towards the end of the war, leaving a well of sorrow in Kitty's heart, and though Kitty had immediately written to her father, like before, her letter had gone unanswered.

Haseeb got up. 'Come,' he took her hand, 'let's put all that sorrow aside for a little while. I'm going to take you dancing.'

'But it's one o'clock in the afternoon,' said Kitty, as he pulled her to her feet.

'Didn't we say we'd make the most of every moment we had together?' he whispered in her ear.

A little while later, Haseeb led her down a street that looked vaguely familiar. It was different in the daylight, the house he'd taken her to once, with the basement jazz club. But now no rain at her feet, no blackout to make her stumble.

'Oh, Haseeb, I don't want to be stuck inside.' Haseeb gave her a gentle squeeze of the hand that meant she needed to be patient.

They made their way through the back gate and she could hear music playing. The garden was full of wilting rose bushes and ragged blue flowers, but there was multicoloured bunting hanging along the fence and red handkerchiefs had been tied to the branches of the shrubs. A trio of musicians was playing swing; they'd somehow even managed to wheel the piano outside. On the cracked patio tiles, a few couples were dancing, while others stood and watched, drinking some kind of pink punch.

'I thought you'd like it,' he said. Kitty ventured a quick kiss on his lips. They were still finding their way back to each other, after so much time apart. She had thought it would be easy, someone she knew so well, so familiar, but neither of them had reckoned on how the war had changed them over the years.

The music made her think of the Taj Mahal Hotel, in Bombay. A new border for India now: the Radcliffe Line, named after a British man who had never before set foot on the marbled floor of a temple or heard the call to prayer from a mosque; who had never been left breathless by the scent of a Saptaparni tree nor walked along the long sweep of Juhu Beach at sunset. Instead, this man Radcliffe drew the new line, emerging like a scar across their land, after spending only five weeks in India. Five weeks to decide all their fates. Millions on both sides took only what they could carry and left behind all that they knew. But they were all aware that the tremors had begun well before the fault line of Partition broke India and Pakistan apart.

She drank punch that left a rose-hip tang on her lips, wanting to dance. Haseeb was a little tentative at first, but after a moment they both relaxed.

As Haseeb twirled her around, her scarlet dress flared out and the piano notes twinkled through the air. Over the fence, an old couple with a garden full of well-behaved flowers were dancing too, shuffling their leather brogues and patent courts together across their orderly garden tiles.

There was soon a sheen of sweat across Kitty's collarbone.

Haseeb loosened his tie a little, his upper lip glistening with moisture. The sun gazed down at them as they revelled. The happiness on Haseeb's face made her heart swell.

'Let's stop a moment,' he said, dabbing his face with his handkerchief.

After they'd caught their breath and downed a glassful of water each, they watched the other dancers moving to a Charlie Parker piece.

'I could stay here all day,' she said, dreamily. She felt the warmth of his arm buzzing against hers. Nearby lavender leaves gently tickled the skin on her bare calves.

Haseeb came closer and whispered, 'But not all night.'

Kitty gave a little laugh, eyes narrowing. 'No, I have other plans for you tonight.'

The piano began to play the first chords of 'Every Time We Say Goodbye' and then the sax and trumpet player joined in. She and Haseeb swayed a little to the music. Then she brought her lips close to his ear.

'Haseeb?'

'Mmmm?' he said in a languid tone.

'Let's go home.'

He lifted his head away from her and looked her in the eyes.

'Back to India,' said Kitty.

'Are you sure?' Haseeb said, grasping her shoulders.

'Let's wait until things are more settled there. But yes, it's where we belong,' she said. What was the point of a free India if they couldn't live their lives there? All this time, everything that had happened, and they had stood on the periphery of it all. With India in turmoil, wasn't it up to them to build a better future?

Haseeb had caught the hope in her voice too. 'And maybe once things settle down, we can go back to Bombay?'

She cocked her head. 'Bombay?' Back to so many painful memories.

'You said you didn't want to start all over again. We know the city, we have contacts.'

'My father wants nothing to do with us.'

'Maybe. But a lot of time has passed. Life has changed for all of us.'

She looked at the people dancing joyfully, then back at Haseeb. India was calling them. Home was calling them.

46

Ruby

'Now, dear, you'll be flying out on 16 May, 2.20 p.m. Or should I say 14.20 hours, as you're an ex-ATS girl?' The woman smiled at Ruby, peering over her navy-framed glasses. The small wooden plaque on the desk read, *Miss Rose Tennant, Assistant to the Head of Operations, Save the Children.* Behind Miss Tennant, there was a photograph of two children in rural clothes, perhaps from Eastern Europe, though it could have been virtually anywhere on the ravaged continent nowadays. Alongside them stood a man in a three-piece linen suit.

'Here you are, dear.' Miss Tennant looked down at the map laid out on the mahogany desk in front of her. Ruby's heart jumped a moment as she glanced at the pink of India, the place that had been such a focus for her in that intense period of time. She wasn't ready for that, but one day, perhaps. Her eyes moved to where the woman's red-painted fingernail pointed. 'You'll arrive in Lebanon. And from there –' she moved her finger – 'you'll stay at our base on the Palestine border. You'll be fully briefed when you arrive. The refugees are flooding in so fast that the team on the ground will be best placed to update you. Understood?'

Although Ruby was probably older than the woman, she'd taken on a teacherly tone that was annoying. Ruby nodded.

'Good girl,' said Miss Tennant, and Ruby wondered how

easy it would be to flick those glasses off that turned-up nose of hers. 'I'm just going to collect your ticket and the rest of your papers. Wait here a moment.'

Miss Tennant walked away, leaving the door ajar. After leaving the ATS, Ruby had tried her hand at being a shopgirl, but as she'd expected, the world had closed in on her. Some days she'd stand there, half-heartedly showing off leather gloves to snooty customers, wanting to scream out loud right there in the department store. The war had shaped her, rebuilt her; it was no good trying to go backwards now.

She pulled out a postcard with the Bengal map on it, the one that Jit had given her. There had been no funeral for her to attend. Instead, she had taken a Parker pen, and on the back, she had written, 'Satyajit Deol, Indian from the first, freedom fighter to the last.'

Ruby traced her finger over those words as she sat there in the woman's office. Keeping your heart wrapped in tissue paper, like keeping your best dress for Sunday, was not living. It was certainly not living freely. You might not make it to Sunday. You might never get the chance to let anyone in.

It won't be the same now, Ruby thought. I'll do things differently. I will be brave this time.

Acknowledgements

This novel wouldn't exist without the hard work and kind support of the many people who helped along the way.

Thank you to:

My editors Anne Meadows and Rosie Shackles, for your deep understanding of my story and characters, your brilliant ideas and endless encouragement. I'm a better writer now thanks to your expertise and insight. Thank you also to Ansa Khan Khattak for your early feedback, which paved the way for the novel's current incarnation.

Kate Green, a dream publicist! It's always a pleasure to work with you and I truly appreciate all the work you put into spreading the word about my own words!

The wider team at Picador including Moesha Parirenyatwa for her utterly captivating book cover design, Rachel Wright for her thoughtful copy-edit, John Sugar in managing editorial, Helen Hughes in production and Eve Lynch in marketing. A special thanks to Isha Banerji at Pan Macmillan India for her insightful feedback.

My agent Jenny Savill and to all the team at Andrew Nurnberg for tirelessly championing *A Thread of Light* near and far.

The wonderful early 'beta' readers and supporters of this novel back when it was known simply as 'Book Two': Wiz Wharton, Carolyn Kirby, Anita Frank, Beverley Jandziol, Corin

Burnside, Manolita Foster, Daniel Aubrey and not forgetting Kate Galley and Suzanne Ewart who were willing to read the novel not once but twice! Your thoughtful feedback and encouragement were invaluable. A special mention also to Julia Kelly whose kindness and support brought me back on track countless times.

The VWG. It was the camaraderie of the writing community that spurred me on during the most challenging moments of this novel, none more so than my wonderful writing friends at the VWG. Thank you for believing in me and my writing even when I wavered. I truly couldn't have done it without you.

Shouma, where to start? From your tireless encouragement for my writing when I didn't think I had it in me, to insisting we go into every bookshop we pass to check if my novel was there, your love and care will always see me through – you are the ultimate main character!

Mum and Dad, I write in your honour and will do so for the rest of my days. My love and gratitude, always.

And thank you from the bottom of my heart to the readers for buying and reading my novels as well as to the booksellers, reviewers and wider book community for sharing my books with others. One of the very best things about being an author is hearing from people who've enjoyed my writing and learnt more about the events that inspired it. I'm incredibly grateful to you all.

Author's Note

One of the reasons I became a writer was to shine a light on the stories that have slipped through history's cracks. While this novel is ultimately a work of fiction and I have occasionally taken artistic licence to fit the story, it's been wonderful to delve into British and Indian history to uncover the many surprising facts and fascinating people that have inspired *A Thread of Light*.

I'm grateful to the British Library archives for my broader research, as well as to the many excellent books on Britain during the Second World War, including *The War on Our Doorstep* by Harriet Salisbury, *London at War* by Philip Ziegler and *Wartime: Britain 1939–1945* by Juliet Gardiner. To help me create Ruby's character, I read Barbara Nixon's excellent autobiography of ARP life, *Raiders Overhead*; Virginia Nicholson's beautiful book *Millions Like Us*, which covers a wide spectrum of women's wartime lives; along with various interesting books about life on the wrong side of the tracks during the war, including *The Secret History of the Blitz* by Joshua Levine.

For insight on India and the Independence movement I turned to *Indian Women's Battle for Freedom* by Kamaladevi Chattopadhyay and Shashi Tharoor's *Inglorious Empire*, among others, and I gleaned more about Subhas Chandra Bose's life from *The Sign of the Tiger* by Rudolf Hartog.

While there is plenty written and recorded about the Second World War and the Indian Independence movement, finding detailed information about Indians who lived in the UK during the 1940s has been more challenging, with many lives sadly now lost in history.

Thankfully, author Rozina Visram's book *Asians in Britain: 400 Years of History* was an incredibly helpful starting point, bolstered by books such as *South Asian Resistances in Britain, 1858–1947*, edited by Sumita Mukherjee and Rehana Ahmed, Mulk Raj Anand's *Conversations in Bloomsbury* and *Indians in Britain* by Shompa Lahiri.

Jit's character is in part inspired by various Indian men whose lives I came across during my research, including Udham Singh, whose story is so compellingly told in *The Patient Assassin* by Anita Anand. Kitty is a composite of various Indian women in the UK at that time, among them Bhicoo Batlivala, an Indian-born barrister, campaigner for India's Independence and fox-hunting socialite who lived in the UK and even appeared in several society magazines including *Tatler*! Mandalji is partly inspired by writer, publisher and freedom fighter V. K. Krishna Menon, who headed up the India League in the UK and went on to become a diplomat for post-Independence India.

While some of the events in the novel are entirely a work of my imagination, including the protest at Bishnupur, many of the scenes are inspired by real-life events, from the Indian delegation to the Houses of Parliament to the cricket match at the Indian Gymkhana in Osterley, West London. Thank you to the team there and in particular Dhirajgar Gosai, who took the time to show me around the grounds and tell me the fascinating stories behind the Gymkhana.

There were few details on the tribunals for Indian conscientious objectors beyond journalist Suresh Vaidya who was jailed at Canterbury prison for a time during the war. Dr Linsey Robb at Northumbria University was able to kindly provide some additional details, and Name Architecture helped with exterior and interior information about the old Fulham Town Hall, both of which helped bring these scenes to life.

I hope you've enjoyed *A Thread of Light*. Thank you again for reading. I would be so grateful if you can take a moment to write a review, which is a huge help to authors like me.

Neema Shah lives in London where she works in marketing. Her debut novel, *Kololo Hill*, was a Foyles, *Daily Mail*, *The Irish Times*, *Cosmopolitan* and *Eastern Eye* pick in 2021. Her writing has won and been listed for various awards, including the Bath Novel Award, the First Novel Prize, The Literary Consultancy Pen Factor and the Eastern Eye Fiction award. She is also a writing mentor and teaches fellow writers about marketing. *A Thread of Light* is her second novel.